KU-650-935

Praise for *The Lazarus Project*

'*The Lazarus Project* is a remarkable book in its own right but one fact about its author keeps rushing from the background to take centre-stage – that fifteen years ago Aleksandar Hemon had only basic English. To have acquired as an adult the mastery required to publish literary fiction puts him in the same boat as Joseph Conrad, but oh how he rows it! Hemon really shines'   *Observer*

'If Woody Allen finds humour in despair, Hemon reverses the process . . . We should thank Hemon for humanizing our world, and reminding us of the beauty that triumphs over our frailties'   *New Statesman*

'*The Lazarus Project* is Hemon's most satisfying book to date . . . sonorous and ambitious – a polyphonic lament for the destruction caused by a century of war, pogroms, migration and ethnic cleansing'   *Metro*

'The best evocation of an immigrant experience you're likely to read. Hemon writes with fresh exactitude and real panache. This is a fantastic novel. Witty, intricate and delightfully realised, it is a study of displacement and solitude, of our yearning for and ambivalence towards that most tricky of notions: home'   *Waterstone's Books Quarterly*

'Charged with fury and empathy, Hemon's sentences seethe and hiss, their dangerous beauty matched by Velibor Božović's eloquent black-and-white photographs, creating an excoriating novel of rare moral clarity'

Booklist – starred review

The Lazarus Project

Aleksandar Hemon was born in Sarajevo. He has lived in Chicago since 1992. He was awarded a MacArthur Foundation 'genius grant' in 2004 and is a regular contributor to the *New Yorker* and *Granta*, among other publications. His three books, *The Question of Bruno*, *Nowhere Man* and *Love and Obstacles*, are also published by Picador. *The Lazarus Project* was a finalist for both the National Book Award and the National Book Critics Circle Award.

The Lazarus Project

ALEKSANDAR HEMON

WITH PHOTOGRAPHS BY VELIBOR BOŽOVIĆ
AND FROM THE CHICAGO HISTORICAL SOCIETY

PICADOR

First published as a Riverhead Book 2008 by
Penguin Group (USA) Inc., New York

First published in Great Britain 2008 by Picador

First published in paperback 2009 by Picador
an imprint of Pan Macmillan Ltd
Pan Macmillan, 20 New Wharf Road, London N1 9RR
Basingstoke and Oxford
Associated companies throughout the world
www.panmacmillan.com

ISBN 978-0-330-45842-9

Copyright © Aleksandar Hemon 2008

The right of Aleksandar Hemon to be identified as the
author of this work has been asserted by him in accordance
with the Copyright, Designs and Patents Act 1988.

The picture credits on p. 294 constitute
an extension to this copyright page.

3 5 7 9 8 6 4 2

A CIP catalogue record for this book is available
from the British Library.

Printed and bound in the UK by
CPI Mackays, Chatham ME5 8TD

This is a work of fiction. Names, characters, places, and incidents either
are the product of the author's imagination or are used fictitiously,
and any resemblance to actual persons, living or dead, businesses,
companies, events, or locales is entirely coincidental.

While the author has made every effort to provide accurate telephone
numbers and Internet addresses at the time of publication, neither the
publisher nor the author assumes any responsibility for errors, or for
changes that occur after publication. Further, the publisher does not
have any control over and does not assume any responsibility for
author or third-party websites or their content.

Visit www.picador.com to read more about all our books
and to buy them. You will also find features, author interviews and
news of any author events, and you can sign up for e-newsletters
so that you're always first to hear about our new releases.

For my sister, Kristina

And when he thus had spoken, he cried with a loud voice, Lazarus, come forth. And he that was dead came forth, bound hand and foot with rags, and his face was covered with a cloth. Jesus saith unto them, Loose him and let him go.

The time and place are the only things I am certain of: March 2, 1908, Chicago. Beyond that is the haze of history and pain, and now I plunge:

Early in the morning, a scrawny young man rings the bell at 31 Lincoln Place, the residence of George Shippy, the redoubtable chief of Chicago police. The maid, recorded as Theresa, opens the door (the door certainly creaks ominously), scans the young man from his soiled shoes up to his swarthy face, and smirks to signal that he had better have a good reason for being here. The young man requests to see Chief Shippy in person. In a stern German accent, Theresa advises him that it is much too early and that Chief Shippy never wishes to see anybody before nine. He thanks her, smiling, and promises to return at nine. She cannot place his accent; she is going to warn Shippy that the foreigner who came to see him looked very suspicious.

The young man descends the stairs, opens the gate (which also creaks ominously). He puts his hands in his pockets, but then pulls his pants up—they are still too big for him; he looks to the right, looks to the left, as though making a decision. Lincoln Place is a different world; these houses are like castles, the windows tall and wide; there are no peddlers on the streets; indeed, there is nobody on the street. The ice-sheathed trees twinkle in the morning drabness; a branch broken under the weight of ice touches the pavement, rattling its frozen tips. Someone peeks from behind a curtain of the house across the street, the face ashen against the dark space behind. It is a young woman: he smiles at her and she quickly draws the curtain. All the lives I could live, all the people I will never know, never will be, they are everywhere. That is all that the world is.

The late winter has been gleefully tormenting the city. The pure snows of January and the spartan colds of February are over, and now the temperatures are falseheartedly rising and maliciously dropping: the venom of arbitrary ice storms, the exhausted bodies desperately hoping for spring, all the clothes stinking of stove smoke. The young man's feet and hands are frigid, he flexes his fingers in his pockets, and every step or two he tiptoes, as if dancing, to keep the blood going. He has been in Chicago for seven months and cold much of the time—the late-summer heat is now but a memory of a different nightmare. One whimsically warm day in October, he went with Olga to the lichen-colored lake, presently frozen solid, and they stared at the rhythmic calm of the oncoming waves, considering all the good things that might happen one day. The young man marches toward Webster Street, stepping around the broken branch.

The trees here are watered by our blood, Isador would say, the streets paved with our bones; they eat our children for breakfast, then dump the leftovers in the garbage. Webster Street is awake: women wrapped in embroidered fur-collar coats enter automobiles in front of their homes, carefully bowing their heads to protect the vast hats. Men in immaculate galoshes pull themselves in after the women, their cuff links sparkling. Isador claims he likes going to the otherworldly places, where capitalists live, to enjoy the serenity of wealth, the tree-lined quietude. Yet he returns to the ghetto to be angry; there, you are always close to the noise and clatter, always steeped in stench; there, the milk is sour and the honey is bitter, he says.

An enormous automobile, panting like an aroused bull, nearly runs the young man over. The horse carriages look like ships, the horses are plump, groomed, and docile. Electric streetlights are still on, reflected in the shop windows. In one window, there is a headless tailor's dummy proudly sporting a delicate white dress, the sleeves limply hanging. He stops in front of it, the tailor's dummy motionless like a monument. A squirrelly-faced, curly-haired man stands next to him, chewing an extinguished cigar, their shoulders nearly rubbing. The smell of the man's body: damp, sweaty, clothy. The young man stomps each of his feet to make the blisters inflicted by Isador's shoes less painful. He remembers the times when his sisters tried on their new dresses at home, giggling with joy. The evening walks in Kishinev; he was proud and jealous because handsome young fellows smiled at his sisters on the promenade. There has been life before this. Home is where somebody notices when you are no longer there.

Responding to the siren smell of warm bread, he walks into a grocery store at Clark and Webster—Ludwig's Supplies, it is called. His stomach growls so loudly that Mr. Ludwig looks up from the newspapers on the counter and frowns at him as he tips his hat. The world is always greater than your desires; plenty is never enough. Not since Kishinev has the young man been in a store as abundant as this: sausages hanging from the high racks like long crooked fingers; barrels of potatoes reeking of clay; jars of pickled eggs lined up like specimens in a laboratory; cookie boxes, the lives of whole families painted on them—happy children, smiling women, composed men; sardine cans, stacked like tablets; a roll of butcher paper, like a fat Torah; a small scale in confident equilibrium; a ladder leaning against a shelf, its top up in the dim store heaven. In Mr. Mandelbaum's store, the candy was also high up on the shelf, so the children could not reach it. Why does the Jewish day begin at sunset?

A wistful whistle of a teapot in the back announces the entrance of a hammy woman with a crown of hair. She carries a gnarled loaf of bread, cradling it carefully, as though it were a child. Rozenberg's crazy daughter, raped by the pogromchiks, walked around with a pillow in her arms for days afterwards; she kept trying to breast-feed it, boys scurrying at her heels hoping to see a Yid tit. "Good morning," the woman says, haltingly, exchanging glances with her husband—they need to watch him, it is understood. The young man smiles and pretends to be looking for something on the shelf. "Can I help you?" asks Mr. Ludwig. The young man says nothing; he doesn't want them to know he is a foreigner.

"Good morning, Mrs. Ludwig. Mr. Ludwig," a man says as he enters the store. "How do you do today?" The little bell goes on tinkling as the man speaks in a hoarse, tired voice. The man is old, yet unmustached; a monocle dangles down his belly. He lifts his hat at Mrs. and Mr. Ludwig, ignores the young man, who nods back at him. Mr. Ludwig says: "How do you do, Mr. Noth? How is your influenza?"

"My influenza is rather well, thank you. I wish I could say the same thing for myself." Mr. Noth's walking stick is crooked. His tie is silk but stained; the young man can smell his breath—something is rotting inside him. I will never be like him, thinks the young man. He leaves the cozy small talk and walks over to the board near the front door to browse through the leaflets pinned to it.

"I could use some camphor," Mr. Noth says. "And a new, young body."

"We're out of bodies," Mr. Ludwig says. "But we do have camphor."

"Worry not," Mrs. Ludwig says, cackling. "This body will serve you well for a long while."

"Why, thank you, Mrs. Ludwig," Mr. Noth says. "But do let me know if some fresh bodies come in."

Next Sunday at the Bijou, the young man reads, Joe Santley stars in *Billy the Kid*. The Illinois Congress of Mothers offers a symposium on "Moral Influence of Reading"; at the Yale Club Dr. Hofmannstal is talking on "Shapes of Degeneracy: The Body and Morality."

The camphor jar and hat in his left hand, Mr. Noth struggles to open the door with his right one, the stick moving up and down his forearm. Mrs. Ludwig rushes over to help him, still carrying the bread, but the young man reaches the door before her and opens it for Mr. Noth, the little bell joyously jingling. "Why, thank you," Mr. Noth says and attempts to lift his hat, the stick poking the young man in his groin. "Pardon me," Mr. Noth says and walks out.

"How can I help you?" Mr. Ludwig says from behind the counter, even more coldly, for the young man is much too loose and comfortable in his store. The young man returns to the counter and points at the rack with lozenge jars. Mr. Ludwig says: "We have all kinds of flavors: strawberry, raspberry, menthol, honeysuckle, almond. Which would be your pleasure?" The young man taps his finger on the jar with nickel-sized white lozenges, the cheapest kind, and offers a dime to Mr. Ludwig. He has money to spend on pleasure, he wants to show them. I am just like everybody else, Isador always says, because there is nobody like me in the whole world.

Mr. Ludwig glares at him; for all he knows the foreigner might have a gun in his pocket. But he weighs a throng of lozenges on the small scale, takes a few out, and slides the rest into a waxed bag. "Here you go," he says. "Enjoy." The young man deposits one of the lozenges in his mouth right away, his stomach howling with anticipation—Mr. Ludwig hears the howl, looks toward Mrs. Ludwig. Never trust a hungry man, his eyes tell her, particularly a hungry man who does not take his hat off and buys candy. The lozenge is apple sour, the young man's mouth awash with saliva. He is tempted to spit it out, but the lozenges entitle him to linger in the store, so he frowns and keeps sucking it, strolling over to the leaflet board to look at it again. At the International Theater, Richard Curle is in his new musical gambol, *Mary's Lamb*. Dr. George Howe and Co. promise a certain cure from knotted veins, blood poison, blisters, and nervous debility. Who are all these people? Dr. Howe's face is on the leaflet—a grim man he is, a venerable black mustache on his white face. Olga's veins are constantly swollen; after work, she sits down and puts her feet up on another chair. She likes to lance his blisters. Mother used to soak her varicose legs in a tub of hot water, but she would always forget the towel. He would be the one to fetch it, wash her feet, and wipe them dry. Her soles were ticklish; she would squeal like a schoolgirl.

The lozenge is nearly entirely melted now and has become bitter. He bids good-bye to Mr. and Mrs. Ludwig, to which they do not respond, and steps out. The horses are clip-clopping, snorting out plumes of vapor. He nods at three women, as they pick up their pace passing him, ignoring him; their arms are linked, their hands warm in muffs. A thick-necked man chewing a cigar stump buys a paper from a boy, who then shouts: "Famous Gunman Shot in Fight!" The young man tries to look over the newsboy's shoulder at the headlines, but the newsboy—hatless, with a scar across his face—scampers away, hollering: "Pat Garrett, the Lawman Who Shot Billy the Kid Dies in a Gunfight." The young man's stomach growls again, and he takes another lozenge. He is glad he has a few more left; he enjoys possessing them. Billy. That's a nice name, a name for a fretful, yet happy, dog. Pat is weighty, serious, like a rusted hammer. He has never known anybody named Billy or Pat.

SHORTLY THEREAFTER, he walks up to Chief Shippy's door, another lozenge dissolving under his tongue, the bitterness scorching his throat, shrinking his tonsils. He waits for the lozenge to disintegrate completely before he rings the bell; he can see a shadow moving behind the curtain. He remembers a childhood evening when he played hide-and-seek with his friends—they were hiding, he was seeking; then they all went home, without telling him; he kept looking for them well into the night, shouting into the darkness full of their shadows: "There you are. I can see you," until Olga found him and took him home. A daggerlike icicle breaks off from a high eave and falls to the ground, shattering. He rings the bell; Chief Shippy opens the door; the young man steps into the murky hall.

At nine o'clock clock sharp, Chief Shippy opens the door and sees a young man with a foreign cast of features who wears a black coat, a black slouch hat, altogether looking like a working man. In the brief all-comprehensive glance he gave his caller, William P. Miller will write in the Tribune, Chief Shippy took in a cruel, straight mouth with thick lips and a pair of gray eyes that were at the same time cold and fierce. There was a look about that slim, swarthy young man—clearly a Sicilian or a Jew—that could send a shiver of distrust into any honest man's heart. Yet Chief Shippy, never to be unsettled by malevolence, invited the stranger into the comfort of his living room.

They stand right at the living room door, the young man unsure whether to enter deeper. After a long moment of ominous hesitation—Chief Shippy flexing his jowls, a confused sparrow chirping just outside the window, a scraping step upstairs—he thrusts an envelope into Shippy's hand.

"He handed me an envelope with my name and address on it," Chief

Shippy will tell Mr. Miller. *"I did not wait to examine the envelope any further. The thought struck me like a streak of lightning that the man was up to no good. He looked to me like an anarchist. I grabbed his arms and, forcing them behind his back, called to my wife: 'Mother! Mother!'"*

Mother Shippy comes rushing in, with all the natural force *Mother* implies. She is stout and strong, with a large head; in her haste she nearly tumbles. Her husband is holding the hands of *a Sicilian or a Jew*, and, in horror, she presses the palm of her hand on her chest and gasps with a boom. "Search his pockets," Chief Shippy orders. Mother pats the young man's pockets, her hands trembling, his sour smell making her stomach churn up. The young man fidgets and tries to wrestle away, grunting like a sinewy beast. "I think he has a pistol," Mother vociferates. Chief Shippy drops the stranger's hands and quickly draws his revolver. Mother dodges and wobbles toward a tapestry that featured—William P. Miller does not fail to note—*Saint George killing a squirming dragon.*

Chief Shippy's driver, Foley, who has just arrived to drive him to City Hall, runs up the front stairs, alarmed by the sounds of scuffle, pulling out his revolver, while Henry, Chief Shippy's son (*on leave from the Culver Military Academy*), surges downstairs from his bedroom in his pajamas, clutching a shiny, blunt saber. The young man wiggles out of Chief Shippy's grasp, steps away for a long instant—Foley opening the door with a gun in his hand, Henry stumbling down the stairs, Mother peeking from behind the dragon—and then lunges at him. Without thinking, Chief Shippy shoots at the young man; blood gushes so hard that the burst of redness blinds Foley, who, being well trained and aware of Chief Shippy's dislike of drafts, is slamming the door shut behind him. Startled by Foley, Chief Shippy shoots at him, too, and then, sensing a body rushing at him, wheels around like an experienced gunfighter and shoots at Henry. *The vile foreigner shot at Foley, shattering his wrist, and then at Henry, the bullet piercing his lung.* Consequently more bullets are fired by Shippy and Foley, seven of which hit the young man, his blood and brains spurting and splattering on the walls and on the floor. *Throughout the struggle,* William P. Miller writes, *the anarchist had not uttered a syllable. He fought on doggedly with that cruel mouth shut tight and the eyes colored with a determination terrible to behold. He died without a curse, supplication, or prayer.*

Chief Shippy stands frozen, holding his breath, exhaling with relief as the young man dies, the gun smoke slowly moving across the room, like a school of fish.

I am a reasonably loyal citizen of a couple of countries. In America—that somber land—I waste my vote, pay taxes grudgingly, share my life with a native wife, and try hard not to wish painful death to the idiot president. But I also have a Bosnian passport I seldom use; I go to Bosnia for heartbreaking vacations and funerals, and on or around March 1, with other Chicago Bosnians, I proudly and dutifully celebrate our Independence Day with an appropriately ceremonious dinner.

Strictly speaking, the Independence Day is February 29—a typically Bosnian convolution. I suppose it would be too weird and unsovereignly to celebrate it every leap year, so it is an annual, chaotic affair taking place at some suburban hotel. Bosnians come in droves and early; parking their cars, they might run into a fight over a parking space for the disabled: a couple of men swing their crutches at each other, trying to determine who might be more impaired—the one whose leg was blown off by a land mine, or the one whose spine was damaged by a beating in a Serbian camp. While waiting in the vestibule, for no discernible reason, to enter the preposterously named dining hall (Westchester, Windsor, Lake Tahoe), my fellow double-citizens smoke, as numerous signs inform them that smoking is strictly prohibited. Once the door is opened they rush toward the white-clothed tables with an excess of glasses and utensils, driven by a poor people's affliction: the timeless feeling that plenty never means enough for all. They spread the napkins in their laps; they hang them on their chests; they have a hard time explaining to the wait staff that they would like to eat their salad with the main dish, not before it; they make disparaging remarks about the food, which then turn into contemptuous contemplation of American obesity. And pretty soon whatever meager Americanness has been accrued in the past decade or so entirely evaporates for the night; everybody—myself included—is solidly Bosnian, everybody has an instructive story about cultural differences between us and them. Of these things I sometimes wrote.

Americans, we are bound to agree, go out after they wash their hair, with their hair still wet—even in the winter! We concede that no sane Bosnian mother would ever allow her child to do that, as everybody knows that going out with your hair wet commonly results in lethal brain inflammation. At this point I usually attest that my American wife, even though she is a neurosurgeon—a brain doctor, mind you—does the same thing. Everybody around the table shakes their head, concerned not only about her health and welfare but about the dubious prospects of my intercultural marriage as well. Someone is likely to mention the baffling absence of draft in the United States: Americans keep all of their windows open, and they don't care if they are exposed to draft, although it is well known that being exposed to severe airflow might cause brain inflammation. In my country, we are suspicious of free-flowing air.

Inevitably, over the dessert, the war is discussed, first in terms of battles or massacres unintelligible to someone (like me) who has not experienced the horrors. Eventually the conversation turns to funny ways of not dying. Everyone is roaring with laughter, and our guests who do not speak Bosnian would never know that the amusing story is, say, about the many dishes based on nettles (nettle pie, nettle pudding, nettle steak), or about a certain Salko who survived a mob of murderous Chetniks by playing dead, and now is dancing over there—and someone points him out: the skinny, sinewy survivor, soaking his shirt with the sweat of lucky resurrection.

In the official part of the evening, cultural diversity, ethnic tolerance, and Allah are praised, and there is always a series of prideful speeches, followed by a program celebrating the brain-inflammation-free arts and culture of the Bosnian-Herzegovinian people. A choir of kids of uneven height and width (which always reminds me of the Chicago skyline) struggles with a traditional Bosnian song, their hearing and accent forever altered by American teenagehood. They dance, too, the kids, under the approving gaze of a mustached dance coach. The girls are wearing headscarves, silky, ballooning trousers, and short vests foregrounding their nascent bosoms; the boys wear fezzes and felt pants. No one in the audience has ever worn such clothes in their lives; the costumed fantasies are enacted to recall a dignified past divested of evil and poverty. I participate in that self-deception; in fact, I like to help with it, for, at least once a year, I am a Bosnian patriot. Just like everybody else, I enjoy the unearned nobility of belonging to one nation and not another; I like deciding who can join us, who is out, and who is to be welcome when visiting. The dance performance is also supposed to impress potential American benefactors, who are far more likely to fork out their charitable money in support of the Association of Bosnian-Americans if convinced that our culture is nothing like theirs so that they can exhibit their tolerance and help our unintelligible customs (now that we have reached these shores and are never going back), to be preserved forever, like a fly in resin.

So on March 3, 2004, I was seated next to Bill Schuettler, the man who was clinking against his empty beer bottle with a dessert spoon, following the irregular, uneven rhythm of the dance. The patriotic people of the organizing committee wanted me to impress

Bill and his wife with my writerly success and personal charm, since the Schuettlers were board members of Glory Foundation and thereby controlled all kinds of glorious funds. Bill had not read my columns—indeed, it seemed that the only thing he ever read was the Bible—but he had seen my picture in the *Chicago Tribune* (twice!) and was therefore duly convinced of my importance. He was a comfortably retired banker; he wore a navy-blue suit that gave him an aura of admirality. He had sparkling cuff links that rhymed with the rings on his wife's arthritic talons. I liked his wife—her name was Susie. When Bill wiggled out of his chair and wobbled toward the bathroom, Susie told me she had read several of my columns and enjoyed them—it was amazing, she said, how different the things you knew well looked through the eyes of a foreigner. That's why she liked reading; she liked to learn new things; she had read many books. In fact, she liked reading more than sex, she said, and winked, demanding my complicity. When Bill came back and sat stiffly between us, I kept talking to her, as through a confession-booth partition.

Both of them were in their seventies, but Bill seemed fully fit for death, what with his hips replaced, the indelible age blots on his face, and an urge to acquire a comfortable condo in eternity by spending his money charitably. Susie was not ready for the infinity of Florida; she had the voracious curiosity of a college junior. She showered me (and my ego) with questions and would not relent.

Yes, I write those columns in English.

Yes, I think in English, but I also think in Bosnian; often I don't think at all. (She laughed, throwing her head back.)

No, my wife is not Bosnian, she is American, her name is Mary.

Yes, I did speak English before I got here. I have a degree in English language and literature from the University of Sarajevo. But I am still learning it.

I was teaching English as a second language, and *The Reader* asked my boss to recommend someone who could talk about the experience of the newly arrived immigrants. She recommended me, so I've been writing the column since.

No, it is not called At the Home of the Brave, it is called In the Land of the Free.

I don't teach English as a second language anymore. I just write the column for *The Reader*. It doesn't pay much, but a lot of people read it.

I am hoping to write about a Jewish immigrant shot by the Chicago police a hundred years ago. I stumbled upon it while doing research for my column.

I am applying for grants so I can work on my book.

No, I am not Jewish. Neither is Mary.

Nor am I Muslim, Serb, or Croat.

I am complicated.

Mary is a neurosurgeon at Northwestern Hospital, in surgery tonight.

Would you like to dance, Mrs. Schuettler?

Thank you.

Bosnian is not an ethnicity, it's a citizenship.

It's a long story. My great-grandparents came to Bosnia after it was swallowed by the Austro-Hungarian Empire.

A century or so ago. The empire has long vanished.

Yes, it is hard to understand all that history. That is why I would like to work on that book.

No, I did not know that Glory Foundation accepted applications for individual grants. I'd be most happy to apply.

And I'd be happy to call you Susie.

Would Susie like to dance?

In a sprightly step we joined the rather stupid but simple dance, whereby people hold hands high up, forming a circle, then move sideways, two steps to the right, one step to the left. She picked it up fast, while I, distracted by the sudden grant possibility, was confused and did my one-step-right-two-steps-left, stepping on her toes quite a few times. My elderly lady friend withstood my anti-rhythmic assaults stoically, until I nearly broke her foot. She dropped out of the circle, her foot fell out of her shoe, she grimaced in pain, skittering one-leggedly. The stocking was bunched up at her big toe; she had a small heel and a swollen ankle. I failed to grasp her fluttering hands, then went down on my knees to pay proper attention to her injured foot, which she unhelpfully kept moving around rapidly. To everyone watching, it seemed that we were dancing with abandon—she a one-footed belly dance, I exalting at her moves—and the Bosnians clapped their hands, and they shrieked with joy, and a flash went off.

When I looked up, I was blinded by another flash, and I could not see the photographer. The dancers were circling around us, the floor slippery with sweat. Susie and I were the showstoppers; a young man with a seriously unbuttoned shirt dropped on his knees and, leaning back, shook his hairy chest at Susie. She seemed to have quickly switched from pain to pleasure, getting rid of her other shoe to succumb barefoot to the orgiastic chest-shaking. I crawled out of the circle, pressed down by a sense of gooey idiocy.

Later on, all the Bosnians in the organizing committee were delighted and praised me for giving Susie a good old time, for now that she and Bill had been exposed to the ecstatic joys of Bosnian culture, a hefty check was doubtless in the offing. I failed to mention to them the prospect of individual applications, which beat in my chest like a brand-new heart. For I was, you see, kept by my wife. In my country, money has a man's face, but Mary was the serious wage earner in the family, and, let me tell you, neurosurgeons make a lot of money. I contributed to the Field-Brik marital budget symbolically: the lousy English-teaching pay, until I got fired, plus not much per column. A beautiful grant took shape in my mind, a glorious grant that would allow me to spare our marriage from the expenses and exertions of my research and scribbling. While the dancing crowd was congealing into another dance, I commenced plotting an easeful lunch with Susie—Bill would be busy in his church or with whatever he wasted his last years on; I would be charming, dispensing amusing stories, laying down before her my project, my ideas, my writerly heart; she would be attentive and acquiescent. At the right moment I could perhaps present to her the picture of our bonding dance; she would laugh, throwing her head back, I would laugh with her, maybe touch her hand among the wineglasses; she would feel young again, and subsequently make sure that my grant proposal was approved. Whereupon I could show Mary that I was not a wastrel or a slacker or a lazy Eastern European, but a person of talent and potential.

Let me be honest: I am not a strong-willed guy, nor am I someone who does not take a long time to make decisions—Mary could easily bear witness to that. But on the Bosnian Independence Day, I immediately set out to work on fulfilling my plan. First, I needed to get a hold of the picture of Susie and me, and with not all too restrained determination, I sought the photographer out in the crowd. Over the claret fezzes and jiggling bosoms, over the loosened ties and minds, over the hopping children and ruined pieces of cholesterol-happy cake, I looked for the light. I pushed through the crowd, elbowing old ladies and teenagers, and finally found the photographer facing a grinning family, each smile frozen in expectation. After the blaze-off, the tableau ungrinned and disassembled, and here I was facing Rora.

Rora. Good fucking God. Rora.

It happens to me all the time: I run into people I used to know in my previous, Sarajevo, life. We yelp in surprise; we kiss or slap each other on the back; we exchange basic information and gossip about common acquaintances; we make firm promises about getting together soon or staying in touch. Afterwards, a tide of crushing sadness always overwhelms me, for I instantly recognize that whatever had connected us has now nearly entirely dissolved; we only make gestures, get through the ritual of recognition, and pretend it was only through our negligence that we had been parted. The old film of the common past disintegrates when exposed to the light of a new life. Of such things I also wrote.

Well, when I recognized the photographer as Rora, I did yelp in surprise and I did step toward him to kiss his cheek or slap him on the back. But he moved aside and ignored my advance, merely mumbling, *Šta ima?* as though we were passing each other on the street. I have to say I was perplexed by that; I introduced myself. I am Brik, I said. We went to the same high school. He nodded, obviously finding me silly for thinking that he would not remember me. Still, he had no intention of embracing the past and slapping it heartily on my back; he held his Canon camera, the flash facing down, like an idle gun. It was not a digital camera, the awkwardness made me notice.

That's not a digital camera, I said.

You know everything, he said. This is not a digital camera at all.

The music stopped; the dancers filed back toward their tables. I was committed to this otiose exchange; I couldn't simply walk away, I could not leave behind all this Bosnian independence and culture business, the past embodied in strangers, the present in foreigners, the schmoozing of Susie Schuettler, the dancing and the kneeling, the escape plan. Funny how when you act once, you cannot stop acting.

I see you never gave up photography, I said.

I took it up again in the war, he said.

I knew from experience that if I—I who had left just before the beginning and missed the whole shebang—were to ask a Bosnian about the war, my question could easily lead to a lengthy monologue about the horrors of war and my inability to understand what it was really like. I was self-trained to avoid falling into that situation, but this time I asked:

Were you in Sarajevo for the whole siege?

No, he said. Just for the best parts.

I came here in the spring of 1992, I said, unasked.

You were lucky, he said, and I was about to object, when a whole family approached him, demanding a photo: the burly, bespectacled father, the burly, short-armed mother, two burly girls with shimmeringly combed hair—they all lined up, stiffened up, and bared their burly teeth for eternal memory.

Rora.

Everybody from Sarajevo had entered your life decades ago; everybody was liable to reenter it with a heavy sack of trivial memories. I knew him well in high school. We smoked at recess in the third-floor bathroom, then threw butts into a de-grilled heating vent, sometimes making bets on who would hit it or miss it. Rora usually had hard-packed Marlboro Reds, much superior to the shit we smoked, which was for some reason always named after various Yugoslav rivers prone to spring flooding. While our cigarettes—it was widely believed—were made from the crumbs swept off the factory floor at the end of a shift, the hard-packed Marlboro Reds had to have been brought from abroad. They tasted like abundance, like the harvest in the milk-and-honey land. Rora was always willing to share his cigarettes, not out of generosity, but rather so he could tell us about his latest travels abroad and show us the pictures of the foreign countries. Most of us still vacationed with parents in dull coastal towns, and we never dared miss school, let alone travel abroad alone. Rora was steadily unreal: he would disappear, clearly comfortable with missing school, inexplicably never getting reprimanded or punished. The word was that his parents had died in a car crash and he lived with his sister who was not much older. And then there were all kinds of far less plausible rumors: his father used to be a spy for the Military Intelligence and his old friends took care of Rora now; he was an illegitimate son of a member of the Central Committee; he was a spy himself. It was hard to take such stories seriously, yet if they fit anyone, they fit Rora. He invariably won the cigarette-butt bets.

He would tell us about the time he had flown to London in a cockpit: when they were high up over the Alps, the pilot let him hold the steering wheel for a little while. In Sweden he had had a guaranteed place in bed with an older woman who showered him with gifts—he would pull apart his shirt and offer us a thumb-thick golden necklace for inspection. She let him drive her Porsche, and would have given it to him if he'd wanted it; he showed us a picture of the Porsche. In Milan he had made so much money playing gin rummy that he had to spend it right then and there or the people he had fleeced would have killed him. So he took them all to the most expensive restaurant in the world, where they ate fried monkey eyes and black mamba kebab and, for dessert, licked honey off the breasts of drop-dead-gorgeous waitresses. He showed us as evidence a photo of the Milan Cathedral. We believed him, even while we sneered at his stories, because he didn't seem to care if we believed him.

The one thing I remembered and missed from the before-the-war Sarajevo was a kind of unspoken belief that everyone could be whatever they claimed they were—each life, however imaginary, could be validated by its rightful, sovereign owner, from the inside. If someone told you he had flown in a cockpit or had been a teenage gigolo in Sweden or had eaten mamba kebabs, it was easy to choose to believe him; you could choose to trust his stories because they were good. Even if Rora lied, even if I didn't always believe what he told us had taken place, he was the only person who could be cast as a character in those stories—he was the only possible cockpit gigolo fond of mamba kebabs. I had my own set of implausible stories, like all of us, featuring people I would like to be, many of my stories variations on the piteous theme of a cool, cynical writer. Besides, Rora's stories were true to our shared adolescent reveries—I had elaborate sexual fantasies which invariably featured the Swedish lady. He lived out our dreams; all of us wanted to be like him because he was like nobody else we knew.

I wouldn't see him much after high school, for he was always away, and I became a studious student of English language and literature. I would run into him on the street, we would shake hands, inform each other that not much had changed in our lives, and then he would outline his most recent trip for me. I would follow his roamings all over Europe on the imprecise, incomplete map in my mind, planting little Sarajevo-youth flags in the European capitals where Rora had cleaned up playing speed-chess and then blew the money on a Gypsy band that played the life out of their instruments all night and all of the day; in the rich towns where he had set straight some haughty Westerner by sleeping with his idle wife and his spoiled daughter on the same night; in the coastal resorts where he would distract tourists with taking their photos while his pickpocketing partner relieved them of their wallets. When he told me about his incredible adventures, I felt the vicarious thrill of facing the world with our impertinent Sarajevo tongue in our insolent Bosnian cheek. Besides, here was a picture of the Gypsies; here you could see mother and daughter; here was my buddy Maron, the greatest pickpocket of Central Europe.

I last saw him in March of 1992. He had just come back from Berlin; I was about to leave for America; everything was falling apart; there was a bizarre early-spring blizzard. We ran into each other on the street as the snow was lashing, and spoke against the howling wind, as in an epic poem. He wore a long, elegant camel-hair coat, his neck snug in a mohair scarf, his curly hair messed up with wet snow. He peeled his lambskin gloves to shake my freezing hand. Both of us were well, given the circumstances; things around us were getting rapidly worse; the weather was bad, the future uncertain, the war certain; other than that, everything as usual. We stood on the street, in front of the stately Energoinvest Company building, the cold was munching my toes, but I listened to him telling me, apropos of nothing, how in Berlin he used to sell pieces of the Wall to the American tourists chasing the shadows of true experience. He had spray-painted a block of plain concrete and broken it into chunks—the bigger pieces were more expensive, and for the biggest ones he provided a certificate of authenticity, signed by himself. He almost got into trouble when cops caught him on the street standing behind a pile of the Wall chunks, a wad of dollars and deutsche marks in his pocket, bargaining with a couple from Indiana who carried empty rucksacks to fill them up with concrete history. He got out of trouble by telling the cops that he was selling *replicas*, which was all right, somehow, with the cops and the Americans. His last words to me were of advice about the U.S. of A. Over there anything is true, he said, and turned away, walking back into a blizzard—or so I like to picture it, creatively, retroactively. In reality, however, he walked me to the Pofalići intersection, where he flagged a cab and I waited for a streetcar. In both versions, he dropped a glove without noticing. I picked it up and took it home, where it was to disappear in the war.

Assistant Chief of Police Schuettler immediately takes charge of the investigation. He speedily dispatches his men to look for clues and witnesses, while he heads over to Chief Shippy's residence. The hallway of the Shippy residence still reeks of cologne, gunpowder, and blood; the stair carpet crawls upward toward the higher darkness. William P. Miller, the *Tribune*'s first pen, is already in the living room, sucking on a cigar, ever dandily dressed. Schuettler nods at him, exchanges a few words with Chief Shippy, who is wincing in pain as Foley is bandaging his forearm. He carefully steps over the carmine blood puddle, shaped like an obscure ocean on the light maple floor, to land on the carpet where the young man's body lays supine. From the floor, he picks up the envelope the young man handed to Chief Shippy. He opens it, reads the note in it, then pockets it. Miller notices, but asks nothing. The chandelier crudely tinkers as someone is walking heavy-footed upstairs. The ceiling is light blue, like the summer sky. "Mother is very upset," Chief Shippy says.

In the young man's coat pocket, Assistant Chief discovers a streetcar transfer issued from the 12th Street streetcar, *suggesting that the assassin was an inhabitant of the South Side Jewish ghetto,* and another one from the Halsted streetcar, dated March 1—he apparently came up to North Side on a reconnaissance mission. There is a slip of paper torn from a calendar pad (date: February 29) with the following numbers: 21-21-21-63; around the 63 is a broken circle, and over this an X. Assistant Chief Schuettler's first guess is that these are the numbers the assassin drew in some kind of anarchist lottery, which was to decide which one of them would commit the crime. His suspicion is confirmed by a bag of white lozenges much akin to poison pills—the young man was clearly willing to die for his misguided cause. Assistant Chief Schuettler also uncovers, folded into the inner band of the anarchist's hat, a piece of cheap scribbling paper with the following sentences:

1. *My shoes are big.*
2. *My room is small.*
3. *My book is thick.*
4. *My soup is warm.*
5. *My body is very strong.*

It is clear that the sentences are a coded description of the stages of the murderous plot. Neither does Assistant Chief find it insignificant that the anarchist has been meticulously shaved, probably that very same morning, and that his hair was carefully cut. His clothes are musty and worn, but he doesn't exude any stench; the man has without a doubt taken a bath recently. *It is not customary with alien men of that class to take care of their persons,* Assistant Chief tells William P. Miller. *It looks as though he didn't expect to come back alive.* "He looks like a Jew to me," Chief Shippy says, as Foley is tearing the end of the bandage with his teeth to tie it up. Assistant Chief unbuttons the man's pants, pulls them down, then does the same with his long underwear; in doing so, he slips on the blood and brains, nearly falling on the body, but quickly regains his balance.

"He's a Jew all right," he announces, leaning over the young man's crotch. "A Jew is what he is."

As nostalgically curious as I was, I had no strong desire to see Rora outside the confines of celebrating our roots, independence, and deracination, but I did want to get from him the picture of Susie and me, because in my overexcited mind, getting the Susie grant was contingent upon the photo. Back at the event, Rora had said he would be happy to let me have it. With a straight, bluffing face I had offered to buy it, hoping he would wave away my bid and promise to give it me for free. He estimated its value at a whopping $100, but I was willing to pay the price. He said he would call me when the picture was done. Perhaps he needed the money; perhaps it was that he could not give it to me for free as a matter of principle. Perhaps it was that I could be featured as a dupe in one of his future stories, just another American he sold worthless crap to.

Be that as it may, some weeks later—it was almost May already, which I knew because I had submitted the grant application on April 1 and I was now getting ready to invite Susie to lunch—I was at Fitzgerald's, an Irish pub in Andersonville, with a pocketful of twenties, feeling the pleasant tingle of vague illegality, staring at the wall with the pictures of various cops and firemen stereotypically clutching their beer pints. Breakfast at Fitzgerald's was my suggestion, owing much to the fact that it was Mary's favorite pub, the place where we connected with her Irish roots by way of imbibing stout. Rora was late, so I worried, as I am wont to, about him not showing up. When I was a kid and played hide-and-seek with other kids, more than once I had found myself seeking my playmates at dusk, looking for them in the bushes and basements and behind cars, chasing shadows, while they were being bathed by their caring mothers, having all left the game without telling me. Consequently, whenever I waited for someone, I spent some time contemplating the possibility of that person never coming. I sometimes imagined Mary not coming back home from the hospital; I imagined her so sick of my writerly ambition and the accompanying underemployment that one day she would just decide not to return from work and leave me hanging there until I recognized that my parasitic existence was no longer acceptable to her. This time I was sitting in the window of Fitzgerald's, facing the empty space across the table, expecting Rora to stand me up, habitually anticipating humiliation. The waitress came by every once in a while to check if I was still hoping for a breakfast mate. I should have never told her that I was expecting somebody.

But then I saw him coming down the street, tall and skinny, his dark hair impeccably curly, in a leather jacket new and shiny, his sunglasses reflective and cool. He stuck out in the morning Andersonville crowd embarking upon their day's work of achieving perfection. I recognized him then; that is, I finally comprehended what I had known but had never been able to formulate: he had always been complete. He had finished the work of becoming himself, long before any of us could even imagine such a feat was possible. Needless to say, I envied him.

He flirted with the waitress, speaking first French to her, then German; she was from Palos Heights and thus unresponsive; he ordered a well-done cheeseburger without uttering please or thank you. I wanted a waffle, they didn't have waffles, so I ordered a medium-well-done cheeseburger. Then we turned to small mumbly talk in Bosnian: he had lived in Edgewater for many years; my habitat had been Uptown since Mary and I had gotten married. I said, It's a miracle that we hadn't run into each other sooner. He asked, Did you know you could get the freshest seafood in the city at the hardware store next to Miracle Video? A Bosnian Rora knew was a fishmonger, supplying ocean creatures to the best Chicago restaurants; the Bosnians who wanted octopus fresh from Florida could just call him and he would drop the order off at the hardware store, owned by a certain Muhamed. There were buckets full of fish splashing in the back of the store, just under the chainsaws— the place smelled of ocean and turpentine.

And here was the feeling familiar from the high school bathroom: it seemed for a moment that this drab, disciplined, soulless world could accommodate exquisite aberrations like the black mamba kebab or a hardware store offering buckets of octopus. Out of my recently acquired habit of American reasonability I challenged him, suggesting that he might be brazenly embellishing, but he calmly proposed that I go there right now and see for myself. I demurred, naturally, and chose to believe. There was no need for a confirmation photo either, because I could see the hardware store through the window.

The cheeseburgers arrived in all their greasy splendor. I waffled through mine; we kept guzzling coffee until my ass was sore with fidgeting. I told him my story: I was here when the war started; I had odd jobs, until I finally started teaching English as a second language. Then the column gig came in; I wrote about the experiences of my students, not at all unlike my own: looking for a job, getting the Social Security number, finding an apartment, becoming a citizen, meeting Americans, dealing with nostalgia, that sort of thing. The column did pretty well, though it paid very little.

People liked it because it was honest and personal and they found the quirky immigrant language endearing. Three years ago, I married an American woman, and she was great.

It was the speech I often delivered to people who break awkward silences at dinner parties by asking flaky questions. I never thought they would care about particularities, so I never told them that Mary and I had met at a singles night at the Art Institute, where loneliness, transnational as it is, had brought us together. We got quite drunk, Mary and I, sat on the stairs of marble, and slurred about life, art, and poetry. I impressed her by mauling Larkin ("In everybody sleeps sense of life loved according to live . . ."), then almost screwed it all up by trying to grope her too soon. She was tipsy enough to be forgiving; we tottered to the lake appropriately adorned with baby waves, sat on the sand of Oak Street beach until cops told us it was time to go home; we went to hers. I proposed a year later in front of Monet's breathtaking water lilies. She was beautiful; my breath was taken; we were still lonely; she said yes. Our first child's name was to be Claude or Claudette, or, we joked, Cloud and Cloudette. When she cooked her stews she wore an apron with a water-lily pattern. Sometimes I thought I had made it all up.

The party inquisitors were often given to gushing over the neatness of my immigrant story; many would recall an ancestor who came to America and followed the same narrative trajectory: displacement, travails, redemption, success. I couldn't bring myself to tell them that I had lost my teaching job and that I was pretty much supported by Mary. She liked the narrative trajectory too, for her people also had a history of displacement and replacement, though I was pretty sure that she was disappointed that my success stage seemed to have been suspended. Still, she mailed the column clips to her parents in Pittsburgh, who obediently put them up on their fridge; she suggested that I was greatly talented and would one day write a great book. They couldn't wait for it to happen, my in-laws. I think they believed that I did not want to have kids before I finished my book, and they could not wait for grandkids. In any case, she was great, very supportive. I was very happy, I assured Rora, because she was great, Mary Field was. She was a surgeon who never cried over dead patients. And her family was great, too. They were Irish-American.

Rora told me about an Irishman he met in the war. His name was Cormac, and Rora ran into him in the Tunnel, where they got stuck because a crate of wine bottles broke somewhere in the darkness ahead of them. While the smugglers were salvaging the wine that was intended for the black market, the two of them waited and talked. Cormac was entering Sarajevo for the first time. Cormac's plan was to organize the Pope's visit to the besieged city. They sat on the cold ground, in the clayish, sepulchral murk, smelling the swill, and Cormac told him he had already talked to the Pope on the phone and His Holiness had agreed to come, with only one condition. I took a great picture of Cormac, Rora said, once we got through: his face muddy, grinning like a lunatic, happy to have emerged from the underworld.

I could not detect the connection between what I had been saying (what was it?) and the Pope story, but of course I wanted to know what His Holiness's condition was. The waitress dropped off the check and, before passing it on to me, Rora said to her: "Ah, that is too much. Can we negotiate?" The waitress seemed tired and emaciated, her flaxen hair slipping the grip of a couple of clips, but she smiled. He was a big charmer, Rora was. In my country, charmers used to be as endemic as land mines were now.

What was the condition? I asked.

What condition?

The condition the Pope had.

Oh, that they end the war, Rora said. Cormac was coming to Sarajevo to tell the people that if they stopped fighting, the Pope would come to visit them for a couple of days.

How did he get the Pope on the phone?

He got the number from that singer, Bono. He's buddies with the Pope.

After the breakfast, Rora wanted to have more coffee. We went to Kopi Café, a venue reeking of patchouli and former-colony teas. I was already nearly blind from caffeine, but I could not say no, as I still hadn't gotten the photo. A twerpy waiter, his short little arms ravaged with baroque psoriasis, took our order. Rora presumptuously ordered a double espresso for both of us and gave a precise set of instructions as to how to prepare them. The waiter listened to him in disbelief, tapping his pen against the notepad, until Rora said, sternly: "Write it down." A scabbily dressed man trembled in the corner; a yuppie in a full-fledged suit was ordering his grand latte; the espresso machine hissed like a geyser. On a bookshelf along the wall there were travel books about far-off lands: Spain, Norway, Swaziland, China, New Zealand, Ireland.

What could I do? I drank my watery double espresso (the waiter having clearly ignored the instructions) and, my hands shaking, I finally asked Rora for the photo. I did not mention what I intended it for. It was black-and-white and the glorious absurdity of my predicament was well manifested: kneeling like a klutzy knight in front of an aged lady, touching her shriveled knee with my left hand. I have to say, however, that my face was beautiful. Noble, I dare suggest. There was some honest innocence behind the veneer of panic—I could imagine Susie liking the picture. And the fact it was black-and-white made it all look old and wise, belonging to a different, vanished, therefore better, world. I liked that picture a lot—that was me in it, as I envisioned myself. I demanded the negative.

You haven't paid me, he said.

You haven't given me the negative, I said.

He gave me the negative; I paid him. Leaning forward, he looked at my face, as though to assess what I would look like in a portrait.

I would like to do photos of you, Brik. You would look good, he said.

Why?

Why not? Every face is a landscape. Besides, maybe they'll want to publish a picture next to your column. Or you might need it when they publish your book.

OTHER THAN GATHERING courage to call up Susie Schuettler, I had nothing better to do. The following week, I posed for Rora, like an honest tourist, in front of various Chicago landmarks: the Picasso, the Art Institute, the Hancock Building, the Magnificent Mile. We also did some dark and narrow back alleys, some cheerful parks, then walked to the Oak Street beach. The day was cold; the lake was the lichen color it acquires when the winds are northwesterly. I confess I was pursuing the nobility visible in the kneeling photo as I postured pensively, frowning, freezing. I gazed at the watery horizon; in a thoughtful profile I contemplated the vast eternity the lake implied. I sat on an embankment wall, focusing on my facial muscles, on the angle of my chin, on my lips being open just enough to suggest a sagacious enunciation on mortality. It could have been excruciating with all the joggers-by stopping to kibitz, particularly since I was constantly asking myself why I was doing it at all. It would have been painful, if it hadn't been for Rora dispensing stories with intractable disinterest, as though he wanted to return the favor by way of enlightening and entertaining me. Not once did he ask me about my life, plans, or experiences, but I remembered that it was the Bosnian manner: nobody asked you anything, you had to make your story be heard. Rora mumbled when he spoke, swallowing the vowels and slurring the consonants in that particular Sarajevo way. I loved the sound of it; it always recalled for me the faint rattle of the first streetcar of a spring day, when the air is humid enough to muffle the city sounds.

He was a Baš Čaršija boy, grew up in the old town. His was an old merchant Muslim family that had always lived in and owned stores in Sarajevo; they had never married anyone born outside the city, so they had no country cousins. I can't stand nature, Rora said to me, as I was leaning for the camera on a leafing tree. I couldn't tell the difference between a cow and a sheep, he said. Both are wild beasts as far as I am concerned. He was ten when his parents died; an aunt took care of him and his sister. Azra, his sister, was a good, obedient child, went to school, studied, helped her aunt with house chores, but he just slept and ate at her house, he said. The Čaršija raised him; he started smoking at the age of eleven; he was making money playing cards at the age of twelve. Sometimes he would talk his sister into mischief. Once, they filled up with water the worshippers' shoes left outside the mosque, and then watched the men slop and slip around the mosque courtyard. As an adolescent, he led stray foreign tourists to a side entrance of the Gazihusrevbegova Mosque, instructing them to leave their shoes, coats, and cameras outside, lest they insult Islam. He promised he would watch over their belongings, but as soon as they entered, he vanished with the loot, leaving the robbed tourists to wander barefoot on the cobblestoned streets. He would sell the booty to Rambo, a seasoned Čaršija criminal at the age of twenty or so, whose father used to be Rora's father's best friend. At the beginning of the war, Rora would join Rambo's unit, because it was one of the few Bosnian units with weapons. Before the war, Rora had extended his services to many a foreigner who wanted a picture taken in the midst of the illustrious Sarajevo history. He would guide them around and photograph them in front of fourteenth-century synagogues and fifteenth-century churches and mosques from the Middle Ages which had all actually been built a hundred years ago; he painted broad pictures of bloody battles that had never taken place;

he brought tears to their tourist eyes by telling them tales that, he claimed, everybody in the city knew: two young lovers had hurled themselves from that minaret; in that store, the legend had it, magic carpets were woven by the blessed hands of a young man named Ahmed, until one day he wove one for himself and flew away to a distant land, never to be seen again. Tourists loved the ghosts; the stories inspired them to pull the wallets out of their traveling pouches and tip him in hard currency.

This guide and photographer experience helped Rora when he slipped through the Tunnel out of the siege in '94. He caught a ride to Medjugorje with a reporter from the *Washington Post* who wanted to write a story about the tens of thousands of pilgrims coming to see the place where the Virgin supposedly announced herself to undefiled shepherd girls—engrossed in the pursuit of eternal salvation, the good Christians failed to notice the slaughter of Muslims a few dozen miles away. Rora thus ended up in Medjugorje, undercover as a Catholic Croat who called himself Mario. He could speak a few languages, never parted with his camera, so he got himself a job leading herds of worshippers to the place where the shepherdesses saw the Mother of God; he took pictures of them glowing with spiritual arousal. Now, Rora had heard of Jesus—*Isus Krist*—for he was a famous person, like Madonna or Mel Gibson, but he had never been inside a church, knew little about the Christian—or any—theology, and cared even less. The silly rituals and soulhealing nonsense, however, were ever easy to pick up, and it took him about a day and a half to learn how to push the buttons of exaltation. The tourists wept under the cross as Rora declaimed what he had picked up from the brochure, with some embellishments. They loved it, all those good people from the Philippines and Ireland and Mexico; touched by the spirit, they tipped him generously.

One day, he was leading a platoon of elderly American pilgrims, fresh out of Indianapolis. With his gigolo experience and Čaršijaaccented English he charmed the clean pants off their Catholic asses. When they reached the annunciation site and the pilgrims shed the conventional tear, they implored Rora to lead the prayer in his language, the request implying an Indiana-sized tip. Rora had heard prayers before, he was well aware that *Isus Krist* featured in them, he knew the sound well, but knew none by heart. Still, he fell down on his knees, put his hands together, bowed his head—an embodiment of piety—and prayed:

Pliva patka preko Save
Isus Krist
Nosi pismo navrh glave
Isus Krist
U tom pismu piše
Ne volim te više

When I was a boy, there was a division of labor between my parents: my father told stories about his fairy-tale childhood populated by clever domestic animals; my mother sang songs or recited nursery rhymes. One of those nursery rhymes was about a duck swimming across the river Sava with a letter on its head reading: I don't love you anymore—*Ne volim te više*. The letter always perplexed me and I spent sleepless nights on its exegesis: Why did the duck carry it on its head? What was the significance of the river? Who was the addressee? Who was not loved anymore? Rora's prayer was that same nursery rhyme, with the incongruous addition of *Isus Krist,* and it was while I listened to his story that I understood the rhyme's inherent cruelty, which was connected in my mind to the inherent cruelty of Mr. Christ's cult.

For I remembered being forced to go to church by my grandparents. They lived their traditional Ukrainian lives in the Bosnian countryside and my parents would ship me out of Sarajevo to spend summers with them. All I ever wanted to do was read, but I often had to help with farmwork, water the cows, or fetch my grandfather, who couldn't find his way back home from the fields. On Sunday mornings I would have to get up at the crack of dawn and they would make me wear my long pants, white shirt, and clip-on tie and we would walk to church, which was four high hills over. In church, only the old folks had seats, while I had to stand, thirsty, tired, and bored, my feet hurting, my ass sucking up the sweaty underwear. Worst of all was the funereal air, the sickly solemnity: the choir wailing songs of suffering, crucifixes everywhere, candles expiring before icons, their smoke sooting up the walls, the hands of the oldest people trembling on the handle of their walking sticks, the younger going down on their knees, growling from the ache in their joints. Everything in the church bespoke death, the heavy-clothed, airless, blind and deaf and decaying death. More than once I peed in my pants. (Why is it that churches have no bathrooms? Did Mr. Christ have no bladder?) At least once I passed out. There was vomiting, there were nosebleeds, too, but there was never any mercy—all suffering was insignificant in comparison to the crucified gymnast's, and nobody cared about me. I would have nightmares for a week; over the phone, I begged my agnostic-cum-Communist parents to protect me from my grandparents' spiritual zeal, but they never would, for the dangers of staying alone at my grandparents' house while they were at church, what with all the knives and matches and garden tools available, concerned my parents far more than my martyrdom—they worried about the preservation of my body far more than that of my soul. My salvation came when I figured out that I could smuggle books into church: behind everyone's back, in the darkest corner, I strained my eyes to read, say, *In Desert and Wilderness,* imagining myself roaming the vast, bright spaces of freedom, while everyone else in church acknowledged their sins and contemplated the flimsiness of their earthly existence. Not only did the book do away with bodily discomforts, but I also found intense pleasure in the fact that I was enjoying it unbeknownst to all of the kneeling worshippers. Therefore I appreciated, tremendously—indeed, orgasmically—the image of the oblivious American pilgrims on their knees, struggling to imitate Rora's incantation, the loveless duck slowly gliding across the river.

BY THE TIME he told me the duck-prayer story, we were shooting in Uptown: the junky liquor stores; the rusty El overpass at Lawrence; the loitering gangbangers, their pants halfway down their tough asses; the boarded-up Uptown Theater; the run-down old hotels serving as halfway houses and mental institutions; the crews of crazies roaming the streets, dazed and drooling. After 9/11, these crazies became as patriotic as everyone else, I said. They had little American flags sticking out of their matted hair; there was a barefoot guy who put a sticker reading UNITED WE STAND on his forehead—his multiple personalities united for the war on terror. Belief and delusion are incestuous siblings.

There was a crazy guy in Sarajevo, Rora said, who jogged all over the city under siege whenever the shooting slowed down. In an undershirt and red shorts he ran and ran, and people tried to catch him and save him, because the Chetniks never really stopped shooting, but nobody could catch him, he was pretty fast. He would stuff a plastic lemon in his mouth, and when he didn't have a lemon he would scream like the *sheitan*. If you asked him, he would say he was training for the Olympics. Then one day, Rora said, he ran with a bunch of people across the airport tarmac as the UNPROFOR and the Chetniks shot at them. But they shot at the crowd, and he was far ahead of them, the plastic lemon in his mouth, so he made it across. Then he ran all the way to Kiseljak. And now he is in Saint Louis, Rora said.

As we walked down Lawrence, a bus disgorged a gaggle of high school kids right in front of us. I could not understand their yelping—the only discernible words were "I was, like . . ." They proceeded toward the El entrance. A couple of boys, one of whom wore the Mexican national soccer team jersey, leapt over the bar without sliding his fare card and ran upstairs in long strides. The rest of the kids roared in excitement, becoming even louder as they heard the train above their heads coming to a halt in the station.

Stand right here, Rora said, and pushed me so I faced the row of kids waiting to purchase their fare cards at the machine. Now look at the camera. A little to the side. That's it. Don't look at them, look at the camera. Good.

I wanted my future book to be about the immigrant who escaped the pogrom in Kishinev and came to Chicago only to be shot by the Chicago chief of police. I wanted to be immersed in the world as it had been in 1908, I wanted to imagine how immigrants lived then. I loved doing research, poring through old newspapers and books and photos, reciting curious facts on a whim. I had to admit that I identified easily with those travails: lousy jobs, lousier tenements, the acquisition of language, the logistics of survival, the ennoblement of self-fashioning. It seemed to me I knew what constituted that world, what mattered in it. But when I wrote about it, however, all I could produce was a costumed parade of paper cutouts performing acts of high symbolic value: tearing up at the sight of the Statue of Liberty, throwing the lice-infested Old Country clothes on the sacrificial pyre of a new identity, coughing consumptive blood in large, poignant clots. I kept those pages, but shuddered at the thought of reading through them.

Naturally I told Mary everything about my book before I had anything I could show her. In my country, it is bad luck to talk to your wife about your dreams, but, as always, I wanted to impress her. She was, as always, fairly supportive of my literary ambitions, but the reasonable, concrete woman that she was could not help but cut gaping holes in the Lazarus canvas I had painted for her. She found my idea of a Lazarus who struggled to resurrect in America a tad pretentious, particularly, she said, since my own American life was nothing to complain about. I had to know a lot about history to write about it. And how could I write about Jews when I wasn't one? It was much too easy for me to imagine my book failing and Mary leaving me for a successful anesthesiologist whose eyebrows she had long admired across the surgical table. Much too often I avoided thinking about my Lazarus project, as though my marriage depended on it. Naturally, the more I tried to avoid it, the more I thought about it, the more I needed to do it. And now the Susie grant hovered on the horizon of glorious possibilities.

Therefore I desperately needed to discuss it with someone. After a long morning of posing and listening to Rora, I could no longer keep my mouth shut. We were having coffee at a newly opened Starbucks that smelled of fresh toxic paint and some extraordinary *shittychino*. Severely caffeinated again, I talked to him about Lazarus Averbuch, his short life and long death. After Shippy had shot Averbuch, Chicago was in hysterics, because people here still remembered the Haymarket Massacre and the trial and execution of the alleged anarchists who were allegedly responsible for the bloodshed. And there had also been the assassination of President McKinley, by a Hungarian who claimed to be an anarchist. America was obsessed with anarchism. Politicians ranted against Emma Goldman, the anarchist leader, called her the Red Queen, the most dangerous woman in America, blamed her for the assassinations of European kings; patriotic preachers raved against the sinful perils of unbridled immigration, against the attacks on American freedom and Christianity. Editorials bemoaned the weak laws that allowed the foreign anarchist pestilence to breed parasitically on the American body politic. The war against anarchism was much like the current war on terror—funny how old habits never die. The immigration laws were changed; suspected anarchists were persecuted and deported; scientific studies on degeneracy and criminality of certain racial groups abounded. I had come across an editorial cartoon depicting an enraged Statue of Liberty kicking a cage full of degenerate, dark-faced anarchists bloodthirstily clutching knives and bombs.

I was not entirely sure he could follow my monologue, for he said nothing, asked no questions. Still, I told him the story of Wawaka, a town in Indiana that received a letter threatening it with complete destruction unless the good Wawakians paid up seven hundred and fifty dollars. The letter had been posted in Brooklyn and signed "Anarchists," so the little town rose up in arms and sought foreigners to get rid of them. But they couldn't find any in Wawaka, so they stopped trains passing through town, which otherwise would not have made a stop, and thus happily managed to lynch a couple of unlucky Mexican farmhands.

Finally, Rora spoke up and told me about a Bosnian who had recently been killed by the San Francisco police. The Bosnian had been smoking on the patio of a nonsmoking Starbucks and refused to leave the premises before he finished his cigarette. When the cops arrived, complete with wailing sirens and Kevlar vests and cool shades, he told them, in polite, restrained Bosnian, that he would be happy to leave, but only after he had finished his cigarette. They couldn't understand him, and they wouldn't wait for someone to interpret. Ever in a hurry to enforce law and order—for law and order never have time to spare—they choked him to death in front of a disinterested choir of healthy grand latte guzzlers. His name was Ismet; he had been in a Serbian camp, snapped after the war; Rora knew his sister.

Lazarus came to Chicago as a refugee, a pogrom survivor. He must have seen horrible things; he may have snapped. Was he angry when he went to Shippy's house? Did he want to tell him something? He was fourteen in 1903, at the time of the pogrom. Did he remember it in Chicago? Was he a survivor who resurrected in America? Did he have nightmares about it? Did he read books that promised better, new worlds? I speculated and rambled; Rora was sipping his fifth espresso. Out of the blue I suggested that we drive down to

Maxwell Street and look at the places where Lazarus had once lived, perhaps he would want to take some pictures. Why not, Rora said. Rora made his decisions quickly, without hesitation.

We crossed erected bridges on our way to Maxwell Street, passed arbitrary stop signs, drove by ghastly warehouses that were to be converted into ghastly lofts; we followed a Peoples Energy truck into Chicago's New Great Neighborhood, where the ghetto once stood. Nothing from the days of Lazarus survived. Among glassy buildings and condemned church spires, there were colossal crane skeletons. Money castles rose over the space where the Maxwell Street Market used to be, where in Lazarus's times peddlers had peddled and liquefied rot had clotted in the gutters, where the streets used to teem with people and gossip used to spread like flu. Here children had grown up; here families had lived on different floors of the same tenement, sorted by generations, yet often dying out of order—children first, grandparents last. Here the English language taught by charitable churchgoing American ladies had been transformed by their students into a sonorous mess of Old World inflections. Here lunatics, alongside socialists and anarchists, had stood on the corners in wait for various messiahs, all ranting about the fast-approaching better future. Here it was now, the future, it had arrived; here was the vacuum of profitable progress; here it was. We drove down Roosevelt, the former 12th Street. Here Lazarus used to lodge in a cramped tenement house with his sister, Olga. Now there were vacuous junk-littered parking lots, portable shit-booths, and dispirited weeds. Past Ashland, just before the spanking-new Cook County Jail, meaningless fences and condemned houses clustered; in front of the only two uncondemned houses, two thoroughly rusted cars were parked. On the eastern horizon, the dark beacon of the Sears Tower loomed. We didn't even stop the car; we drove through the debris of the present without touching it, no pictures taken, no film exposed.

Do you know the joke, Rora said, where Mujo goes to America, settles there, and then starts inviting Suljo to come, too? But Suljo's reluctant. He doesn't want to leave his *kafana*, his friends, his daily routines. Mujo is persistent, writes to him all the time. Come, he says, it's all milk and honey here. Suljo writes back and says, That's all well and nice, but I like my life in Bosnia; I don't have to work much; I have plenty of time to drink coffee, read newspapers, take walks, whatever I want whenever I want it. In America, I would have to slave all the time. I am good here, Suljo says. You wouldn't have to work much here, Mujo writes. The streets are lined with money, all you have to do is bend over and pick it up. All right then, Suljo says, I'm coming. So he comes to America, Mujo shows him his house, they eat, drink coffee, talk about the old times, and Suljo says, I am going out for a walk to see a little bit of your America. He goes out for a walk, comes back. Mujo asks him, How was it? Well, Suljo says, you were telling the truth. I was walking down the street and there was a sack full of money, it looked like at least a million dollars. A million dollars? Mujo's flabbergasted. Did you pick it up? Did you? he asks him.

Of course I did not, Suljo says. You don't expect me to work on my first day here.

WE WENT UP NORTH THEN, to Lincoln Park, to Chief Shippy's former neighborhood. The rich still lived there, but the address where Shippy's house used to be was no longer in existence. Ludwig's store was long gone, too, as was the Halsted Street streetcar line which took Lazarus to Lincoln Park. The streets were now named after German poets, presently not widely read in the neighborhood; old ladies with blown-dry remnants of hair walked toy dogs; slim blondes strode in pursuit of physiological happiness. There was no particle of the Lazarus story to be photographed, nothing, and Rora took no pictures. So many things had vanished that it was impossible to know what was missing. Girls in heavenly-blue and sun-yellow shirts were playing soccer on the Parker High School field. We parked the car and watched them.

You should go back where he came from, Rora said. There is always a before and an after.

The tallest girl on the blue team leapt and scored a goal with her head; her teammates huddled around her for a while, then scattered around the field to their original positions. She might remember the goal she scored on this cold day for many years, I imagined. She might be able to recall all the lilting names of the huddle girls: Jennifer and Jan and Gloria and Zoe. But there would always be the one whose name she could not remember; and she would call Jennifer and Jan and Gloria and Zoe, twenty years from now, and ask them about the name of the sweet, scrawny girl with bony knees and hopeless braces who played at the fullback position. No one would ever remember: Jan would think that her name could be Candy, Zoe would corroborate it, but Jennifer and Gloria would strenuously disagree. Every once in a while, she would see someone on the street who would remind her of the hypothetical Candy. She would never approach the scrawny woman; she would never see her again, never remember her true name, but she would never forget Candy.

Rora was right: I needed to follow Lazarus all the way back to the pogrom in Kishinev, to the time before America. I needed to reimagine what I could not retrieve; I needed to see what I could not imagine. I needed to step outside my life in Chicago and spend time deep in the wilderness of elsewhere. But that method of writing a book would be entirely different from what Mary had expected, or what I had planned to do, with or without the Susie grant. Mary would not like me going away, particularly because she had suggested that it would do us good—especially her—to go on a vacation; possible dates had floated on the surface of our dinner conversations, then sunk into the after-dinner stupor. And I certainly didn't want to beg her for money, again, and go through the whole debasing process of proving that my plans, hopes, dreams are not overly indulgent. I realized that I had fantasized myself into a corner with the Susie grant. Everything depended on it all of a sudden though there was no reason to believe that it could work out, even if I had spent some sleepless nights rewriting it to dubious perfection. Many times, I had called the offices of the Glory Foundation—instead of calling Susie, as I had initially planned—to ask when the decision might be made, and every time I called it was clearer to me that my chances were slim.

All I conceded to Rora, however, was that now would not be a good time for me to go. It would be too expensive, I would like Mary to come with me, and she could take no time off. I don't think I should go, I said. I had plenty more research to do in the libraries, many more books to read about Lazarus and anarchists and the sumptuous palette of American fears. Maybe in two, three years, there was no rush; nobody was waiting for my book to arrive. The world would be exactly the same with my book as it was without it. Rora did not argue; I drove him home. The Lake Shore high-rises cast long, mawkish shadows into the oncoming waves; he said nothing.

He produced a particular kind of silence: it was not heavy, not accusing, not demanding. I imagined that was the same kind of silence as when he waited for a picture to appear on the photographic paper sunk in emulsion. I was learning that I liked such silence, as I liked his sounds and stories. And from such silence an improbable memory emerged: he and I in kindergarten; we are straddling our enchanted pillows, our brawny mustangs; we are Indians, chased by cowboys, riding west. All the other kids are asleep, curled into backbreaking shapes, their mouths angelically agape. We spur our downy beasts on toward the painted sunset on the dormitory door, behind which our careless caretakers are smoking, sipping coffee, and gossiping.

There are moments in life when it is all turned inside out—what is real becomes unreal, what is unreal becomes tangible, and all your levelheaded efforts to keep a tight ontological control are rendered silly and indulgent. Imagine Candy showing up at your door and she is nothing like what you remember; she is angry because you could not remember her, although you were asking around about her. You wonder how she got here, how you reached this uncanny moment; you realize you have no idea who she is but she is as familiar to you as your own soul. You cannot comprehend her journey to your door because it is not a story she or anybody can tell but a nightmare of random events. I had no reason to believe that Rora and I shared any early-childhood experience; for all intents and purposes, I might have been remembering a dream. That was beside the point: I recognized the false memory as something that bound us now, and I understood that not only did I have to find a way to go to Kishinev as soon as possible, but that Rora had to come along. It seemed to me that if he didn't come along I would never see him again, and I needed him around, for his silence, for his stories, for his camera.

All night I tossed and turned, racing and stumbling through thoughts and dreams, replaying and revising my many-times-imagined schmooze-lunch with Susie, occasionally becoming conscious enough to listen to Mary's breathing. She threw her arm across my chest once, asked me if everything was all right. It was, I said. Her arm lay heavy on me for a long time and I could not breathe but I did nothing about it. Ismet and Lazarus and Rora, and ducks and mosques and Jesus and Susie and the runner with the lemon in his mouth, and Shippy and Bush and the crazy with the UNITED WE STAND sticker on his forehead—they all left their somnial traces in my feverish mind. As it dawned, I began rehearsing my ultimate speech to Susie: I decided to drop the charming shtick and level with her, to tell her that I needed the grant money desperately; in my dizzy head I tabulated the expenses of the now-imperative journey to Kishinev, all the things the writing of the book required, how I would always be grateful for her support. I had not informed Mary about the Susie grant, for I did not want her to know that I failed, if I failed, but before I fell asleep again, I decided that telling her everything would somehow make the grant approval more likely.

And at the breakfast table, as I was telling her that I wanted to go to Eastern Europe to sort out what I wanted to do with Lazarus, to figure out how to do it, Mary was called away to take a bullet out of someone's brain. When Mary left for the hospital, I sat paralyzed with despair in the living room, the Schuettlers' number on a piece of paper in my hand, until I inhaled deeply, dialed the number, and closed my eyes as their phone was ringing. Bill picked up the phone; it took a few degrading repetitions before he could hear my name properly. Once he did, I introduced myself and asked for Susie; she was not in; she was with her book club; she would be back in the afternoon. I said I would call later and was about to hang up, when he exclaimed: "Brik! Yes! You are Vladimir Brik! Of course! We were just talking about you at the board meeting yesterday," whereupon he told me that they had approved my grant proposal unanimously and that someone would be calling me today to deliver the news. I actually said, "I love you!" to him, which, I am happy to say, he completely ignored.

After I hung up, I sat down on the floor and spent a considerable amount of time rubbing my sweaty palms against my pajamas. Thick apprehension descended upon me, for now it was clear, there was no way back, no excuses, no escape from writing the book. I could not think of what I was going to do, and I was frighteningly alone with it. I sat there, waiting for the molasses of fear to thin out so I could call Mary and share the happy news. But instead, without thinking, I called Rora and told him I might go to Ukraine and Moldova to do some more research on Lazarus. I was just granted funds for my Lazarus project and I could use the money for the trip. I would love it if he came along with me. I would pay for his ticket and expenses. He could take photos. I didn't know how he would use them, but I could put some of them in my book when I wrote it. And I said, to my own surprise, we could maybe go to Sarajevo, too, see what's happening at home.

Why not, he said. I've got nothing else to do.

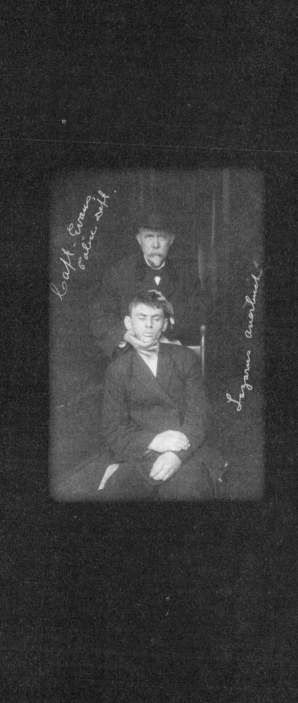

Capt. Evans
Police Dept.

Suzanne Overbeck.

Meanwhile, Assistant Chief Schuettler's best men, Detectives Fitzgerald and Fitzpatrick—known all over town as the Fitzes—canvass the neighborhood around Lincoln Place. Soon they learn that an *outlandish* young man ran into the Nicholas Brothers real estate office, a block away from Chief Shippy's residence, and inquired with a clerk there what had happened at Chief Shippy's and whether the gunman was known. The *outlandish* stranger was five feet eight inches tall; twenty-three or so years old; weighing about 145 pounds. He had a flat forehead and alien hair; he wore a black overcoat of the kind that anarchists favor. The man was, *without a doubt,* a foreigner.

That same afternoon, *the assassin* is identified by Gregor Heller, a fellow employee at the South Water Street Commission House, where they both worked as egg packers for W. H. Eichgreen, a commission merchant. Heller had noticed his absence from work and once he heard about the terrible crime, he went straight to the police. He positively identifies the body as belonging to Lazarus Averbuch. Heller is also able to provide the address of Averbuch's residence: 218 Washburn Avenue, a second-story flat. Although there is no reward promised, Assistant Chief Schuettler assures

Heller that he can reasonably expect a few dollars from Chief Shippy himself for helping to crush the snake's head. Heller walks back home, already spending the money in his head: a scarf for Mary, new socks for himself.

The Fitzes, with William P. Miller *exclusively* in tow, break into the second-story room at 218 Washburn and seize a curly-haired foreigner, who confesses instantly that his name is Isaac Lubel. But they need and demand more than that, so Fitzgerald begins interrogating him *vigorously*, throwing him to the floor, pounding the man in the face, kneeing him in the kidneys, roaring at him all along, which frightens Lubel's wife *nearly into hysterics* and sends their children into *convulsions of screams*. Between the punches and kicks, through his bloody teeth, Lubel manages to tell them that the Averbuchs live across the hallway.

Fitzpatrick flings the door across the hallway open and startles a woman setting the table for supper. With a plate in each hand, as if about to juggle them, she identifies herself as Olga Averbuch. "What is Lazarus Averbuch to you?" Fitzpatrick asks. "My brother," she says, her voice trembling, the left plate sliding out of her grip and smashing against the floor. "Lazarus is my brother. What he do?" Fitzpatrick sucks at his teeth and says nothing. Through the open door she can see Lubel curled up on the floor, a finger-shaped trail of blood coming down his neck. Fitzgerald shakes his head as if to suggest that the problem is too complicated to explain. "What he do?" she asks again. "You've got nothing to worry about," Fitzgerald says. "We shall sort it all out."

The place is furnished with only *the bare necessities*. The kitchen contains *a stove with a moribund fire and a small kitchen cabinet: an odd cup, a solitary pot, a tiny, slender vase*. On the table there are cold leftovers of a meat dish, a hardened loaf of rye bread, and a pot of coffee—Fitzgerald takes a sip, then spits it out; Fitzpatrick smashes the vase against the floor. The bedroom has a small table with a *cheap* violet-blue covering, two *common* chairs, a bed and a narrow cot, a *well-oiled* sewing machine, a mirror and a washbasin, and a wardrobe with a litter of clothing reeking of naphthalene and the stove smoke. *The only article of tawdry finery Olga Averbuch possessed,* William P. Miller will write, *is an old a purple velvet skirt.*

The detectives ransack the place *with the passion of soldiers fighting a just war.* The plate in her hands, Olga watches them impassively. They dig up things from under the bed: books, bundles of rags, and a cardboard suitcase from which they shake out a manuscript and a batch of letters in Russian; they confiscate it all. They flip through the *subversive books*; Fitzpatrick reads the titles aloud: *The Story of a Bad King, In the Land of the Free, Saving Your Mind and Body, What the Constitution Teaches,* etc.

"Never met a kike before who could read English," Fitzgerald says.

The Fitzes load all the confiscated books, along with Olga, into the car. Fitzgerald drives to the central police station, while Fitzpatrick and Miller cheerfully take a streetcar. They discuss baseball and observe the passengers, Miller fertilizing their acquaintance with casual flattering, hoping he can harvest a scoop. By the time the two get to the station, Assistant Chief Schuettler is already interrogating Olga with the help of Fitzgerald, who keeps smoking, his sleeves rolled. She occasionally coughs, politely putting her small hand over her mouth. "We already know everything," Assistant Chief tells her, "so feel free to tell us everything." Olga implores him to let her speak to her brother, and Assistant Chief promises that she will see him later. "Everything will be sorted out. We all have our common interests in mind." Olga is convinced that, whatever it may be, it is all a regrettable mistake, and that if she answers the questions sincerely everything will be cleared up. Fitzgerald's forearms are hairy—the hair stretches outward, even on his knuckles, as if he combed it.

Schuettler lets Olga talk—he appreciates babbling suspects—interrupting her occasionally, carefully, with a reasonable question. Miller speedily takes notes, hunched over his notebook in the corner, still sucking this morning's cigar. This is good stuff.

She claims Lazarus is a good boy, always kind to everybody.

She can speak four languages, but her brother can speak all these and French and Polish besides. He studied English at a night school at 12th Street and Jefferson.

English, Yiddish, German, Russian.

He has never mentioned Chief Shippy's name in her presence. She's never heard him talk about anarchism.

Many of their friends are curly-haired.

Their father was a merchant in Kishinev, Russia. She insists he was not a revolutionary nor did he belong to any secret society. He was a religious man.

They survived the Easter pogrom in Kishinev, in 1903.

There was another one in 1905.

She is convinced there will be many more. It is a custom there to kill Jews.

They were the only Jewish family in four blocks. Their neighbors gathered outside their house and yelled: "Kill the Yids!" They banged and threw stones through the windows. There were policemen among them. They beat them, broke Father's ribs. He nearly died. He died later.

Schuettler looks at Miller, who looks at Fitzgerald, who looks at Fitzpatrick. "Policemen," Schuettler says. Olga looks at her wringing hands.

Bitter tears are streaming down the Jewess's cheeks, William P. Miller writes, and underlines *bitter tears,* twice.

"Take her to see her brother," Schuettler orders.

The Fitzes escort Olga to Bentley's morgue. Miller and Hammond, a *Tribune* photographer Miller urgently summoned, scurry behind them. They walk down the street from the police station, she between the Fitzes, asking every few steps: "Where is he? Where is it we going?" "He is in a better place," Fitzpatrick says, and Fitzgerald chuckles. The walls in the morose rooms are adorned with solemn paintings: a mother praying over the body of her son; a family of four having dinner at a table, the fifth chair empty; a dark forest at sunset. The news has already spread around town, and hundreds have come by to view Lazarus's body that afternoon. Many are still there: common citizens with their hats pushed high on their heads, scruffy idlers and pomaded socialites, weeping churchwomen, off-duty firemen and mail carriers with bags full of undelivered mail, policemen of every rank, some of whom have angrily struck the body or spat on it; several citizens bribed Georgie, the lame morgue attendant, to take a look at the Jew's member; a demented woman had to be escorted out because she claimed the corpse opened his eyes and looked at her. Now the onlookers stand lined up in the long morgue hall, anticipating Olga's shock and pain, watching her with gloating curiosity. Oblivious to the surroundings, she walks slowly. She moves quietly between the detectives, her dress too sweat-damp to rustle. It is only when they open the door of the room that she begins to hold back. Men are gathered around the chair where Lazarus sits, and she is relieved to see he is alive. She sighs and grips Fitzpatrick's forearm. But one of the men is holding Lazarus's head; her brother's eyes are closed, his face ashen; her heart stops, frozen. Fitzgerald urges her on; Fitzpatrick says, as if delivering a punch line: "Happy to see him? Give him a kiss . . ." The crowd titters, transfixed by Olga stepping toward Lazarus, as if she were mounted on cothurni: a short, reluctant step back, then two awkward steps forward to touch his lifeless cheek, whereupon she collapses, unconscious. The crowd gasps.

The Fitzes carry her to the side door opening into the alley, where they unbutton her dress and allow her to breathe the cold air. The detectives smoke, while Miller monitors Olga's feelings, as well as her chest. "That must've been a big surprise for you, girlie," Fitzpatrick says. They hear the booms of the photographer's flash inside.

THE MARCH 3 morning edition of the *Chicago Tribune* is led by William P. Miller's story. *The terrible deed of yesterday morning,* he writes, *was planned and carried out to death by a dreamlike Jewish boy whose mind was distorted with the inflammatory ideas of remedying social conditions and so-called injustices, promulgated by Emma Goldman and other leaders of "liberal thought" in America. The condition of his mind is further revealed by the fact that last week Lazarus Averbuch planned to commit suicide with another young Jew, one who is identified only as the "curly-haired man" and is thought by police to have helped in the murder attempt upon Chief Shippy. Assistant Chief Schuettler declined to name the suspect, but from sources intimate with the investigation, the* TRIBUNE *has learned that his name is Isador Maron.*

Indeed, the police cast a wide net in their hunt for the curly-haired man.

Bruno Schultz, a bartender at the H. Schnell Saloon, 222 Lincoln Avenue, identifies the assassin as a man who had visited the saloon on a number of occasions in the past three weeks, several times accompanied by a curly-haired man.

Several men of Russian Jewish type—at least one of them curly-haired—visited the Von Lengerke & Antoine sporting goods store, 277 Wabash Avenue, last Saturday afternoon. They wanted to buy revolvers, Von Lengerke tells the police. But being of apparent anarchistic type and demeanor, no encouragement was given to them, and they left the store in a rage.

Another curly-haired suspect was arrested at 573 12th Street, a couple of blocks away from Averbuch's home. The suspect gave the name of Edward Kaplan. Neighbors said he had been at home all day and had acted in a particularly nervous way, seemingly expecting something. The arrest was made after a detective overheard the message given to Kaplan over a crossed telephone wire. ("The jig is up," someone said. "Get out of town.")

Joseph Freedman, despite being rather bald, was arrested on a Halsted streetcar for anarchist talk, at the request of several patriotic passengers. A policeman happened to be on the same car and managed to stop the crowd from indulging their rage with a lynching of the suspect.

Harry Goldstein was arrested in the ghetto on information furnished by the White Hand Society, an organization of patriotic Americans formed to combat anarchism. G. G. Revisano, a lawyer representing the Society, submitted to Assistant Chief Schuettler a long list of sundry Chicago anarchists, compiled by the Society.

Anton Stadlwelser (scant blond hair) was arrested at home. The detectives seized a loaded revolver, $136, a silver watch, forty two-cent stamps, twenty one-cent stamps, a stuffed parrot, a small jar with a lizard preserved in liquid, a Confederate one-hundred-dollar bill, four Colombian 1902 half-dollars. Stadlwelser was unable to explain how he came into possession of such items and is to be detained indefinitely on various suspicions.

The conspicuously curly-haired Isador Maron is sought by the Fitzes. He is said to have been prowling about the Averbuch house, *possibly oblivious to the tragic end of his fellow anarchist.* Out of Isaac Lubel the detectives beat another confession; yes, Isaac coughs it out along with clots of blood, he has seen Maron knocking on Olga Averbuch's door, but not in the past couple of days. The Fitzes talk to the Maxwell Street peddlers, to the whores and thieves, to the agitators and ranters; they spread the word among their ghetto informants that Maron is not only a dangerous anarchist but a homosexual as well, and worth at least thirty dollars to them. They visit Olga at her workplace—she is a seamstress in Goldblatt's sweatshop and cannot afford to miss a day's work—and tell her, so everyone can hear, that if Maron comes by she must instantly inform them. "And this before any necking or fucking," Fitzpatrick says. After they leave, Mr. Goldblatt calls Olga over to his office, gives her some money, and suggests that she stay at home for a while, at least until the affair blows over. Things, he says, will get better.

She walks home through the frigid drizzle, her bones light with hunger and the sense that everything is turned inside out; her legs hurt. Why was Lazarus at Shippy's house? Isador took him to those anarchist meetings, but she thought it was all just angry talk— young men like angry talk. He could not have become part of some crazy conspiracy. He was always prone to fantasies, always with one foot in some other world, but he would never do anything about it; he was a dreamer. She did not listen to him when he told her about his ideas, thoughts, fears, stories he was planning to write; she was always too tired. He had no anger, no violence in him. He would never hurt anybody. She used to go look for him in the evenings. She would shout his name, until he hollered back from the woods or the back alley, wherever he was waiting for her to come and get him—he did not see well at dusk. He was a child when she left him behind, he wasted his boyhood in a refugee camp in Czernowitz, he landed in Chicago as a young man. How did she miss it all? When was it that she'd lost him? How did he become who he was? Who was he?

DESPITE ALL *the encouraging success, we have yet to learn about the evil among us that needs to be exterminated,* Assistant Chief Schuettler confides in William P. Miller. *It is almost impossible,* Assistant Chief says, *to pick up a man and determine whether or not he is an anarchist. We know, however, that such men are generally half-crazy individuals of foreign descent and of considerable degeneracy. We must follow them and learn their habits from the moment they reach this country so as to pre-empt their atrocities.*

There are, however, a few setbacks: the mysterious numbers 21-21-21-63 turn out to be a receipt for the purchase of three dozen eggs, twenty-one cents each, issued by South Water Street Commission House. The five sentences that Assistant Chief believed to have been coded instructions are an exercise from an English-language class at the Maxwell Street Settlement House. Indeed, Mr. Brik, a teacher there, describes Lazarus Averbuch as *a faithful and persevering student of a very good character*. The informers infiltrating various anarchist, socialist, and unpatriotic societies provide little on Averbuch or Maron: though they were spotted absorbing detrimental and degenerate ideas at various lectures and readings, they paid no dues, were not outspoken enough to be conspicuous, had no confirmable connections with the fanatics that run those conspiratorial packs. It is clear that their failed plot had well-hidden, deeper-than-usual, possibly worldwide roots.

Assistant Chief Schuettler is tireless, for the very notion of freedom is at stake. He immerses himself, with the help of a translator, in Averbuch's papers. He discovers that the manuscripts—pages and pages of passionate, clearly troubled, handwriting—contain a bloody tale, written in the first person, of domestic tragedy in Kishinev. The story begins by describing the married life of the narrator. Poor though they may be, the newlyweds are happy: flowers are blooming on the windowsills, warm kasha is on the table; they partake in frivolous fun at the county fair, go for evening walks by the river, its surface occasionally broken by a hungry carp. But the sky falls down when he returns home one day and finds his beautiful wife in bed with a wealthy young doctor. As they beg him for mercy, the husband shoots his wife and the doctor dead. On the run from the law, he crosses borders, moves from country to country under false names, until he boards a ship to America—and the manuscript ends before he reaches these shores. To Assistant Chief's mind, the narrative has all the earmarks of a confession of a double crime committed in Russia, exhibiting Averbuch's cunning, murderous proclivities and foreshadowing a life of anarchism and crime in Chicago.

The letters are mostly from his mother, whose handwriting is terse and flattened, the blank space between lines carrying immense weight. *I look at the pictures of you, my son, and remember how good-natured you were as a boy. Don't despair,* she writes, *but be brave and work hard. Know that we think of Olga and you, ceaselessly.* Mother's letters are rife with indications that Lazarus had spoken about America in bitter tones. He seems to have found the circumstances in Chicago almost as bad as in Russia, his hopes betrayed. His disappointment and murderous anger, Assistant Chief observes, are almost palpable.

He sends the Fitzes to fetch Olga Averbuch once again. William P. Miller bears witness to Assistant Chief Schuettler prodding Olga about the men under arrest as they are paraded in front of her. She sobs without pause, occasionally forced by Assistant Chief's yell to look up; he does not let her use her handkerchief to wipe her tears; she is not allowed to fix her uncoiling hair. She does not recognize anyone, but upon firm questioning by Fitzgerald, Fitzpatrick holding her hands behind her back to bend and push her forward, she does concede that Stadlwelser looks familiar. He is taken away, professing in vain his innocence.

Olga is allowed to sit down. Assistant Chief lowers his voice and tells her, with his hand on her shoulder, his fingers just slightly pressing into her flesh, that he knows the letters from Mother Averbuch are veiled messages, that he has found traces of invisible ink between the lines.

"Lazarus is good boy," Olga says feebly.

"We know everything," Schuettler whispers in her ear, his breath spreading down her neck, as she cringes. "You cannot hide anything from us."

He lets silence and the uncertainty it implies work on her for a long moment, whereupon he demands in measured, determined utterances that she confess her brother killed his wife and a doctor in Kishinev, that he escaped from the law to America.

"But Lazarus is nineteen years," Olga cries. "He is never been married. He is never been with girl."

Schuettler circles around her like a hawk, pitilessly repeating his questions, as she keeps retorting: "Lazarus is good boy," until she slides off the chair to the floor and lies there, lifeless. William P. Miller bends over her, touches her pulse, then brushes off a tentacle of loose hair from her face so as to look at it more closely. *She is beautiful in her own Semitic way.*

BEFORE HE DISMISSES HER, Assistant Chief informs Olga that, given the likelihood of further anarchist attacks, the authorities believe her brother had best be inconspicuously disposed of in a potter's field. Olga listens to him in grievous disbelief; she begs him to allow her to bury her brother according to Jewish custom, but Schuettler tells her, his hand heavy on her knee, that forty Jewish undertakers have already refused to handle the body and no rabbi is willing to conduct the service for a murderer. "You lie," she cries. "Is not true." This is not the time, he tells her in a forgiving, avuncular voice, to doubt the benevolence of the authorities, nor is it the time to think about oneself. She ought to atone for her brother's crime by making a sacrifice for her coreligionists, who will surely benefit from the absence of fuss. And the people of Chicago will most certainly appreciate her commitment to law and order.

"Think of others, of their disrupted lives," he says. "Imagine how they might feel. This is the time for sacrifice."

It was never in my nature to take a straight path anywhere: our first stop would be Lviv, Ukraine. Lazarus had almost certainly never been there, but my paternal grandfather was born in Krotkiy, a nearby village; I remembered the stories about his childhood visits to Lviv and I wanted to spend several days in the city. Then we would hire a driver to take us south to Chernivtsi, where Lazarus had spent time in a refugee camp after the pogrom. On our way there, I thought we could stop by Krotkiy. The Susie grant required no specific itinerary or activity report; I could do whatever I wanted, as long as I eventually showed them something for it. As far as Rora was concerned, it was all the same to him, we could go anyplace, do anything, we could just keep going forever. I began to wish again I could be him.

On the flight from Chicago to Frankfurt, we monitored a herd of visibly virginal young women, part of a Christian group on its way to missionary work and guilt-inflicting deflowerment some-where in the East. They sang songs of Jesus and eternal life; they clapped hands and hugged each other frequently—Rora ogled them; I habitually hated them. There were also American soldiers, presumably on their way to Iraq via a base in Germany: crew cuts,

trimmed mustaches, manly eyebrows, thick necks. They were check-
ing out the virgins, relishing their last hours before returning to a
life of manual self-abuse, trigger-happiness, and a possible limb-
by-limb entry into eternity. Rora took a picture of a row of soldiers
sleeping with their blankets over their heads. They looked like
ghosts to me, like hostages to Rora.

When the virgins succumbed to slumber and the uncovered soldiers took to beer drinking, Rora told me, in a droning whisper,
how he joined Rambo's unit. Back then Rora believed in a Bosnia
in which everybody lived together; he loved Sarajevo and wanted to
defend it from the Chetniks. He could have escaped to Milan or
Stockholm or wherever; instead he volunteered for Rambo's unit—
there was no Bosnian Army at the beginning of the war, so those
who had guns got together to protect their homestead. He knew
Rambo and Beno from Čaršija. But before they confronted the
Chetnik aggressors and bled in the battle, Rambo and Beno helped
themselves to the goodies available in the city, where law and order
had evaporated overnight. Rambo called it requisition, but it was
pillaging and pilfering. I may sometimes be a thief, Rora said, but
I am honest: I do not rob neighbors. He told me about the early
days of the war, about all the intrigues and assassinations and a few
poignant stories about the people we both knew: Aida was shot by
a Chetnik sniper; Lazo was taken away to Kazani by Caco to have
his throat slit; Mirsad had his brain taken out by a piece of shrapnel . . . But, to my eternal shame, despite my compassionate attempts to keep my eyes open, despite, even, pinching myself under
the blanket to stay awake—I fell asleep. I was subsequently simultaneously both inside and outside the dream in which the soldiers
and the virgins were shopping naked at Piggly-Wiggly, singing
Jesus nursery rhymes; then there were Aida and Lazo and Mirsad
and some other obscure people, singing in English: "Hoydee-ho,
haydee-hi, all we want is not to die."

Having slept on the flight from Frankfurt to Lviv as well, I truly woke up only once we were in Lviv, outside the airport, when the side mirror of a passing truck knocked me in the head because I stood too close to the curb. *Good morning, Mr. Writer!* said Ukraine. Rora touched my cheek and turned my head slightly to assess the damage and then shook his head. It was unclear to me at the time whether he was concerned about my injury or was savoring my clumsy stupidity.

We took a cab from the airport to the grandly misnamed Grand Hotel; I had negotiated the price of the ride in my obsolescent, grandparental Ukrainian with a little dictionary at hand. The car was an old Volga, reeking of diesel and the U.S.S.R. We progressed and then regressed through the city; it seemed that we took the same streets a few times—there could not have been three casinos with the identical neon signs in Lviv. The driver's head was cubical, vines of hair creeping up his neck; there was a gray swirl around his bald spot, not unlike a satellite picture of a hurricane. I wished Rora would photograph it, but there was not enough light. He had decided, without consulting me, not to bring a flash on this trip. The flash is for weddings and funerals, he said. What needs to be photographed will be photographed.

In 1991, the summer before I left Sarajevo, I had a place in Kovači, up the hill from Baš Čaršija. Everybody was waiting for the war to come, and almost every night I was startled out of sleep by a violent noise, by heavy rattling and revving. I would sit up, convinced that Serbian tanks were advancing upon us, my heart pounding, my first thought, *Here it is.* Once or twice, I hid under the bed. It was usually just a truck going downhill, much like everything else at the time. For the rest of the night, I would toss, as if on a barbecue grill, parsing night noises, imagining in detail all the possible and probable catastrophes.

Your nightmares follow you like a shadow, forever. Mary once turned on the dishwasher in the middle of the night—sometimes she would do things around the house after coming home late from the hospital. Something in the machine rattled and screeched, and I was halfway down the stairs before Mary caught up with me and led me back to bed. I put my head on her bosom; I could hear her heart beating, steadily, calmly, against the dishwashing cacophony; she scratched my head gently until I passed out again.

What startled me in the Grand Hotel room in Lviv was a street-car clanging by in concert with a passing bus. All fears are memories of other fears, so my first thought was, again, *Here it is.* But the streetcar passed, and the room was silent, the silence mucous. I had faded watching the ember-letters Rora wrote in the dark with his cigarette, but now he was absent. I turned on the TV and flipped through channels: images of breast-bloated women and serious-balding men; commercials that brought us happiness in the form of a detergent that made bloodstains disappear; shrill voices going through a Babel repertoire—everything was familiar and incomprehensible. I stopped flipping when I heard Madonna sing "Material Girl." At our wedding Mary and I had danced to that song, played by a mistuned, morbidly enthusiastic band. The singer on TV was a matronly woman in a curtainlike, glittery dress, awkwardly swinging her thick hips between chairs and tables, while a toreador-mustached man, all tension and sinews of an erect penis, twisted and pressed luridly against her sides. It was clear that the couple was Ukrainian, the way it is clear that it is morning in the morning. And a frightening possibility of a parallel universe presented itself to me—a universe in which there was a Ukrainian Madonna, with exactly the same voice, and exactly the same me listening to her, recalling my wedding night, while everything else was entirely, horribly, different. I watched, mesmerized, the ontological warp flickering in my face, and only with great effort did I manage to continue for another round of channel flipping. I finally realized I was watching a karaoke show when I saw Madame Madonskaya and Monsieur

Penischuk talking in Ukrainian to a puffy-haired sap who apparently revered them as stars. There's an accomplishment for you—becoming a karaoke star. I could be a karaoke star.

Rora walked out of the bathroom, glanced at the TV disinterestedly, and switched on the light: for a moment, the two narrow cots and the socialist-fifties furniture were overlit like a prison cell, until a couple of bulbs hiccupped and died; the air stank of lead-based paint and suicide. How do you get to be a karaoke star?

The karaoke show ended. I could not sleep, so we went out for a stroll. The darkness was overtaking everything, and we had no map; we simply sought the less dark streets, guided by the rare, arrhythmic streetlights. Even the lit streets seemed abandoned under the pressure of the advancing murk.

My grandfather had chicken blindness; he could see nothing in twilight, sentimental sunsets were invisible to him. Dusk often caught him out in the fields, where he went to fetch the cows and bring them back home. A crew of his grandchildren would be dispatched on a search mission, and we would find him staring into a darkness visible only to him. One of us would grasp his hand and take him home, while the rest led the cows dropping a trail of fresh turd behind them, as though planning to return to the same sweet pastures tomorrow.

He eventually became completely blind. He had always been a slow man, but after he had sunk into the aquarium of darkness, he became even slower; now time flowed differently for him. We would take him for a walk to the hives, where he sat listening to the tranquilizing buzz of working bees. That was a distance of fifty yards or so from the house, but it took him forever. He put one foot an inch in front of the other, not lifting it, shuffling through dirt and grass and chicken shit. Shortly before he died, he would not even leave the house—we would take him to the front door, his legs and limbs so weak and tired that the threshold was much too high. He would stand there, facing the vast landscape of nothingness.

After he lost his sight, he became entirely removed from the present: he could not remember our names, did not know us as his grandchildren. We became the Briks he had left behind in Ukraine to come to Bosnia in 1908: Romans and Ivans and Mykolas and Zosyas. He would talk to us, ask us questions we had to make up answers for (Did Ivan shake the bee swarm off the apple tree? Has Zosya fed the ducks?). Sometimes, he would snap out of his death-rehearsal slumber and yelp: "Why did you leave me in the woods?" It was very funny—nothing is as funny to kids as adult discom-bobulation—and then we would have to walk him around the kitchen, inch by inch, then return him to the sofa on which he was spending his final years. The circuit around the kitchen was his journey home. Once I took him for a kitchen walk, to the cupboard and back, a total of three yards that took us an eternity to cover. And suddenly we were in Lviv, he was nine, I was his father, we had gone to church, and now he wanted after-church rose candy as promised. When I said I couldn't give it to him, my grandfather cried like a child. I returned him to the sofa, he turned toward the wall, prayed, and wept, until he fell asleep.

So, here I was in Lviv again. We should look for some candy, I said to Rora.

In Sarajevo under siege, Rora said, there was no electricity for months. When it came back, all the lights not turned off weeks ago would go on, all the radios and TV sets would start blasting, build-ings would light up, coming awake. You could see the city in a different light, flashing out the weirdness of war: burnt cars like crushed cockroaches in the streets, dogs trotting away toward the safety of the shadow, couples making love in the darkness, sud-denly recognizing the haggardness of their bodies. But after a few minutes the frail electrical system would collapse, and the darkness returned. It was for the better, for if the lights stayed on, our friends from the hills could pound us and kill us at night as well, picking out all the lit targets, Rora said. We dreamt of light, but hoped for darkness.

Have you ever seen a fleet of tracer bullets in the night? he asked me.

No, I said.

It's a beautiful sight.

Early in the war, Rambo's unit would go to requisition whatever was left in the stores. They went out at night, the truck's headlights extinguished, smoking strictly prohibited. We were cleaning out a shoe store in Marin-dvor one night—I'll remember it for the rest of my life, Rora said. We carried out boxes of goods: high-heel shoes, children's sneakers, steel-toe boots, sandals, anything. I got a pair of stiletto-heel boots for my sister, but she never wore them. Rambo stood with the silver gun glintless in his hand, his adjutants' rifles pointed up at the windows of the buildings around, in case some unwise witness-wannabe peeked from behind the curtain. There were no lights in those homes and the curtains blacked out the windows, so when some concerned citizen spread his curtain apart, Rora could see, from a hundred yards away, the white of his eye sparkling. Rambo would shoot at it and the eye would disappear. What does not need to be seen will not be seen.

I CALLED MARY from Lviv the next day, after some aimless morning ambling. It was early in Chicago, but she was not home; I had visions of a telegenic doctor amusing her with medical double entendres; it took a few tries before she answered her cell phone. She had just finished a surgery; it was hot as hell in Chicago; she was going to Pittsburgh for the weekend. George and Rachel were going to Rome in a couple of weeks, she said; they had never been out of the country, but Rome was Mom's dream. Dad agreed to go, because Mom had always wanted to see all the churches and pray with the

Pope. Dad was worried about the fact that he couldn't speak Italian, and he was worried about the Europeans. (I was the only European George the Dad knew, the obvious implication being that if all other Europeans were like me, there was reason to be worried.) Mary missed me; the hot summer made her pissy; she was working a lot; she was thinking about taking a long leave of absence when I came back. How was the Lazarus thing going? She was not happy I was away, I could hear it in her voice. "It's going well," I said. "I'm making a lot of mental notes." "Great," she said. "I'm so happy for you." I told her Lviv was depressing; I told her about the natives not using deodorant, the women not shaving their legs, which ought to have discouraged her possible jealousy. I told her about the darkness, the filthy streets, and the Soviet architecture; about the slapdash currency-exchange booths attended by sweat-shirted goons laundering money by hand; about the decrepit man in Cossack attire, with an acrid, corpsy smell, selling fresh-off-the-press copies of *The Protocols of the Elders of Zion*. I told her about the weak water pressure in the hotel and how hard it was to take a shower. I listed enough grievances to make her feel that I was working hard, that the trip was nothing if not challenging. We ended the conversation loving each other.

It seemed that we loved each other better when there were large swaths of two continents and an ocean between us. The daily work of love was often hard to perform at home. While she was in the hospital, I longed for her, and when she came back, she was too tired to attend to my needs and desires. I would get into complaining about her coldness and distance, about our marriage requiring more than reading the newspaper together on Sunday mornings. She was tired, she would say, because she worked a lot; someone had to earn some money. I would reassert that I wanted to write and was preparing to do so, and I would list all the things I had gone through in my life, all of my contributions to our marital unit. Every once in a while, we would find ourselves screaming into each other's face, whereupon I would start furiously breaking things—I had been especially attracted to vases, for they flew well and shattered nicely.

One morning in Chicago I had tiptoed to the kitchen with the intention of making some coffee. While customarily spilling coffee grounds all over the counter, I spotted a can in the corner whose red label read SADNESS. Was there so much of it they could can it and sell it? A bolt of pain went through my intestines before I realized that it was not SADNESS but SARDINES. It was too late for recovery, for sadness was now the dark matter in the universe of still objects around me: the salt and pepper shakers; the honey jar; the bag of sun-dried tomatoes; the blunt knife; a desiccated loaf of bread; the two coffee cups, waiting. My country's main exports are stolen cars and sadness.

When I stepped out of the post office from which I called Mary, sadness seemed spread wide and thick all over Lviv: a couple of boys were washing a white Lada in the middle of the street; a man wearing an obsolete Red Army hat stood over a blanket stretched on the pavement on which the complete works of Charles Dickens were spread out; a Darth Vader–like Orthodox priest glided along the street, his feet invisible under the long black robe. The buildings with the high Austro-Hungarian windows and reserved ornaments were begrimed with a thick layer of despair.

And I could see then that Lazarus griped to Olga about the meaninglessness of his egg-packing job, and she implored him to be patient, begged him not to write to Mother about it and worry her with his disappointments. But he was sick of living in the ghetto, exhausted by the cold in Chicago. People here snarl and frown a lot, he wrote; he had seen neither a smile nor the sun in months. What is life without beauty, love, and justice? Be patient, his mother wrote him back, it is just the beginning, think about the good things ahead of you. Many people want to go to America; you are lucky, you and Olga are together, you have a job. He wrote back about the crowded streetcars, about the Chicago beyond the ghetto, where streets were lined with gold, about his friend Isador, who was smart and funny. He worried about his mother's health, her heart, her varicose legs; he was saving money to buy her good shoes. Do not stand on your feet for too long, Mother. And do not be oversad, for you must take care of your heart. Olga and I need your heart. I want to rest my head on your chest and hear your heart beating.

In a park by a church, kids in holey canvas shoes played soccer with a deflated ball, the smallest one in a shirt with *Shevchenko* stamped on its back. A cluster of old men convened around a bench, watching a chess game. I wondered what happened to Lazarus's mother after his death. Olga probably wrote her a letter, the letter must have traveled for months, the letter that said Lazarus was no more. As it traveled, Lazarus was still alive for her: she worried about his working so hard, about him walking out in the cold with his hair wet, about his congenital sadness. She hoped he would marry a nice Jewish girl; she had a feeling Isador was a ruffian. Then she got the letter from Olga and read it and reread it, arguing against it, thinking up misunderstandings that could be undone so he could be restored to life. She asked Olga for his picture, demanding of her that she deny the words of the previous letter, still talking about Lazarus as though he were alive. Oh yes, he got a job as reporter for the *Hebrew Voice,* she would say to Madame Bronstein. And his boss thinks he has a great future ahead. She probably did not live long after Lazarus, her heart finally giving out.

And did the biblical Lazarus have a mother? What did she do when he was resurrected? Did he bid her good-bye before he returned to his undeath? Was he the same son to her undead as he was alive? I read that he sailed to Marseilles with his sisters afterward, where he may or may not have died again.

A crowd disembarked from a streetcar at the Rinok stop; I followed three young women who linked their arms and walked across the square in unison, toward a place that called itself Viennese Café, toward Rora, who was there refueling on espressos and cigarettes while waiting for me. I let the three graces get ahead; I stopped to listen to a group of singing pensioners who stood in the middle of the Rinok, belting out an old Ukrainian song: squat old ladies clutched their grocery bags; old men, their pants short enough to expose the disarming combination of brown socks and sandals, entangled their hands on their rotund bellies and looked up when reaching for the high notes. From what I could understand, the song was about a wounded Cossack who was nursed to health by a young lassie, but then cruelly left her once he could ride again; he quickly forgot her, but she never forgot him. Hear my sorrow across the steppe, the pensioners sang. Hear my sorrow, may it break your Cossack heart.

I did not want to tell Rora about my conversation with Mary; I wordlessly joined him at the table. The three graces were holding their cigarettes in an identical manner: their palms facing upward, the cigarettes downward, the fingers slightly bent, the smoke crawling around their long painted nails. Rora took a picture of them, and the click made the blondest one turn toward us, her face pale, her cheeks rouged—she smiled, and Rora smiled back. The waitress came in her fake-lace-hemmed white apron and black skirt and I asked her if they had any rose candy. She did not know what it was, what I meant by it, and my Ukrainian was not good enough to explain, the dictionary forgotten in the hotel room. A Viennese coffee, then, I said. And one more for him.

Rora put his black Canon down in his lap, then under the table. He snapped a picture of the graces' legs, covering the click with a false cough.

Why did you take that picture?

That's a stupid question, Rora said. I take pictures.

Why do you take pictures?

I take pictures because I like to look at the pictures I take.

It seems to me that when people take a picture of something, they instantly forget about it.

So what?

So nothing, I shrugged.

They can look at the picture and remind themselves.

But what do you see when you look at a picture you took?

I see the picture, Rora said. What's with these questions?

When I look at my old pictures, all I can see is what I used to be but am no longer. I think: What I can see is what I am not.

Drink more coffee, Brik, Rora said. It will pick you up.

The waitress came by with our coffees, so I drank more of it. Each of the three graces looked at us at least once and Rora smiled each time.

Do you know the Lazarus story from the Bible? I asked Rora.

Can't say that I studied that particular section, Rora said.

Well, Lazarus is dead and his sister is friends with a certain Jesus Christ, the local prophet and miracle worker, so she asks him to do something about it. So Mr. Christ does his gimmick, goes to the cave where the dead Lazarus is stashed away. He calls him forth and Lazarus rises from his death. Then he totters back into life and vanishes. And Mr. Christ becomes even more famous.

That's not much of a story.

It is rather weak, I agree. But Lazarus went to Marseilles with his sisters afterward. Now that's a story. I wonder if he had a new life there. Perhaps he never died again. He might still be around, still undead, entirely forgotten, except for being the white rabbit in Mr. Christ's magic show.

What the fuck are you talking about? Rora said. How is that related to anything?

I have been thinking about the Lazarus stuff.

Stop thinking, Rora said. Have some coffee.

We sipped coffee in silence. Hear my sorrow, may it break your fucking heart, I hummed to myself. But I could not be quiet.

I talked to Mary, I said.

That's nice.

My in-laws want to go to Rome and hang out with the Pope.

Nice, Rora said. I could tell he wanted me to shut up, but I went on. It could well be that I had already ingested too much coffee.

My in-laws are very religious, I said. I had to get married in a Catholic church. I refused to do it, but Mary would not hear about it. I knelt under a cross, the priest sprinkled me with water.

Not only did I kneel before the nailed gymnast, but the Fields, the biggest Catholics in goddamn Pittsburgh, made me bow my head many a time, whereby I pretended to contemplate the frightening evanescence of my earthly existence. I remember the first Christmas we spent at the Fields'; Mary and I had just been married and I officially inducted into the family, Mary's love vouchsafing me despite my unreliable foreign background. We sat at a round table, and the Fields uttered their grace and then passed, counterclockwise, the ham and the gravy and the mashed potato. I accepted it all and then passed it on. It brought tears to my eyes, that circle of familiarity. So I bowed my head at every subsequent Christmas, for back then it all seemed worth a little pretending. Mary and I, George and Mrs. Field, sometimes the Pattersons would be there; they read from the Bible, while I, bookless, patiently counted the ham slices, admired their even thinness. And later I would join the effortless dessert talk, no issue ever pressing, complimenting the apple pie ("Rachel, this apple pie alone was worth coming to America!" I would cry, everybody earnestly laughing). Mary and I would hold hands between our plates, I would make statements featuring the first-person plural ("We like to keep our book on our chest when we read in bed"), and endure teasing questions about possible babies. After dinner we would take long walks, discussing

matters of little importance at a slow pace, the cold gnawing at our
cheekbones. George would sometimes make me lag behind so he
could ask me trick questions pertaining to my financial instability,
but Mary would save me from his scrupulous grip. Yet, I often felt
at home; there was comfort in those rituals.

So you are Catholic? Didn't know that.

I am nothing, I said. God knows God is no friend of mine. But
I envy people who believe in that crap. They don't worry about the
meaning of life and things, whereas I do.

Let me tell you a joke, Rora said.

Mujo wakes up one day, after a long night of drinking, and asks
himself what the meaning of life is. He goes to work, but realizes
that is not what life is or should be. He decides to read some phi-
losophy and for years studies everything from the old Greeks on-
ward, but can't find the meaning of life. Maybe it's the family, he
thinks, so he spends time with his wife, Fata, and the kids, but finds
no meaning in that and so he leaves them. He thinks, Maybe helping others is the meaning of life, so he goes to medical school,
graduates with flying colors, goes to Africa to cure malaria and
transplant hearts, but cannot discover the meaning of life. He
thinks, maybe it's the wealth, so he becomes a businessman, starts
making money hand over fist, millions of dollars, buys everything
there is to buy, but that is not what life is about. Then he turns to
poverty and humility and such, so he gives everything away and
begs on the streets, but still he cannot see what life is. He thinks
maybe it is literature: he writes novel upon novel, but the more he
writes the more obscure the meaning of life becomes. He turns to
God, lives the life of a dervish, reads and contemplates the Holy
Book of Islam—still, nothing. He studies Christianity, then Juda-
ism, then Buddhism, then everything else—no meaning of life
there. Finally, he hears about a guru living high up in the mountains somewhere in the East. The guru, they say, knows what the
meaning of life is. So Mujo goes east, travels for years, walks the

roads, climbs the mountain, finds the stairs that lead up to the guru. He ascends the stairs, tens of thousands of them, nearly dies getting up there. At the top, there are millions of pilgrims, he has to wait for months to get to the guru. Eventually it is his turn, he goes to a place under a big tree, and there sits the naked guru, his legs crossed, his eyes closed, meditating, perfectly peaceful—he surely knows the meaning of life. Mujo says: I have dedicated my life to discovering the meaning of life and I have failed, so I have come to ask you humbly, O Master, to divulge the secret to me. The guru opens his eyes, looks at Mujo, and calmly says, My friend, life is a river. Mujo stares at him for a long time, cannot believe what he heard. What's life again? Mujo asks. Life is a river, the guru says. Mujo nods and says, You turd of turds, you goddamn stupid piece of shit, you motherfucking cocksucking asshole. I have wasted my life and come all this way for you to tell me that life is a fucking river. A river? Are you kidding me? That is the stupidest, emptiest fucking thing I have ever heard. Is that what you spent your life figuring out? And the guru says, What? It is not a river? Are you saying it is not a river?

I laughed a bit. I see what you mean, I said.

You see nothing, Rora said and pointed at the neon sign glaring CASINO beyond the Rinok. We should go gambling.

Gambling would feel good, I thought, although I was no gambler. On a whim, I volunteered to bankroll a hundred euros of the Susie money for Rora to gamble with. If he won, we could split the money, I suggested, he agreed, and off we went.

A BISON-NECKED BEAST, apparently hiding hams in the sleeves of his faux Armani suit, stood at the metal detector and demanded that Rora leave his Canon case in the checkroom, pointing to the sign forbidding weapons in the casino. I was willing to turn away and seek some other avenue of abandon and distraction, but Rora stepped aside, thereby suggesting that I deal with the bison man. I stepped forth and spoke; my Ukrainian, spoken with an American (rather than a Bosnian) accent, implied a store of good, hard currency to be blown. I proposed to the bison that I hold on to the camera case while my friend gambled, promising that I would not open it or even touch it. He opened it and took out the Canon and the lenses, setting them down on the floor. I saw Rora cringe, about to object, possibly violently, but the bison stood up, letting Rora pack it all back in and hand it over to me.

There was nothing gray in the room: the blazing-green felt; the red and blue and white chips; the pink shirts and raven-black vests of the two lonesome female croupiers. It was early evening, no gamblers were present. The croupier at the roulette table had her hair pulled tightly back to make her face wide and her eyes bigger, but she looked forlorn and lifeless. The blackjack woman said: "Hullo!" She was small-shouldered, her twiggy arms emerging like tongues from the puffy sleeves. Rora went straight to the blackjack table, sat across from her, and grinned. She smiled back and straightened up the chip stacks as Rora showed them the hundred-euro bill and pushed it through the slot. Some kind of a boss sat in a high chair in the far corner, a human watchtower, redirecting his searchlight gaze toward Rora and the dealer who was giving him the chips.

I had never seen Rora gamble, but it seemed to me at first he was not very good; he barely looked at his cards, getting repeatedly busted, and very quickly lost half of his chips. I was getting all fidgety but stayed put because Rora did not stir. Rora and the dealer were not talking, but she occasionally arbitrarily tittered, her gaze stuck to the cards, hidden from the watchtower. It seemed that Rora was more interested in getting laid than winning.

But then he got on a roll. The stack of chips rose in front of him, as he made large bets and kept winning. The dealer stopped smiling; she raised her index finger without lifting her left hand from the table edge—the watchtower man saw the signal. I was euphoric for a moment because I broke the secret code; I was in on the workings of the casino underworld, and imagined a photograph: a close-up of that hand. The watchtower walked into the light cone, put his hands over his crotch, his face in the dark. He had steely rings on all of his fingers, certainly for the purpose of breaking jaws and cheekbones. Rora lost a couple of hands but then went through an improbable winning series, turning his heap into a mountain. The watchtower murmured something into the dealer's ear, and called over the croupier and the two switched. The croupier had a faint mustache and a thin, sharp jaw; she was not going to bat eyes at Rora, who leaned back and sighed, as though the whole winning ordeal was hard on him. He stretched his neck like a fighter, then angled forward to plant his elbows on the ledge, his hands together as for a prayer, and he put in a large bet.

As I was falling asleep on the plane, Rora had told me of the time he escorted Miller to an interview with Karadžić. In the lousy Ukrainian casino, I recalled the story—or the dream I had dreamt. The Chetniks stopped him at the last checkpoint before they got to Karadžić, and one of them put a gun into his mouth, all the way to the tonsils. Rora assumed they couldn't kill him, because Rambo made clear to his Chetnik business partners that Miller and Rora were under his protection and that killing them would hurt the commerce. The guy who put a gun into his mouth was probably bluffing, for the sake of Miller more than anybody else. Nevertheless, Rora said, for a moment I saw a gleam in his eyes— the what-if gaze. I had known that gaze: this was what you waited for in your opponent: you wanted him to think that nothing bad could really happen, that his daring would make everything go right for him. That was when you raised the bet and took the enemy down. But it was an entirely different game if you had a gun down your throat: the taste of grease, burnt powder, and death.

And the face was ugly: a wrinkled forehead, asymmetrical brows, small, round, red-webbed eyes, and a pimple right in the corner of the left nostril.

The bison moved to stand beside the dealer, the watchtower on the other side of her, both clearly hoping to menace Rora, who did not heed the fists over their crotches. I feared not pain or death, though now expecting one or the other or both seemed perfectly reasonable; nor did I fear being robbed to the bones. It was in fact exciting. The bison went on around the table and stood next to me, probably to see whether I was giving Rora signals.

And then all the lights went out, and my bowels sank—we were about to get swallowed by the darkness. The bison pinched the skin under my shirt and viciously twisted it; the pain was surprising; the abrupt absurdity of the assault was terrifying, but I giggled. Starting toward the door, I stumbled over a chair and fell, and the lights went on, as though the whole purpose of the blackout was my fall. Everyone except me was still in their pre-blackout position, including Rora.

I am going to cash out, he said in Bosnian. The men understood and nodded, approving of the wisdom of his decision. No one said or did anything that would suggest that the blackout had taken place. Rora pushed a little stack of chips toward the dealer, for a tip; I got up and straightened the chair.

I had to help Rora with his chips to the cashier, struggling to hold on to the camera, dropping some of the chips on the thickly carpeted floor, but not even considering picking them up. Rora had made fifteen hundred euros. You could buy yourself a hard-working peasant for that kind of money in Ukraine. There was something deeply satisfying about the fact that the Susie money begot more money. The bison walked us to the door, kindly wishing us good night. *Dobra nych,* I said. It was only outside on the rainy Lviv street that I nearly passed out from the combination of fear and exhilaration.

. . .

AT VIENNESE CAFÉ, I guzzled down the most expensive Armenian cognac they had in stock, as Rora confidently explained to me it was all about counting cards, nothing but simple mathematics. But you don't want them to see you counting, you must never appear to be thinking at all. You are better off if they think you don't know what you are doing.

Miller was crazy about poker; it was part of his Americanness. He played with other foreign correspondents, but then he ran out of poker buddies. Rora was pitching himself as a fixer to Miller, so he promised him a regular poker game. He knew Rambo was a gambler, too, and that playing with Miller would appeal to him—a Sarajevo warrior playing tough poker with an American war reporter—so he set up a game. Rora was at the table; Beno, ever a capable killer but never very bright, was there, too, as security; there was a guy from the Bosnian Special Police, whose purpose was to make Miller feel safe, although he lived with his head up Rambo's butt; there was a Government Guy, who loyally watched Rambo's back. Everyone except Miller knew that Rambo was going to win. Rora wisely got himself out of the game by losing his money quickly. He considered it an investment, for the purpose of the game was to establish a relationship between Rambo and Miller from which Rora could benefit. He described to me different hands in detail, all the bluffs, all the raises, until only Rambo and Miller were left playing: Rambo with a large pile of dollars, Miller with a smaller one and a full house in hand, kings over queens. It was a setup, for Rambo had four jacks. They kept raising until Miller put down his watch and gold chain and, in the end, his future earnings. He was drunk, too, having brought a couple of bottles of Jim Beam to the table, and he gave Rambo his word that he would pay him if he lost. In some other game, in some city not under siege, no one would accept such a promise, but Rambo and everyone present and even the drunk Miller knew that dying in Sarajevo was the easiest thing in the world, even if you were an American reporter—a misunderstanding, an accident, a sniper shot. Miller lost, of course, and Rambo had him in his pocket. Afterward, Miller did little favors for him: a little package delivered to a friend; a story in American papers about Rambo, heroically fighting against the Chetniks; passing on drugs to other foreign reporters; connecting TV crews with Rambo, etc. It all worked out well for Rora: he was off the front line now, no more trenches or night actions for him, because Rambo let him be Miller's fixer so he could keep an eye on him.

You're making up these stories, I said.

I wish, he said.

You should write it all down.

I took photos.

You must write it down.

That's what I have you for. That's why I brought you along.

After the autopsy is performed by the esteemed Dr. Hunter, Assistant Chief Schuettler shows the report to William P. Miller, who is rather touched by the newly found professional intimacy between Assistant Chief and himself:

Body of a man, about 20 years old, 5 feet 7 inches tall, weighing about 125 pounds, somewhat undernourished.

Over the left frontal eminence puncture wound one-fourth inch in diameter.

Puncture wound over the left side of the chin.

Puncture wound in the right eye.

Puncture wound two inches above the clavicle on the right side.

Puncture wound two inches to the right of the left nipple.

Puncture wound at the lower angle of the left scapula.

Puncture wound in the medial line of the back of the head.

And beneath skull at this point a bullet was found.

The cranium is of peculiar formation. The hair is dark, the skin is of dark complexion. The nose is not of pure Jewish type but has a Semitic cast.

From other evidence, however, it is clear that the man was a Jew.

No filling in the teeth. Hands well formed, indicating manual labor.

In removing the skull cap, the skull was found to be exceptionally thin. Three bullet wounds were found to have punctured the brain.

The puncture wound in the proximity of the left nipple was found to have pierced the heart.

Other organs normal.

The thin skull cap, the large mouth, the receding chin, the low forehead, the pronounced cheekbones and the oversized simian ears all indicate a well-marked type of degeneracy.

In our opinion, said unknown man came to his death from shock and hemorrhage following bullet wounds of the body.

"They are creatures of a different world," Assistant Chief says, pensively, as though he was working on the thought while Miller was reading. Assistant Chief's office is dark—only a desk light is on—and the windowpanes are drumming under wind assaults.

"Indeed they are," William P. Miller says.

THE EMPTY STREETS crawling between the dark buildings; the unwieldy carriages pulling through thick sheets of rain and deep puddles; the disoriented, freezing drunks and the late-shift workers—all are flashed into brief existence by a thunderbolt. The storm is punishing Chicago, whipping its citizens with hatred.

Here it is, Olga thinks. For an instant, the shards on the floor glitter like remote celestial bodies. The petrified rye loaf appears on the table, then it vanishes. The fire in the stove is still expiring with nauseating smoke; cinereous flakes slip through the cracks in the stove and land on Olga's hair and face, light as breath. She feels the weight of her hands in her lap, and when lightning cleaves the dark space, she sees them as skinned little babies. They perish, and the only thing left is the damp coarseness of her dress. The thunder roars away, ending with a spiteful last grumble. No point in lighting the lamp, for the wafture would extinguish it.

Dear Mother,
Our Lazarus is asleep, but out of that sleep we may not awake
him.

She cannot send a letter home until the proper burial, unless
Kaddish is said. They will dump him into a hole in the ground, like
a beast. Will they even put him in a casket? Will they wash him or
did they leave it to the rain? Will the *politsey* kick his corpse into the
grave? Will they piss into it? She leaps out of her chair and makes
two steps forward, one step back on the shards. The forks and
knives and the cups clink and crackle. The noise makes her furious;
she grabs a fork as if to stab someone, but then stands with her
hand half-raised, the spikes of the fork pointed at the darkness. The
rain is scudding against the windowpane. In the far corner, in the
deepest darkness, something watches and listens.

Dear Mother,
There is no good way to say this: Lazarus is no more.

No. Nothing.

Dear Mother,
It seems we can never escape grief. We have lost Lazarus. What
have we done to deserve so much suffering?

Her dress reeks of doleful sweat and policemen's cigars, her
stockings are torn, the heel is broken on her left shoe. He cried
when he lost one of the calf-skin gloves he received as a bar mitzvah
present. Lazarus in his silly boy-sailor suit. He used to be afraid of
sparrows. Lazarus at the bar mitzvah, reading from the Torah, haltingly. Why does the Jewish day begin at sunset? Lazarus teaching a
stray dog to fetch in the refugee camp in Czernowitz, the dog

watching him with confused disinterest. And then the way he pushed his ears forward with his fingers and jutted his lower jaw to look like a monkey. The depth of his laughter when Mr. Mandelbaum did his tricks: an egg would disappear then reappear behind Lazarus's jug ear. He refused to acknowledge the first gossamer on his chin. The taste of his curls when she kissed them: sweet and salty, sometimes bitter. His cold face in the morgue; no heartbeat in his chest, nothing.

Dear Mother,
Your last letter made us so happy. We're more than fine: I
have a new job as a legal secretary and Lazarus is working for the
Hebrew Voice *as a reporter. He is contemplating getting*
married.

It would be a waste to throw away the desiccated rye bread. She should steam it. She will never eat it. A vague smell of the forgotten carrion coats everything in the room. The place is hollow without Lazarus, the objects in it stand excluded from her world, uninvolved in her woe: an empty basin, a shawl hanging over a chair, a stolid water pitcher, the sewing machine, its belt occasionally rattling. She cannot bear to touch them; she stares at their shapes, as if waiting for the moment when they will break open and reveal the hard pit of sorrow that is inside every cursed thing. Here it is. Here sat Lazarus Averbuch, a nineteen-year-old boy. Here he ate his kasha, taking crud out of his left eye with his thumb, yawning and exposing his gums and incisors, like a cat. Here he put the tin bowl into the sink and here it clanged against the brim. Here he pinned the picture from the *Daily News*: a throng of Jewish girls exercising on the roof of a building, reaching for something in the sky.

Did the *politsey* search the outhouse?

She rushes down the stairs, past the slumbersome *politsyant* in the hallway who does not leave his chair. She trudges through the storm, the backyard morass, the frigid mud squeezing into her shallow shoes; she slips but she doesn't fall; her hair sags with rain. Bending over, she pushes the rock that keeps the outhouse door closed and flings it open; the stench is horrid—the storm released the putrefaction vapor, the shit rose with rainwater. Here was the English-Russian dictionary he liked to take to the outhouse. She gropes for the dictionary and touches its spine, which is sticking out like a minikin mountain range. She always warned him it would be too cold to sit here and read, but he never listened; he would come back, coughing and sniffling. Last week she wiped his nose; he winced and whined like a child. The book is warm, as though Lazarus has just held it, his life still radiating out of it. Her knees give in and she sits down with a sob, her left buttock over the shit-hole. Lazarus, she cries, pressing the book against her bosom. My little brother. All the lives he could have lived. She used to help him study; she read English words to him and he would respond with the Russian equivalents; just on Tuesday, they were going through the letter L:

Look

Loom

Loose

Loot

Lop

Lopsided

Loquacious

Lord

Lore

Lose

Lost

Lot

Loud

Louse

What could these mysterious words tell her now? She moans, rocking back and forth as if praying, as if becoming nothing on her way to nothing.

Lout

Lovable

Love

Lovely

Lover

Low

Lower

Lowland

Lowly

Lord, what have I done?

Olga, is that you? Olga?

She yelps with horror, coils up to protect the good book and her heart from whatever it is that is speaking to her. The voice is sourceless and hoarse, coming from the darkness around her. More lightning, her feet are freezing. With unbearable relief she considers the possibility that she has lost her mind.

Dear Mother,
Lazarus is dead, and I am mad. We're fine otherwise and think
of you a lot.

Olga, it's me, Isador, the voice says. I am down below.

The splashing underneath is unmistakably real.

Isador?

It's me, Olga. I am down in the shit. I am dying here.

What in the world are you doing down there?

I love swimming in shit. What do you think? They are looking for me all over the city.

Olga is staring into the stinking black hole; bile rises through her chest and she retches.

How do you know they are looking for you? How did you get in there?

I was coming to see you when the police arrived, so I hid. Good people had told me to stay away from the law.

If you did nothing wrong, there is no reason to hide, Olga says without conviction.

I was told I am the curly-haired accomplice to the crime, Isador says. Except I am not curly-haired and there is no crime.

Did you want to kill Shippy?

Don't be a fool, Olga. Why would I want to do that?

What was he doing at Shippy's doorstep?

I don't know. Listen, I have to get out of here. I am freezing and starving. The shit is rising.

It was all your anarchist nonsense, all the angry talk. What was wrong with the life he had?

We just wanted better things. We were just reading and talking, Olga. I am going to die here.

You are lying, Isador. You enticed him.

Olga, you know me. I ate at your table. He was my brother. You are my sister.

I am not your sister. I had a brother and you led him to death.

He was his own man. He made his choices.

You took him to listen to the Goldman woman, to all those red troublemakers; you fed his heart with anger. Let your anarchist sisters get you out of shit.

She cannot see him and she does not know how deep below he is. She never looked into the hole in daylight. Everything has become a different reality. Isador used to be just another loudmouth boy, and now he is the most wanted anarchist in Chicago.

There is police everywhere around, one in my hallway, she says. They are waiting for you here. If I don't go back soon, they'll come looking for me.

I have not eaten anything in two days. Rats are walking all over me. I am going to die. I don't want to die.

I can call the police and they can get you out.

Isador is silent; the storm has rumbled away. The outhouse door has a heart-shaped hole; the draft is browsing through a pile of newspaper patches. Olga's skull itches under the wet sworls of hair.

Give me one reason why I shouldn't call them, she says.

Lazarus was innocent and was killed by the police; I am innocent and will be killed by the police. Two reasons. If you want more I am sure I can dig some out of this shit.

Olga cannot feel her toes and fingers, and her heart is turning into ice, too. Why not just stay here and fall asleep and put an end to it all? Everything should stop. Lord, why did you leave me in these dark woods?

Olga, please. Just help me get out of the hole and bring me some food and a blanket.

You can't stay in the outhouse forever.

Let me just get through the night. We'll think of something.

I hate you, Isador, all your world-changing, all the grandstanding. You don't live in this world. Why couldn't you just let us be?

All I have ever wanted is to live in this world with some dignity. Help me out, Olga. Please.

She puts the dictionary down and reaches inside the darkness until Isador's slimy hand grabs her wrist, nearly pulling her in.

Plague on you, Isador, on you and your kind, she says. The dictionary slips into the hole, hits Isador in the face, splashes, and sinks.

What was that? Isador gasps.

IN HER BED, Olga pulls the covers over her head, fending off the cold and shit stench, knowing that neither would ever again abandon her body; it will be a miracle if she does not get brain inflammation. She took a blanket and the dry bread loaf to Isador, both hidden under her dress. "Busy bowels, eh?" said the *politsyant* with a smirk of disgust. He doesn't seem to be too bright, but Olga worries about him going to the outhouse. Don't worry, Isador said. They don't shit with Jews.

There he is now, Isador, beshitten on the absurd throne, wrapped in a flimsy blanket, thinking up free worlds in which everybody has indoor plumbing. I just hope I don't have to relieve myself, Isador said, but she didn't laugh. She will never laugh again. She has washed herself over the basin, scrubbed her hands many times, but the stench is pasted against the walls of her nostrils.

Here is Lazarus coming home with Isador and three dozen eggs in a newspaper cone, not one of them broken. They slowly deposit them into a bowl, arguing over whatever it is that they heard at the Goldman woman's lecture. Isador flails his arms with silly seriousness; Lazarus is like a clumsy fledgling.

Isador is in the outhouse; policemen are everywhere around; Lazarus is dead; I stink of shit and sorrow; there is an endless storm outside; I am lost in a foreign country. Overall, not a bad lot.

Dear Mother,
I don't know how to begin

She turns to the side, slips her right hand under the pillow, hears straw crepitating in it. Isador could sneak out before dawn, when everybody is dead asleep; the storm must have been exhausting. If I fall asleep and wake up dead, I could be rid of this sickening grief.

Look

Loom

Loose

His face was so angry in the morgue, so tense, his lips frigid and sharp. What made him angry? He talked about anarchy and liberty, police and justice and America. Because a few possess everything, he said, the many possess nothing. We are the many, this is the life of the many. Do you know, Olga, that I do not feel anything in my fingertips after work? When I write, I cannot hold the pen. Whatever I touch feels like an egg. He daydreamed about being a reporter for the *Hebrew Voice*. He would travel the world and write about it. He cut bread with long, slow moves, as if sawing it. His arms were so bony, his elbows were like featherless wingtips.

Isador cracks one of the eggs against the table edge and, before it can dribble out, he drops the yolk and the white into his mouth. His long throat swells briefly with a gulp. He would be handsome if he weren't so obtuse. Lazarus tries to crack his egg, but smashes it against the table instead.

Lose

Lost

Lot

Loud

She hears knocking on the door, leaps out of bed, because there are two short and two long knocks—the way that Lazarus, conspiratorially, likes to do it. She opens the door and there he is: tall and shabby, shoeless, with holes in his socks, his suit hanging on him like a blanket. The scrawny sternness of his face stretches out into an ear-to-ear smile. She gasps with joy and gushes into tears, hugging him around his biceps. She presses her cheek against his chest, his heart is beating, one of his buttons leaves an impression on her ear. Where were you? she asks him frantically. Why do you play hide-and-seek with me? But he says nothing, kisses her head, and shrugs her off. He slumps into her chair, breaks off a piece of rye bread, and, with his mouth full, shakes his head despondently, as if to say, You have no idea what I've been through. She falls on her knees in front of him, lays her palms on his thighs to calm him down. Low Louse, he says, his eyes unsteady like mercury bubbles. Loom Lopsided Lord Lost. Lower Lowland Lowly.

Nobody in Lviv was going to have memories of us, not the casino bruisers, nor the waitress at Vienna Café who pricked up her ears at my obsolescent Ukrainian, nor the young ladies who smiled at us, beaming signals of availability. The only person who might remember us was the driver I hired to take us to Chernivtsi. I had gone to a taxi stand at the bus station and talked to the youngest, healthiest-looking driver with the best car. His name was Andriy and he drove a blue-and-rusty Ford Focus; he had a moony face and bright, open eyes that bespoke either deviousness or innocence, possibly both; he seemed sober and wore a wedding ring. He wanted a hundred dollars of the Susie money, plus food and gas; it would take five to six hours. I told him I would like to stop by the village—Krotkiy—where my grandfather was born. That would be a hundred and twenty, Andriy said. Other drivers, undershaven and cantankerous, stood around, listening to the negotiation, snorting with approbation, one of them attempting to offer a lower price. Andriy just glanced at him scorchingly and the man retreated.

It was still dark the following morning when he threw our bags in the trunk and shook our hands, sealing the covenant. Rora was looking at him over his sunglasses—apparently predawn Lviv was not lightless enough for him. I took the passenger seat, and as I was pulling the belt down to buckle up, Andriy grabbed my hand and said: "Not necessary." I tried to explain he should not take it personally, but he said again, sternly: "Not necessary." I was going to trust him with my life; Rora chuckled in the back. If it is your time to go, it is your time to go, he said. I don't want to go, I said, but did not buckle up. The Ford Focus smelled of feces.

We left the city on a poorly lit road, heading east, seeing only a horse cart with a cage full of rabbits, the man holding the reins slouching like a refugee. A boxy truck rumbled from the opposite direction and left us in a cloud of nocturnal dust; we must have been raising clouds behind us; once the dust settled it would cover our tracks.

Had Lazarus lived, would he have become Billy Averbuch? Would his children have become Avery or Averiman or, who knows, Field? Would he have begotten a latter brood of Philips and Sauls and Bernards and Eleanors, who would have begotten Jameses and Jennifers and Jans and Johns? Would his anarchist proclivities, receding chin, and simian ears have been tucked deep inside the family history, inside the glorious American dream? There are so many stories that could be told, but only some of them can be true.

RAMBO LIKED TO take Miller for a ride down the streets of Sarajevo. He would hop in the six-cylinder Audi he had requisitioned from the Bosnian Parliament's prewar car fleet, get Miller in the passenger seat, and drive, unbuckled, at insane speeds. They did it for the thrills: Rambo swerved and skidded through the debris, corpses, running civilians, sniper hail, and Miller would look at his watch for the time; they drove from the headquarters in Radićeva, down to Stup, where the unit fought. The Audi was riddled with bullet holes, but somehow no bullet ever hit them; they were taunting death, and had a hell of a time doing it. Miller loved it; Rambo let him drive every once in a while, and he would nearly pass out from the adrenaline rush. They drove at night, too, with the headlights out; Rambo claimed he was so good he could do it blind, and driving in the complete darkness of a Sarajevo night was much like that.

And when Rora was in Scania, Sweden, once, he played gin rummy with a guy who got all beside himself when he heard that Rora was from Sarajevo. The man barely noticed that Rora skinned him alive. He took Rora home in his Bentley, large as a house, the seats made of leather so fine that you could hear the spirits of the slaughtered calves sigh—he needed to show him something, he said. The man collected old cars; he had Ford Ts and the Nazi editions of the Volkswagen and a Bugatti that could still race. But the collection was not what he wanted Rora to see: on his garage wall, lit like an altar, was a steering wheel and a horn, the kind that used to be used for talking to the driver from the backseat. They came from the automobile in which the archduke and archduchess had died in 1914 in Sarajevo: in the backseat of this car World War One had begun, the first casualty the pregnant archduchess. The man was drunk and high from losing a lot of money; he talked fervently about the driver's sweat absorbed by the steering wheel, about the archduke's last breath, about the hard, German, throttled consonants stuck in the horn. Those ancient microscopic residues were all that was left of the man who was going to be an emperor. The steering wheel of the empire was last touched by an anonymous, terrified driver, who must have thought that they would blame him for everything, the man said, crying. (I looked at Andriy's hands firmly gripping the Ford's steering wheel, two knuckles on his left hand bruised—he must have punished the price-lowering colleague.) To Rora it seemed that somebody had scammed the Swede, because you could find that kind of antique-looking crap anywhere. Rora used to know a tailor in Berlin who fashioned old war uniforms; and there was a guy in Milan who wrote sixteenth-century love letters; and he had heard of a blacksmith in Amsterdam who cast ancient samurai swords. But he let the man believe what he needed to believe.

And Rora's uncle, Murat, was drinking with his buddies the night before he was supposed to travel to Mecca for the hajj. He missed the flight, so when he woke up, hung over, he caught a cab on the street and when the driver asked him, "Where to?" he said, "Saudi Arabia." The driver drove him to Mecca, it took them a few days. But then Uncle Murat didn't think that it would be right if the driver went back alone, so he paid for his lodging and food and they worshipped at the Kabba. On the way back they bought some cheap carpets in Syria, some fine demitasse in Turkey, resold them in Sarajevo, and made a little money.

And so Rora went on, one story after another. I had never heard him talk so much; it was as though moving through the verdant, depopulated landscape prompted his stories; indeed he would take photos, lazily, without interrupting his narration. Even Andriy seemed mesmerized by his voice, with the steady stream of soft, epic, Slavic sounds. I wanted to write some of those stories down, but the Ford Feces leapt over potholes, my forehead steadily banging against the side window as Andriy passed trucks, entirely uninterested in the oncoming traffic.

I used to tell stories to Mary, stories of my childhood and immigrant adventures, stories I had picked up from other people. But I had become tired of telling them, tired of listening to them. In Chicago, I had found myself longing for the Sarajevo way of doing it—Sarajevans told stories ever aware that the listeners' attention might flag, so they exaggerated and embellished and sometimes downright lied to keep it up. You listened, rapt, ready to laugh, indifferent to doubt or implausibility. There was a storytelling code of solidarity—you did not sabotage someone else's narration if it was satisfying to the audience, or you could expect one of your stories to be sabotaged one day, too. Disbelief was permanently suspended, for nobody expected truth or information, just the pleasure of being in the story and, maybe, passing it off as their own. It was different in America: the incessant perpetuation of collective fantasies makes people crave the truth and nothing but the truth—reality is the fastest American commodity.

Once upon a time Mary and I were at a wedding in Milwaukee. Her cousin, who worked for the governor of Wisconsin, was getting married, and we shared a table with eight other people, all couples invested in state politics. As it happens at weddings, they all started talking about their fateful encounters: Josh and Jennifer met at their gym; Jan and Johnny were a college couple, broke up, later found themselves working for the same law firm; Saul and Philip met at a toga party, by a keg of Miller Light. Everybody was happy now, you could tell, the table laden with bliss and future, no sardines of sorrow served.

So as to contribute to the discourse of momentous attraction, I told them about the Cold War rabbits. It was Rora who had told me this story once upon his return from Berlin. All along the Wall, I/Rora said, there were grass-covered minefields, so there were a lot of free-running rabbits, too light to set off a mine, no other beasts to prey upon them. At mating time, the hormone-crazy rabbits would smell a partner on the other side, and they would go crazy, producing the pining-rabbit sound, trying desperately to find a hole in the Wall. The rabbits would drive the guards out of their minds, but they could not shoot them because they had to save their bullets for the humans trying to defect. Everybody in Berlin knew that the rabbit-mating season was the worst time to attempt to escape across the Wall, because the rabbits made the guards very trigger-happy.

Outrageous though it may have been, I always found the story funny and poignant—the unnaturalness of the Cold War, the love that knew no boundaries, the Wall brought down by horny rodents. It required no effort for me to suspend my disbelief and admire

Rora's narrative embroidery. But my Wisconsin audience stared at me with the basic you're-okay-but-strange smiles, waiting for a more potent punch line. Whereupon Mary said: "I find that hard to believe." She was hurt and annoyed, I know for a fact, because I didn't tell our own falling-in-love story (the sand between the toes, the reflections of Chicago shimmering on the lake, the waves licking the breakers), but it was rather humiliating to be publicly distrusted by your own wife. Josh asked: "Why didn't the rabbits find a mate on their own side of the Wall? Why would they only be interested in a rabbit from the other side?" I had no answer, as it had never crossed my mind to ask Rora such a question; the story and its reality disintegrated right before me. What's worse, I felt that Mary was speaking from across the wall that divided us and that all the verifiable reality was on her side. Never could I tell that story in Mary's presence after that.

Rora was good with the audience, as judged by my unflagging, unquestioning, decades-long interest in his stories, this journey included. He could measure the intensity of my involvement; he could balance suspense, withhold information, manage asides, read my face, qualify my laughter. It was pleasant, I have to say, to be subjected to such studious storytelling. I used to be reasonably good myself, but now I feared distrust, the listeners' questioning gazes likely to bore into my hollow heart.

Anyway, an edentate man led a bloated, mouth-foaming goat down a road webbed with knee-deep gullies. Andriy asked him how to get to Krotkiy; he pointed up the hill without a word and up we went. There was a schoollike building at the top of the hill; the fields around were yellow with blooming clover; a gaggle of ducks wobbled toward a puddle. The school was condemned; in front of it, a winged monument to a long forgotten victory had one of its wings broken. Across the road, there was a gateless cemetery; this was where we stopped and disembarked. Rora's black, polished, possibly Italian shoes looked uncannily out of place on the dirt road—he picked a stone out of his leather sole and threw it over his shoulder, as though performing a good-luck ritual. It seemed that we disturbed a world of birds, for they twittered madly, spreading the news that three strangers had appeared.

I knew of no Briks living in Krotkiy; the family memory contained only the idyllic images of pristine Ukrainian landscapes devoid of people with names, as depicted to me by my grandfather; he left these parts when he was nine. I trudged through the unkempt cemetery, looking for any Brik graves. Some of the tombstones emerged from high grass, some were swallowed by thorny bushes; death was experienced here. But there were a few newer tombstones, the marble bright and fresh. Some of them had solemn dun-and-beige pictures of the deceased, below which there were their names and dates: Oleksandr Pronek 1967–2002; Oksana Mykolchuk 1928–1995. The whole life a dash between the two arbitrary numbers. Hoydee-ho, haydee-hi, all I want is not to die.

Is this you? Rora asked, pointing at a tombstone under a cherry tree; the cherries were ripe, perfect red beads. There were two pictures: the woman's face was framed with a black head scarf, her eyes two dark holes. Her name was Helena Brik and she was firmly dead: 1929–1999. The man's name was Mykola Brik; he was born in 1922; he seemed to have died last week: 2004 was at the other end of his dash. His side of the grave was covered with a mound of recently wilted flowers, his picture on the tombstone untainted by rain and birdshit. He's your tribe, Rora said. He looks like you. He certainly did look like me—in fifty years or so: the same large nose and low forehead, the same prominent cheekbones and large, apish ears, the same hirsute eyebrows.

A human face consists of other faces—the faces you inherited or picked up along the way, or the ones you simply made up—laid on top of each other in a messy superimposition. When I taught ESL, I had students who would come to class with a different face every day; it took me a while to remember their names. Eventually, from a certain angle, I could see what was buried under their fleeting grimaces, I discerned the deep faces beyond their acting out the person they imagined themselves to be. Sometimes they would flash their new, American face: the raised eyebrows and the curved mouth of perpetual worry and wonder. Mary could see no deep face of mine, because she did not know what my life in Bosnia had been like, what made me, what I had come from; she could see only my American face, acquired through failing to be the person I wanted to be. I did not know what shadows Rora saw, comparing my face and the one on the tombstone, but I did not think him crazy. Mykola Brik may have been someone who had settled here—here in the narrow passage between my brain and my gaze—before I was even born. Nobody can control resemblances, any more than you can control echoes.

I wondered, but could not see, what this world of Ukrainian peasanthood, the routine and exotic suffering, looked like to Rora. He was a descendant of the Halilbašić brothers who, way back in the sixteenth century, had fought the Morić brothers for control of the Čaršija—songs were still sung about those street battles. His great-grandparents had owned one of the first cars in Sarajevo; his great-aunt was the first Muslim woman in the city to wear pants and had self-published a book of love poetry. Rora's grandfather had his suits done in Vienna, went on the hajj many times, stopping over for a vacation every time: Lebanon, Egypt, Greece. The world had always been available to the Halilbašićs. Whereas my grandfather grew up in the Bosnian countryside, in a mud-wall house the family shared with cattle and chickens—and this was a step up from the life his parents had lived in Krotkiy—leaving it only to go to church. Nobody in Rora's family knew anything about slaving in the arid fields; there had never been any dirt under their nails; they had a street in Sarajevo named after them. What did he see when he looked at those graves and the miserly fields of retarded corn beyond? Rora was smoking, nothing around us moved, except for the hysterical birds high up in the trees. Andriy was passed out in the front seat of the car, impervious to the potential poignance of the moment.

It is so much easier to deal with the dead than with the living. The dead are out of the way, merely characters from stories about the past, never again unreadable, no misunderstandings possible, the pain coming from them stable and manageable. Nor do you have to explain yourself to them, to justify the fact of your life. I could see them but they could not see me: Mykola had a pointed chin; Helena trudged on her varicose legs toward the stove to steam the week-old bread. Splendorous temples were built on the belief that death does not erase the traces of those who lived, that someone up there busies himself with keeping tabs, and is going to send down Mr. Christ or some other delusional prophet to resurrect all of the disintegrated nobodies. The promise is that even when every trace of your life vanishes absolutely and completely, God will remember you, that He might devote a speck of thought to you while reposing between putting up universes. And here they were, Helena and Mykola, rotting uninterruptedly under my feet. For a moment, I contemplated lighting candles for my distant relatives' souls, packed in a wooden box for eternity, roots pushing through their eye sockets.

Rora put out his cigarette on the ground and said, I knew a guy in Sarajevo called Vampir, because his bright idea was to take his ladies to the Koševo cemetery for a fuck. He figured it was clean, nobody would bother them, she would cling to him out of fear, and there were always candles if the chick was a romantic one. So once he and his lady had just finished banging and buttoned up when two cops caught them. What are you doing here? the cops ask. Without blinking, Vampir says, We're visiting my grandfather's grave. Which one is it? the cops ask. So Vampir says, The one over there. The cops look at the tombstone he pointed out, and it belongs to a woman who died at the age of twenty-five. What's this? the cops ask. Vampir looks at them and says, I am shocked, officer. Never did I think that my own grandfather was such a two-faced liar.

THE SUN BEATING into my chest woke me up. The windows of the Ford Feces were solidly shut, no air available. On top of the shit stench, Andriy was smoking—I'd neglected to inquire when I hired him if there was any air-conditioning. I dramatically huffed and puffed, but Andriy either did not care or failed to understand, his squirrel face expressing little. "Could we open a window?" I finally asked with a deliberately weakened voice, lest I insult him. He said nothing, pressed a button, and the window on my side slid halfway down.

Unprompted, I explained my partial Ukrainianness, as though being from the same people, partly, should entitle me to more air. But he pressed the button again, and the window went up, until only an inch or so was left open. Still I went on: I told him about my cousins in Bosnia, England, France, Australia, Canada, about my life in America, where there are lots of Bosnians and Ukrainians. I told him about the churches and delis and credit unions the Ukes had in Chicago, in the part of town called Ukrainian Village. He pricked up his ears. "Is there work?" he asked. "There is always work if you want to work," I said. I told him that at the beginning I had served food at the Ukrainian Cultural Center; I had done data input for a real estate broker; I had worked as a teacher of English. I assured him it was very easy to make money in America. I wanted him to think that my life in America was all about hard work, rather than an embarrassing mixture of luck and despair.

Andriy was clearly contemplating his hypothetical American life: he was imagining himself with a job, making and saving money, buying a house; the corner of his mouth quivered toward a grin.

"Are there women to marry?" he asked.

"Plenty," I said. "My wife is American."

A full-blooded American, she was. She took me to baseball games and held her hand on her heart to sing the anthem, while I stood next to her, humming along. She used the national *we* when talking about the U.S. of A. "We should have never gone into Iraq," she would say. "We are a nation of immigrants." She often craved cheeseburgers. George and Rachel had bought her a car for her sixteenth birthday. She had the bright, open face that always reminded me of the vast midwestern welkin. She was routinely kind to other people, assumed they had good intentions; she smiled at strangers; it mattered to her what they thought and felt. She was often embarrassed; she dreamt of learning a foreign language; she wanted to make a difference. She believed in God and seldom went to church.

"There are a lot of good women there," I said. Fully grinning, Andriy was conjuring up a healthy, fecund American woman in his mind. Then he asked, gloomily:

"And problems?"

"What problems?"

"If you have family and house, you want to protect them. But this world is crazy. Homosexuals, crazy Muslim terrorists, problems."

In a desperate attempt to escape this dialogue, I turned to Rora and asked him, Are you sleeping?

I am listening to you, Rora said. In a week I'll be able to speak Ukrainian, but maybe you should tell him now that I am a Muslim problem.

I ignored the suggestion. The road was straight between the hills, as though they parted for it. Andriy was speeding, disregarding the complicated pothole constellations; the engine was screaming, he might have forgotten to shift gears. My primary problem was to put out of my mind the possibility of the feculent vehicle turning into a ball of fire. I wasn't going to say anything, lest we continue the conversation. Clouds and cloudettes were bunching up over a distant hill, as if getting ready for an assault. Andriy occasionally honked madly at a car crossing to our side to pass a truck, but not for a moment did he consider chickening out. I closed my eyes and started composing a letter I decided I would send from Chernivtsi:

> *Dear Mary,*
> *Ukraine is huge, endless. The steppe seems exhausted from*
> *stretching so far. One feels so small in this place. This must be*
> *how settlers felt facing the prairie.*

But Andriy finally slowed down and shifted gears and the Ford Feces was now purring and rocking, and my letter transmogrified into a dream.

I WOKE UP only because we had stopped. Rora and Andriy smoked outside, the smoke whirling around them; Andriy was laughing as if he were clearing his throat after vomiting.

I am Muslim, I heard Rora say to him, in Bosnian. I have seven veiled wives, forty-three children.

I got out of the car. We were at the bottom of a hill, on top of which there was a spireless, disconsolate church, or, perhaps, a godforsaken monastery. There were only trees around, writhing under the wind; the landscape seemed eminently conducive to monasteries. In my country, monasteries had been turned into sanatoriums for war criminals.

"He says he is Muslim," Andriy said to me, as if letting me in on a joke, hissing with joy. He made a circle with his hand around his head to suggest that if Rora were Muslim his head should have been wrapped.

Why are you laughing? Rora asked him with a grim face.

"He is Muslim." I nodded.

Andriy looked at Rora, then at me, at Rora again, tittering still, giving us a chance to laugh it up with him and stand united in the extended joke. The wind was slapping the tree crowns, like a teacher slapping children. Rora's right hand flew into his left hand straight up like a tower, he produced a roaring-engine sound, then collapsed his left hand, slapping his thigh.

That was me, Rora said, and Andriy laughed even louder, riotously. I am not sure he understood what Rora was referring to, but Andriy was going to tell all of his friends about the crazies he had driven from Lviv to Chernivtsi.

Mujahedeen, Rora said and pointed at himself. Homosexual, he pointed at me, laughing in concert with now hysterical Andriy, slapping him on the back.

Stop it, I said.

We are the problems, Rora said. Big problems.

It took Andriy a while to calm down. Back in the car, I tried to buckle up again, but Andriy said, giggling: "Not necessary." But I defiantly buckled up, and he unsmiled, looked ahead, and did not say a word for a long time.

In a bullet-riddled Range Rover, Rora drove with Miller all around Bosnia. At some point, Miller had to leave Sarajevo more often because New York was sick of yet another story about Rambo and his brave unit. So the two of them would go to Mostar and Goražde and Doboj. Miller was a heavyweight, what with his New York credentials and a bulletproof vest and a word from Rambo preceding him so that he couldn't be harassed too much; sometimes the Chetniks who knew him would even wave him through. Rora had a fake press pass Rambo had arranged, and the name on it was not Muslim—otherwise, he could have been clipped at a checkpoint by anyone sufficiently drunk. Once they were stopped up near Sokolac, and the checkpoint Chetnik was someone Rora had played poker with before the war. He had a long warrior beard and a red beret and spoke with a labored Serbian accent, but Rora recognized his eyes, for into his eyes he had stared across the table blanketed with mixed currencies, reading them. His name was Zlojutro, and he instantly recognized Rora. He checked Rora's pass, then his face, and shook his head dismayingly, as if saying: How stupid of you to try to fool me. He asked Rora: What are you? Rora could either lie and say he was a Serb, which the Chetnik would know was not true, or he could admit he was a Muslim, for which they could accuse him of being a spy—either way, he could be shot. So Rora said, I am a gambler.

It is dark already when the body of Lazarus Averbuch is disposed of in the potter's field at Dunning. *No friend of the young man, nor his sister Olga, are at the burial*; only Assistant Chief Schuettler and William P. Miller are present. *In the driving rainstorm, not unlike the beginning of a biblical deluge,* the body, wrapped in cloth, was rolled into the grave, half-filled with water. After watching clots of mud fill up the hole, the two of them trudge through the darkness as thick and wet as broth, guided by headlights. As the car leaves Dunning behind to take them home, they share their concern for Chief Shippy's welfare; the assassination attempt might nudge him toward retirement, they sigh in simultaneous agreement. The car is warm, the rain lashes the windshield. Miller resists the temptation to doze off, as Assistant Chief talks, rather poetically, *about the world that resists order, about all that needs to be done, now or never, to rid it of evil for good.*

THE AIR IN Sam Harris's Place is turbid with smoke; the stove in the corner is belching and regurgitating; the lamps are so sooty that it seems they are just producing more darkness. William P. Miller's feet are wet, as is his coat and his shirt and his undershirt; he pours rain out of the brim of his hat. There are two men standing at the bar; one of them has a long beard and a yarmulke. The man should not be here; in fact, the saloon should not be open at all, for it is past closing time; the bartender should be wiping or picking up glasses, but that is not what he is doing—there is a whole battalion of steins lined up on the bar. Stroking his pointy mustache, the bartender glances at Miller and signals with his head toward the back.

Guzik is waiting in the back, in the corner away from the light, his hands in his armpits, his thick thumbs straining to meet on his chest. Only as he approaches the table does Miller see a fat, round-headed little man, the size of a child, leaning over his beer on the table. Miller joins them without a word; his wet shoes have already picked up a coating of sawdust off the floor.

"Friend here must take you where you want go," Guzik says. "You know what is my price, his price he tell you. Don't tell nothing to police. This only is for you." The fat little man is quiet, his eyes are bright, with long eyelashes, a boy's face pasted on a watermelon.

"Does your friend here have a name?" Miller asks.

"No. He don't have no name," Guzik says.

"No name," says the fat little man. His voice is high-pitched and hoarse. Miller wonders if his feet are touching the floor at all; he is probably protected from the rising sawdust.

"What's the word on Averbuch? Who put him up to it?" he asks Guzik.

"Ach, friend, who put him up to it. Who put him up to it? Who knows. He was dreamy boy. People here are not happy. They don't go to your part of town, you don't go here. When somebody from here go north, it's problems."

The fat little man nods wistfully, as though remembering the one time he went north without problems.

"What about Maron? Is he a member of Edelstadt?" Miller asks.

"Maron. Maron is snake. He like to tell bad stories about good men. Big snake."

"Okay, but is he a member of an anarchist organization?"

"Anarchist, no anarchist. Everybody is little bit anarchist here, everybody talk a lot—no justice, no freedom, nothing, they say all time. You gonna hear. But killer, no. We live, you live. Everybody must live."

"Yes, of course. What else have you heard?"

"Emma Goldman will come tomorrow. There's going to be meetings, there's going to be some crazy people come with her, there's going to be maybe riots. Emma Goldman don't come here for shopping. There's friends of Red Queen in Chicago. There's people angry. There's people angry at police."

The fat little man shakes his head, then nods again. The flame in the nearby lamp flickers, and Miller suddenly notices that the fat little man has a thin mustache over his lip. "Friend here must take you to one meeting tonight, so you see what is what." He slaps the fat little man on the back as though offering him to Miller.

Miller takes a well-folded dollar bill out of his inside pocket and puts it on the table. Guzik looks at it with a worrisome frown, as though he has never seen anything like that, then lays his hand over it. The fat little man nods and stands up—he is but a couple of inches taller standing.

"Anything else?" Miller asks.

"Maybe," Guzik says. Miller gets another dollar out of his pocket and sets it down on the table next to the other one.

"How about now?" Miller says.

"There's people who do business with students of medicine. Students must study. If they want to study they need dead people.

Dead people are expensive. But there are free dead people in cemetery. Your friend Averbuch is dead people."

"That's a good story," Miller says. "But I just came back from his burial."

"People like good story," Guzik says. "Maybe you look for your dead friend later. Maybe he is gone away."

"I appreciate good stories myself," Miller says. "One more thing. What do you know about Olga?

"What Olga?"

"Olga Averbuch."

"What Olga Averbuch? Olga Averbuch is nothing. But I ask."

"Thanks." Miller gets up to go. "When is the next game?"

"Monday," Guzik says. "Maybe you have good luck this time. Or maybe you learn gamble is bad for you."

"I'll see you Monday," Miller says.

ALL OVER TOWN, *anarchists hold secret meetings, where they further stoke the fire of violent discontent in hope it will consume peace and decency in our city. The* TRIBUNE *reporter was secretly present at one of those intemperate summits last night. In a back room of a common Jewish ghetto tenement, speeches were delivered in myriad accents that could envenom the blood of any honorable citizen. The speakers thundered against various phantom injustices and exchanged distorted views on "the few who possess everything and the many who possess nothing." Various assassins who had taken the lives of distinguished presidents and noble kings were praised. The actions of young Averbuch, whose attempt on Chief Shippy's life is universally endorsed in anarchist circles, were justified by the perceived "misery and degradation, economic exploitation, governmental suppression, lawful brutality, judicial murder, etc."*

Cold though the room may be, there is a lot of passion in the air. The stove in the corner is out; the speaker's breath spouts out of his mouth like gun smoke. The room is barren, apart from the crowd: scrawny, mustached, consumptive, damp-clothed, enraged men, reeking of vinegar and revolution. There are even several women, wearing prissy hats and graceful glasses, yet looking masculine and hairy. The fat little man gets up to applaud along and vociferate agreement with every speaker—"Bravo!" he shouts, as though he were at the opera. Indeed, it would not be surprising if everyone in the room suddenly broke out in song. Where were these people when young Averbuch was being dumped in the ground? William P. Miller's spine tingles with the pleasure of bearing exclusive witness to Lazarus's interment; these men know nothing about his death, nor his life. No matter what happens, no matter who lives or dies, they always see the same thing; their anger coats everything in the same black color, and they like to yodel about it.

Each speaker enumerates the usual collection of complaints; now and then the name of Emma Goldman emerges from the babel. Occasionally, Miller dozes off, but is woken up every time by the fresh zeal of the new speaker. The man clamoring presently has put his hat on the cold stove; he raises his hands up toward the ceiling, so the sleeves slide down and Miller can see the dainty, weak wrists—this man knows nothing of manual labor. He declaims in good English; his sentences contain articles; unlike the typical anarchist degenerate, he is rather articulate.

"For years," the man rattles his hands above his head, "for years they have been maintaining the illusion that no social question exists in this country, that our republic has no place for the struggle of poor and rich. The voices of the deep, the cries of human misery and distress are silenced by the formula saying 'we are all free and equal in this country.' The empty cant of political liberty has been made to serve those in ruthless power. Those who dare to object to the farce of political freedom, those who resist the social and economic slavery are branded criminals."

Miller leans over to the fat little man, who is fluttering on the tip of his toes, extending his little arms to applaud, and asks: "Who's this?"

"That is Ben Reitman," the fat little man squeals. "Great man. Emma Goldman's man."

Miller squeezes the fat little man's shoulder. He feels an impulse to touch his egg-shaped head, his oval torso, the round heat that he exudes—he is so indelibly present, this little man. Miller wonders where Guzik found him.

"Our brother Averbuch has fallen victim to the secret kings of the republic," Reitman goes on, "to the gendarmes and sheriffs of the possessing class. Pure in aspiration and motive, the personality of Lazarus Averbuch towers above our stifling social existence. Purer, indeed, than his executioners and the lying press will ever acknowledge. They have left nothing undone to make him appear a low, vile creature, since it is necessary to lull this nation into the belief that only the basest of men could be guilty of discontent. And Brother Averbuch is more than merely innocent—he is a martyr."

If someone walked in just now and told Reitman that Lazarus Averbuch was in fact outside, alive and well and happy, he would not care, thinks William P. Miller. He would just go on talking about his martyrdom, for a dead Lazarus is much more valuable and useful for this fiery pageant. Nobody in this room misses him. Nobody misses him anywhere.

"And how many martyrs do we need before we understand that we must respond armed with our righteous wrath? The kings of the republic are summoning their baneful forces, writing new laws that would turn masses of people, millions of human beings, into criminals. We know that laws ought to be obeyed only if they come out of people's sense of justice, not because the state needs them to preserve its power. Laws devised for the depravity of power are as worthless as the paper they are printed on."

Miller gets up, pats the tiny fatso on the back as he frantically claps his finlike hands, and bids him good-bye. *Ben Reitman, the* *high priest of anarchy, made his words and deeds plain for all to see last night. The vileness of his violent plans was palpable in these fiery procla-*mations. Of these things I like to write, William P. Miller thinks. *The calenture that is the result of feverish degeneracy burned in his mind as he envisioned a future holocaust in which he wished us all to perish.* Of these things I write, and I am fairly good at it.

I paid Andriy and wished him good luck on his way back, and thus he completed his purpose and exited this narrative. He had dropped us off at a hotel that called itself Business Center Bukovina. Its façade was freshly painted bright beige and implausible raspberry. The stairs leading to the entrance were red-carpeted, but the carpet was filthy; at its low end there lay a mangy dog who raised his head and sniffed the air when we passed but did not move—it appeared blind.

Our room was on the fifth floor and we climbed the stairs, hauling our luggage. On each floor there sat a *baba*, an older, chubby woman in blue cleaning-personnel overalls, glaring at us as we passed. The last one stopped us with a grunt and called us over to her desk. On a sofa behind her, three scantily clad women sat with their legs identically crossed, flashing their miniskirted thighs. They were looking at us unblinkingly, assiduously, as though about to utter a prophecy, and then the one in the middle, lippy and large-eyed, winked and said: "Hi!" Somehow she recognized us as Americans, as we recognized them as prostitutes. We signed something for the *baba* and she handed each of us a slim roll of pink toilet paper, apparently rewarding us for overcoming all the obstacles and successfully reaching the fifth floor.

The room smelled of my grandfather's death—a malodorous concoction of urine, vermin, and mental decomposition. When I turned on the lights a host of cockroaches scurried radially from the center of the room, marked by a stain on the carpet. The blankets on the beds were greasy, the sheets blemished and wrinkled. There was a small TV in the upper-left corner; the walls were much too white, as though blood splatter had been whitewashed with quicklime. Rora opened the window, which overlooked nothing but a gigantic garbage container brimming with glass bottles—its sparkling fullness gave me a momentary pleasure. I always like to see a full garbage container, because I relish the thought of emptying it, the complete unburdening implicit in it.

Do you know the joke, Rora said, where little Mujo asks his mother where children come from, and she says: Well, I put a little bit of sugar under the carpet before I went to sleep and the following morning I found you there. Little Mujo puts a little bit of sugar under the carpet before he goes to sleep. The following morning he finds a cockroach and says: You motherfucker, if you weren't my brother, I'd smash you flat.

I knew the joke; it used to be funny. I stretched on the bed; Rora got hold of the TV remote: a herd of bicyclists climbing a hill; a man in a gray suit with an eternal wheat field behind him, reporting on the harvest prospects; Madonna slithering up the shimmering body of a female dancer, making two steps forward, one step back; an Orthodox Darth Vader, wailing in Church Slavonic; Wolf Blitzer worrying about something imminent and irrelevant with the usual dorky earnestness; a beating heart inside an open, bloody-pink rib cage; a suited man delivering a speech to a crowd, rattling his hands above his head; a wench in the back of a limousine spreading her thighs to be licked by another wench; the bicyclists falling into a bundle of bikes and legs. Here I was in a brothel in Bukovina, very far away from my life.

Lazarus had spent time in Chernivtsi—Czernowitz it was back then—the first place he and I now shared, apart from Chicago. No accounts of his life talk about his refugee years; Czernowitz was but a stop between Kishinev and Chicago. This was his nowhere, yet it was what he would remember. Here he lived at a barrack with other pogrom survivors who escaped from Kishinev to the safety of the Austro-Hungarian Empire. With the survivors he spoke Yiddish and Russian, German with the Austro-Hungarian soldiers guarding the camp. Some of those soldiers must have been Bosnian, he must have marveled at their fezzes, their wide faces and bright eyes. This was how I imagined it. He practiced Hebrew with the Zionists who gathered inside the belly of a bunk bed at the far end of the barrack; he met Isador at a Zionist meeting, then again at a Bund lecture—both of them signed a petition neither of them fully understood. With Isador he slipped through the fence and went to the casinos and the brothels abounding in the border town. The empire sent its soldiers and officers for a rewarding stay in Czernowitz, a town notorious for its licentiousness, before they were assigned to the sterner parts. The border euphoria; the elation of nobody ever being at home; the freedom of no attachments possible; the smugglers, the refugees, the gamblers, the conspirators, and the whores; the illegal crossings and the drunken fights at the beer hall—it was the Sodom of the empire. Here Lazarus lost his first money gambling; here he was flagellated in his dreams by the Kishinev pogromchiks; here he was deflowered; here he first felt adrift in a foreign land; here he learned that humanity is wicked and endless. Later, in Chicago, he and Isador remembered Czernowitz with some fondness and nostalgia; it was the last place where Lazarus was able to imagine the exciting details of a better future: the place where he would live with Olga, the books he was going to read, the job he was going to get, the women he was going to meet. And in Chicago, before falling asleep in the cold Washburn Avenue room, he recalled the tall, handsome Austrian officers tottering drunk and ludicrous, and the harlots that would let go of their arms adorned with sparkling cuff links to pinch his cheeks; he remembered the taste of the cotton candy sold on the Promenade. He frequently had dreams in which his family and friends were all together, all in one place, and that place was always Czernowitz.

Often, before I went to sleep, I remembered—or I should say I tried not to forget. Before I passed out, I recollected particular moments in slumberous tranquillity; I replayed conversations; I reflected upon smells and colors; I remembered myself as I used to be, twenty years before, or earlier that day. The ritual was my nightly prayer, a contemplation of my presence in the world.

It often got out of hand: possible stories sprouted from the recalled instants and images. Take the afternoon in Lviv when I stepped out of the bathroom after a long and torturous time in the trickling shower to find Rora napping, so peacefully invested in his dream that he looked like somebody I did not know. When, fading to sleep that night, I reflected upon his face, I envisioned a story in which I woke up and found him dead in a hotel room we were sharing. I had to call the reception desk and deal with all the logistics of removing his body from the room, from the world. I had to call his sister and break the heartbreaking news, and so I went through his stuff, only to discover that he had a forged Austrian passport with a different name and a plane ticket to Vienna for the next morning. When I called the only phone number I found among his belongings, nobody picked up the phone.

Many of those stories turned unnoticeably into a dream, whereby the narrative went completely haywire and I became but a confused character within it, unable to escape the plot. I could only snap out of it, and if I did, I instantly lost the dream, its reality vanishing the moment I woke up. Occasionally, a violently involuntary memory of a dream emerged in my mind, like a corpse released from the bottom of the lake. Once, with perfect sensory clarity, I recalled the weight of the schoolbag on my shoulder in which I carried, like a puppy, the war criminal Radovan Karadžić.

Part of the recollection ritual was admitting the defeat, recognizing that I could never remember everything. I had no choice but to remember just minuscule fragments, well aware that in no future would I be able to reconstruct the whole out of them. My dreams were but a means of forgetting, they were the branches tied to the galloping horses of our days, the emptying of the garbage so that tomorrow—assuming there would be a tomorrow—could be filled up with new life. You die, you forget, you wake up new. And if I cared about God, I would be tempted to think that remembering was sinful. For what else could it be, what could remembering all those gorgeous moments when this world was fully present at your fingertips be but a beautiful sin? The sour grains of Oak Street sand on my tongue; Lake Michigan changing with each leavened cloud passing over the moon from inky blue to piceous and back; the smell of Mary stored forever in the curve of her neck.

Did the biblical Lazarus dream, locked in the clayey cave? Did he remember his life in death—all of it, every moment? Did he remember the mornings with his sisters, waking up with a sunbeam moving across his face like a smile, the warm goat milk and boiled eggs for breakfast? And once he was resurrected, did he remember being dead, or did he just enter another dream of another life by way of Marseilles? Did he have to disremember his previous life and start from scratch, like an immigrant?

I woke up after the nap, the dream, naturally, vanishing without a trace. So we went for a stroll, Rora and I. Rora liked the light of the setting sun; I liked watching Rora take pictures. The streets were cooling, the buildings darkening, the windows as yet unlit, and so we roamed. Within half an hour, we stumbled upon another

Viennese Café, conceptually identical to the one in Lviv: the same coffee list, the same pastry selection, the same frail waitresses in black dresses and white aprons. We installed ourselves out in the garden and ordered our coffee with the nonchalance of Viennese Café veterans.

There used to be a Viennese Café in Sarajevo, too, inside the hotel called Europa—the red velvet chairs, the Secession adornments on the ceiling; waiters wearing bow ties, their thin mustaches neatly trimmed. It was a kind of place where the elders of the old Sarajevo families met every day, for decades. The waitstaff knew their usual orders and addressed them with reverence. You would have taken only your steady girlfriend there for a slice of Sacher torte, coffee, and schnapps; or she might have taken you to present you to her parents, who were regulars there, to prove she was not of peasant roots but of a family who used to own whole blocks of the city in the days of the empire. The café was destroyed, along with the Europa, early in the war, a couple of direct rocket hits, and I mourned it from afar.

Rora's *dedo*—grandfather—was a Viennese Café regular. Having coffee there every morning was his nostalgic ritual, for he had been a student in Vienna before World War One. He had been supposed to study architecture, but instead enjoyed the life away from Bosnia, the remote province of the empire, where the papers carried reports on Viennese opera galas and provincial kapellmeisters fashioned themselves after Mahler, but where many women were still veiled and everyone in the family strived to marry you off to a bucktoothed distant cousin you had been avoiding since you learned to walk. In Vienna, women found Rora's *dedo* attractively exotic with his soft-consonant accent and his claret fez. Licentious art students, eager to learn about his fairy-tale homeland, sat in his lap and played like kittens with his fez tassel and his curls, while he wrote falsely nostalgic letters home, complaining about the life in Vienna, which confused him and scared him, so much so that he had miscalculated the money he needed for surviving in the wilderness of the imperial metropolis. *Please, send more or I'll die, far from everything I love.* He'd sign off and buy schnapps for the art student and her friends. He would have stayed in Vienna forever, Rora said, if he didn't impregnate one of those art students and have to beat it. He returned to Sarajevo unwillingly; he sulked and drank for a while, until he married and took over the family business, just in time for the Great War. He was devastated when the empire disintegrated; it was as though he had lost his father. So he was a regular visitor at the Viennese Café for decades afterwards; the staff addressed him as Herr Halilbašić. He was prone to dropping German words in the middle of his sentences— *schnapps, Schweinerei, mein Gott*—even during his late years, which he spent studying the Qu'ran and praying five times a day. He could never get over the demise of the empire. It was his first love, his *dedo* would always say.

Love was what I had felt for Mary when she took me to Vienna for our second anniversary, just weeks before 9/11. She had booked a fancy hotel with gilded convolutions on the walls and ceilings; she had Googled the best restaurant in town, bought a suit for me and a chancy red dress for herself to wear for the anniversary dinner. After the dinner, we roamed Vienna; we held hands, the hands were warm, the night was cool, the streetlights glinted. I told her about my family and the empire and their journey to Bosnia, a story she had heard before, but this time it seemed that everything around me was evidence that I had not made it up. Now she had to believe me, that I had had a life, that my family had a history, that it was all connected through a powerful and loving, if perished, empire. We were walking down the Main Strasse, whatever you call it, with a lot of modern shops she would have been interested in had I not been so compelling, when, as if on cue, we heard an angelic voice singing the Ukrainian song my grandfather liked to sing. The singer must have been trained: he rounded his mouth and breathed like a pro, but he was blind, holding a tall white cane in front of himself like a biblical staff. An unshaven man in a filthy checkered jumper stood next to the blind singer; he scanned the crowd, his role to prevent the coins in the hat from being filched away. The song was a heartbreakingly sad one—"*Ridna Maty Moya*" it was called: My Sorrowful Mother. We stood there, squeezing each other's hands as though trying to press through the flesh to the bones and then beyond. She kissed my cheek and neck, and I felt the joy of omni-present love—everything around me speaking about me with affec-tion, and Mary was listening.

A HUMONGOUS tinted-window Mercedes SUV roared down the street, then stopped right in front of the café garden. Out came a brawny driver with black sunglasses, his waist snap-narrow, his biceps like ostrich thighs, his chin menacingly dimpled. He opened the back door and we first saw small leather-shoed feet, from which grew short legs in white khakis followed by a tight torso of an Olympic wrestler. The man wore a cell-phone holster on his belt, much akin to the way Soviet commissars used to wear Lugers. He sat down, pulled out his phone, and slammed it against the table, as though about to begin interrogation, and took up that sitting position peculiar to Slavic men: one hand on the thigh, the fingers nearly touching his groin, the other hand hang-ing over the table's edge, ready to spring into action. He scanned the café and called over a waitress who obediently scurried to his table. Having placed a curt order, he plugged his head into the cell phone; he spoke in brisk, moneymaking sentences. He was, may no one dare doubt it, a businessman. The driver leaned on the vehicle and lit a cigarette.

The rest of us were all aware, perhaps even aroused, that we were privy to possibly criminal transactions; nobody dared stare, yet everybody wanted to see. The café rearranged itself around the businessman: he was the center, while the dumb bodyguard angel marked the border of his domain. I kept looking over to him, for I felt I needed to memorize the menacing frown looming over his small eyes, the dilating nostrils bespeaking anger and disdain, his hairy forearms, his widely spread legs, which he did not seem able to cross due to a weapon tucked in his waist, or a hard-on, or both. Rora kept drinking his coffee and smoking, his Canon quiet in his lap, as though he could not hear the businessman barking power-wielding Russian into the cell phone, as though he were oblivious to the goon leaning on the car and watching.

These people, these gangsters, Rora said, they are the same wherever you go—the same smirk, the same cell phone, the same goon. There used to be a guy named Pseto, a big gangster in Sarajevo just before the war. His business was racketeering. He ran a crew, including a few cops, who would break up a vendor if he did not pay for protection. He had a jewelry shop for money laundering, and sometimes he wore half of his inventory: diamonds and gold all over. He walked down Ferhadija Street with that Sarajevo-street-thug strut, and people would part reverentially. (I could see him: throwing his shoulders and jerking his neck, pursing his lips, the mouth half open to show that he was halfway to being very pissed.) He would walk into a bar and the owner would have to buy drinks for everybody present, as though Pseto were the king. As his headquarters, he used a café called Djul-bašta (I knew exactly where it stood); the owner was blessed with his protection but had no customers other than the people who came to do business with Pseto. He had trained the owner to bring him a short espresso every half an hour by the clock, and he would sit there, drinking coffee all day. Once he made a disobedient cop suck his cock. And when a stupid journalist wrote about the collusion of the police and Pseto, he had sent goons to bring the fool and had him tied to the tree in front of the café. He put a gun at the journalist's temple and told him to bark, so he barked. And he barked all day, was fed pizza leftovers, and had to fetch a stick.

One day, shortly before the war, Rambo came to see him, pulled out his gun, and clipped him right there, Pseto's mouth full of espresso. And then he sat down, Pseto still dying at the next table, and ordered himself a double espresso with a touch of milk.

I REPLAYED RORA'S STORY in the sordid Business Center room, unable to fall asleep, owing to gallons of Viennese coffee, and turn it all into a dream so I can forget about it. Rora, naturally, was asleep—he had trouble neither with coffee nor with the memory-dream transitions. I flipped through channels, spending some time on a skin flick featuring a lot of frantic licking, then another CNN story about another suicide bomber in Baghdad, then the World Series of Poker. I have to confess that I was aroused by the dispirited cunnilingus on the TV screen as well as by the utopian iniquity Rora's story implied, by the plain possibility of the world governed by the depraved triumvirate of power, survival instinct, and greed. Rora had visited, perhaps had even inhabited, such a world, which meant I was but one step removed from it. That would be the true land of the free. In such a country I could do what I wanted—no marriage would matter, I would not owe anything to anybody, I could spend the Susie grant, the infinity of grants, on my pleasures. In such a world I could stop caring what I promised, what I committed myself to, because I would just not care who I was and become somebody else on a whim. And I could do it whenever I wished. I could be the sole meaning of my life.

A harbinger from that utopian land arrived at my door: I heard a coy knock, and when I stood up and opened it, hiding my erection behind the door, there was the pretty-faced prostitute. She had rather striking eyes and very fake long lashes; she was propped on top of high platform heels, thrusting her hefty cleavage toward me. She pulled her top down, exposing her pear-shaped breasts with hardened nipples, and said, in English: "Love." For a moment I thought, Here it is, then, why not? But then I shook my head, and closed the door.

I was still too weak to pursue my pleasures at the expense of others, certainly not at the expense of Mary or this wretched harlot who was probably going to be slapped by her pimp for failing to fuck a God-given American. And I was not unselfish enough not to be tempted by pursuing pleasure with abandon. Forever stuck in moral mediocrity, I could afford myself neither self-righteousness nor orgasmic existence. That was one of the reasons (unspoken, to Mary, or anybody) why I absolutely needed to write the Lazarus book. The book would make me become someone else, go either way: I could earn the right to orgasmic selfishness (and the money required for it) or I could purchase my moral insurance by going through the righteous processes of self-doubt and self-realization.

Mary witnessed my moral waddling; from her high position of surgically American decency she could see me struggling through permanent confusion. She wanted me to emerge from it, to move up the moral ladder, but I kept missing the next slippery rung. She was patient with my not showing her any of my writing, or with my refusing to rise early in order to look for munificent employment. She found triple-X cookies on my hard drive and was appropriately disgusted, but she didn't really think I would have an affair or hire an experimental escort. She tolerated my revulsion for things spiritual, just as she put up with my uninterest in children and home adornments. But what did truly bother her was that I couldn't see that the project of our marriage was the pursuit of a perfect state, the transition from the marriage of bodies to the marriage of souls. I was not pulling my weight (as a matter of fact, I was gaining weight), but she was still stoically forbearing. I did want to be a perfect husband, and I did love Mary, her hands bloodied daily by love, but I never stopped being aware of the possibilities that existed beyond the boundaries of our marriage, of the freedom to pursue gratification instead of perfection.

Lazarus and Isador went to a brothel together. Lazarus had received some money from his mother; Isador convinced him to invest it in deflowerment. They went to Madame Madonskaya's; she pinched their cheeks; the girls giggled as the two of them blushed. Isador picked the one with the largest bosom and went upstairs, leaving Lazarus surrounded by a gaggle of whores, until one of them took him by the hand and led him to her room. Lazarus was scared wordless, he could say nothing. She introduced herself as Lola; she had a dog in her room—a tiny, half-blind mutt who barked at him hysterically. As Lazarus undressed, the dog sniffed at his shins, and he broke into tears.

I turned off the TV and listened to Rora's breathing, conjuring up crashing waves. Outside, a man and a woman were talking and giggling, stumbling on something. A dog barked, then squealed; then there was the sound of glass crashing and shattering. Rora did not stir; the woman's voice trilled with mirth. The dog started howling, screaming, and yelping, all in the midst of breaking glass, and it went on for a while, the tortured whining, until it faded into a whimper. The man and woman had thrown the dog in the garbage container full of bottles and then must have watched it writhing, shredding and slicing itself, trying to escape.

The red flag of anarchy *was dragged yesterday through the pulpits of Chicago. Aroused by the attempt on Chief Shippy's life by a Russian Jew of the terrorist type, clergymen, irrespective of their denominations, denounced the conditions that have resulted in the malignant growth of such a sect. The Tsar of Russia, lax immigration laws, gross ignorance of our lower-class foreign residents, congenital laziness, and degeneracy common in their respective countries, along with the lethal concoction of the saloon, gambling, and atheism, were all mentioned as direct causes.*

At the temple at Indiana Avenue and Thirty-third Street, Rabbi Tobias Klopstock delivered an address extremely bitter in its denunciation of anarchism and its profane pronouncements. "The spirit of anarchy is flaunting itself in its attack against the integrity of our government," Rabbi Klopstock vociferated in front of a substantial crowd of Jews. "It is no surprise that Chief Shippy, as the most relentless enemy of the anarchist golem, was their target. We know it is time to call a halt when America, the land of liberty and freedom, loses itself in godless lawlessness. We Jews, as citizens of this free country, must join our Christian brethren in their opposition to the spread of revolutionary teachings on the soil of America."

From the pulpit of the Holy Heart of Resurrection, Father George

Field bemoaned the barbaric ignorance of the newly arrived immigrants. "Upon their disembarkment, many fall into the hellish pits of anarchism, out of which they have no way of climbing," he thundered yesterday. "For the souls of those who accept neither the hand of God nor the hand of America are lost unless we redeem them with our stern Christian love. Let us pray for the soul of Lazarus Averbuch and hope that he may rise in Christ like his beloved namesake."

IT IS LATE MORNING when Olga limps into the Central Police Station, past a couple of policemen sniggering and exchanging lewd jokes about this disheveled tart, one shoe heel missing. Olga announces to Deputy Sergeant Mulligan that she wishes to speak to Assistant Chief Schuettler. The sergeant laughs and says: "And who might you be, lassie?" But William P. Miller, lingering at the station in hope of a scoop, immediately recognizes she is dramatically distraught; her Semitic features emanate fathomless suffering, her olive skin has a tragic quality—one day, her people will sing songs about her. He whispers something into Mulligan's ear, and Mulligan shakes his large, cubical head dominated by a broken nose. Olga insists she must see Assistant Chief Schuettler, and Miller is already opening his notebook, pulling a pen, like a comb, out of his inside pocket. Olga Averbuch—*strong-headed Jewess, suffering tragedienne*—contains multitudes and stories. He puts on a charming grin and offers to walk her to Schuettler's office, but she does not even look at him. "You must consider having a bath, ma'am," Mulligan says to her back. "You smell like shit."

Last night, the unwieldy, ungainly silence of the city would not allow her to sleep, reminding her of the absence. Lazarus's cheek was like marble, his hair straw-dry. The *politsyant* was murmuring in his sleep when she went to the outhouse, carrying a towel, her long velvet skirt and a knitted scarf in her bosom. He was still asleep when she came back, so that when Isador, reeking of the cesspit, walked by him in woman's clothes, his face tucked into the scarf, he woke up only to utter a comment about stinking foreigners, but was too dazed to notice anything. It was her idea to go see Schuettler, hoping they wouldn't come to pick her up and find Isador in her bedroom, folded painfully inside her wardrobe, behind a suitcase and a pile of rags. This will be good practice, Isador said, for when you are married and I am your lover. On her way to the police station, she imagined the Fitzes beating him with cheerful ardor, as they beat Isaac, presently gasping for air in his bed, his ribs thoroughly cracked. Even if he deserved a good beating, Isador would never live through it; some bones were never meant to be broken.

Assistant Chief Schuettler is under the desk; it appears that he is looking for a cuff link or a dropped coin. She watches his bottom wiggling, until he emerges from the kneeling position, slowly uncoiling himself, like a snake. He looms over Olga, smoothing out his sleeves, as she tries not to lean on her heelless side. "You've come to confess the crimes of your brother, Miss Averbuch? Perhaps denounce his anarchist companions? Or tell us where we can find the young Maron?"

Defiantly she faced Assistant Chief Schuettler, William P. Miller will write. *She in her malodorous, maculate robe, he in his impeccably tailored suit; she with the wildness of the steppe gleaming in her eyes, he with the strength of law and order exhibited in his square, wide shoulders. It was a battle of wills: masculine versus feminine; American versus Semitic; civilized versus anarchist. In no uncertain terms, the suffering woman demanded her brother's body back so that he could be buried according to the ancient Jewish rituals. Howling foul words at Assistant Chief Schuettler, who stood stolidly facing her, she threatened with the wrath of the international Jews and depicted a modern-day apocalypse. With animal passion in her eyes, she promised long years of general terror, decades of anarchy that would destroy our freedom and everything we hold dear. But Assistant Chief Schuettler stared her straight in the eye.* "Miss Aver-

buch," said he, *"my job is to uphold law and order, and for law and order I must do what is best. Let your brother lie in peace, so this tormented city may finally return to tranquillity."* At that the wounded Jewess stormed out, cursing with such foul fury that it would not have been out of place in hell itself.

A *politsyant* with a handlebar mustache slaps Olga's behind on the way out, and she totters out onto the street. Miller watches her, not laughing, even though the policeman nudges him—*like the sister of the biblical Lazarus, she would go to any length to save her brother*. She walks randomly, crossing the street only to cross back again. She finds herself lost in a maze of crates full of chickens and rabbits, then steps in front of a piebald horse dragging a cart of pendant tin pots hysterically banging against one another. The horse looks straight into her eyes, its eyelashes ridiculously long, and neighs, as if greeting her. She stops in front of a candy store, looking into the window and not seeing the pink and the blue and the swirling candy, not seeing the licorice or the sugar cotton. A three-legged mutt runs up to her, as if recognizing her, and sniffs her. A newspaper boy shouts at the corner: "Washington to take the first step in purging the nation of foes to government and individual life!"

Dear Mother,
This letter is coming from a better world: by the time you receive
it, Lazarus and I will be together waiting for you.

Somebody is picking up his change in the store, while the man behind the counter glares out the window at Olga, as if warning her against coming in. She feels bodies passing her, brushing against her outskirts. A hand touches her shoulder and a man behind her says: "Would you like some candy?" Without responding, she strides away, bitterness climbing up her throat—had she eaten anything since yesterday, she would have vomited. "I am a friend," the man says, catching up with her. "I aimed to introduce myself at the police station." His voice is deep, his English un-American. She hurries forward, hobbling, catching with her hip a basket laden with fish, their doll eyes bulging. "I'm very sorry about your brother, Lazarus," the man says, panting a bit. "There are a lot of people who believe"—he scurries after her, losing his breath—"who believe that the complete truth about his unfortunate death has not come out yet." Olga slows down but does not turn back. This might be another *politsey* joke; her other heel is shaky, she can feel it quiver. The man, still at Olga's heel, begins the next sentence with a bass cough: "There are people in this city who believe we might soon witness a pogrom."

Olga turns around. The man has a bowler hat, a tubercular pallor coupled with sickly ruddy cheeks, a collar white enough to indicate respectability.

My name is Hermann Taube. Great delight to have met you, he says in Yiddish.

"What you want from me?" she asks, in English.

Let us converse, he continues in Yiddish. Let us go to a more affable place.

He offers her his arm, but she walks apart from him. Yet when he hops on a Halsted streetcar, she follows him; he pays her fare. As they are moving deeper into the streetcar, he turns and smiles at a detective who ran after them and managed to get on. Olga saw the detective at the police station; she recognizes his new, oversized cap pressing down the tips of his ears. He is conspicuous in his determination to stay close, awkwardly looking past the two of them. The crowd presses Taube's body toward her, but he pushes back against it and makes a quick, barely visible, bow. She imagines his heels clacking.

A fox's glass eyes are staring at them from the neck of a speckled matriarch, rings abundant on her white-gloved hands. How did this woman end up on a streetcar? She looks like a widow. Up in the back there is an argument going on, in Italian it seems, and in the front of the streetcar necks and heads turn toward the ruckus, all curiosity and disgust. It soothes Olga that her companion is not worried about the detective, but she says nothing, and so they ride in silence. It is probably a symptom of her mind decomposing that she feels a certain pleasure in not knowing where they are heading.

Taube helps her off the tram, she accepts his hand, but lets hers be limp and does not thank him. They walk briskly down a tree-lined street, past stately houses, past wrought-iron fences with spikes and curlicue patterns, the detective following them at a distance. When they enter through the back door of what appears to be a tavern, he stops outside. There are loafers smoking at the front door of the tavern, their collars upturned, caps pulled down to the eyebrows. The detective walks between them and orders a beer at the bar. Above a gigantic mirror, there is a glass-eyed boar head.

A stout, blue-eyed woman carrying a file pressed against her chest whispers something to Taube in German. The hallway reeks of beer-soaked sawdust and burnt sauerkraut. Olga follows Taube into a murky maze of offices, the woman right behind her. Through a door ajar she can see a staircase leading to the basement; there are sounds of heavy objects scraping against the floor, but Taube closes the door. She limps up a stairway in Taube's redolent wake— he smells of wax and violets. The staircase is steep, her hip is hurting, so she stops every once in a while. If you find yourself asking: How did I get here? Isador once said, that probably means you are living a life worth living. Isador knows nothing about life.

Taube's is a lawyer's office. Thick leather-bound law books line the shelves; there is an inkwell and a feather pen on the clean desk. He offers her a seat, washes his hands in a basin, then slowly lands behind the desk—there is a copy of the *Tribune* on it, which he rotates and pushes toward her. His motions have well-planned devotion, as if he rehearsed it all and is now finally performing. She is still frightened by the torqued logic of the day, by the burden of the sleepless night pressing down on her spine. Lazarus's death, Assistant Chief Schuettler, the lecherous *politsey,* the shitty Isador in her wardrobe—it all seems unreal in this orderly office: a single carnation in a suave vase on the cabinet, a framed diploma from a Viennese law school on the wall; a pipe on the file cabinet, lying sideways like a tired dog; a weak fly buzzing somewhere along the windowpane, looking for a way out. On the front page of the *Tribune* is a photo of Lazarus in profile, his eyes closed, a dark shadow over his eyes and in the hollow of his cheeks. THE ANARCHIST TYPE the heading says; numbers are strewn around his face. Below it, the numbers are explained:

1. *low forehead;*
2. *large mouth;*
3. *receding chin;*
4. *prominent cheekbones;*
5. *large simian ears.*

Olga wheezes in disbelief; as nimbly as a magician, Taube pulls a white handkerchief out of his inside breast pocket and offers it to her. She declines at first, but he silently insists and she takes it. He picks up the *Tribune* and flips through it as she wipes her nose.

"The anarchist vermin that infest Chicago and our nation are to be exterminated to the last vile individual," Taube reads in his German-inflected English. "Every power at the command of local authorities will be invoked, every loyal citizen will be called upon, to achieve this job of housecleaning. The authors of seditious utterances will be prosecuted. Undesirable foreigners will be deported. Street gatherings of malcontents will be absolutely prohibited. Municipal authorities will deal summarily with unlawful disturbances. No pity will be shown."

Olga does not understand everything Taube reads, but she can sense the agitation beyond his declaratory voice. He flips another page, searches up and down until he finds what he is looking for.

She caressed Lazarus's chin, touched the bullet hole, black as a birthmark. His forehead tasted like some mortuary chemical.

"The methods of anarchists have changed materially in the last twenty years. In the days before the Haymarket riot the anarchists were preaching violence against a class as a whole. They went in for wholesale violence. Their leaders were English and German. But now the Italian and Russian Jewish elements have come to the fore. Their leaders are of a lower, degenerate, more despicable criminal type, but their methods are more dangerous. They preach the murder of the individual. They believe in nihilistic ideas of suicide and assassination."

Why are you reading this to me, Herr Taube? What am I to understand? What do you want?

Taube now speaks in a Viennese German that contains no trace of Yiddish; he lowers his voice, raises his chin.

"I mourn the death of your brother with you, Fräulein Averbuch. I was brought up to believe that if we lose one Jew, we lose the world. And I suffer your loss not only as a Jew but also as one who believes in the rule of righteous law."

Olga becomes aware of the smell her body exudes—she scrubbed herself time and again last night but still feels beshitten.

"There are men in this city, Fräulein Averbuch, all well-established members of society, who are duly apprehensive about the current atmosphere, as it could easily lead to uncontrollable violence. Such a development would endanger what they have been working for for a long time and would likely impede the further progress of their less-fortunate brethren. Being of Semitic origin, they are outsiders themselves in their circles, so they do not wish to emphasize their kinship connections with alleged anarchists. At the same time, they are not impervious to the travails of the poor and the innocent."

Olga blows her nose mightily into his handkerchief to punish him for his opacity.

"Well do we all know things have been changing: what blood libel was in Russia, anarchism could become in America. Many of us who escaped pogroms and came here know that it starts with editorials and ends in massacres. We have friends who are happy to see a more realistic picture of Hebrew life, but there are also patriotic Americans who cannot tell the difference between a decent, loyal citizen and a vile anarchist. Your brother's unfortunate fate might have confused many more good Americans. Alas, he is undeniably dead now, entirely unable to help us with the truth as we are left to deal with the consequences.

Who are you, Herr Taube?

His is a voice of practiced reasonability; he has conducted business negotiations before. He goes on in his lawyerly German.

"I am an attorney representing a group of interested citizens, Fräulein Averbuch. We have reasons to believe that the police are looking for one Isador Maron. His is a well-known name among the reds, a notorious adherent to the abject teachings of Emma Goldman. It seems clear that he is the main culprit, the one who exposed your brother to Goldman's humbug, who mesmerized him with the black hand of anarchy. It would benefit everybody involved if he were forced to face the consequences of his words and deeds.

I don't know how I could help you with that, Olga says. She keeps speaking Yiddish, but Taube does not register her spite.

"The police are under the impression that you and Maron were more than just acquaintances. They need to talk to him. He might perhaps clarify that your brother's death was but a matter of misunderstanding. Until then, your brother's memory will continue to be besmirched."

I do not know where Maron is. I do not know him that well.

Her fingers are entangled in the handkerchief, until she notices Taube glancing down at her hands; she lets go of it. Lying does not come easy to her, particularly since turning Isador in is not an unreasonable, untempting possibility. Everything, this, should stop.

She spreads the handkerchief in her lap, then carefully folds it and dabs her cheeks to suggest she is done crying.

They killed Lazarus, she says. Whose fault can that be? His? Isador's? Emma Goldman's? They did not even have the decency to tell me how exactly it happened. What do you want from me?

"Olga—if I may—Olga, you surely want to lay your brother to rest according to our time-honored customs. I've read the autopsy report. He was riddled with bullets. I do not wish to upset you further, but he did not die a peaceful death. We have to do something or he will never have peace. Nor will we."

Who are we?

"Olga, do try to understand. Right now, the police might be willing to believe that the crime against Chief Shippy and the laws of this country was committed by enraged degenerates. Freedom is a business much easier to run if the authorities have a useful enemy, and anarchists appear to be more than happy to be cast in that role. Should the authorities run out of patience, they may succeed in convincing themselves—and many others—that all Jews, regardless of their loyalty and patriotism, are the enemy. I do not need to tell you what that would mean. You lived through the Kishinev pogrom."

I don't know who you are, what your business is. I do not know who you are representing. I have no reason to trust you or believe you.

"I am representing certain honorable individuals who would like to help you, both out of a sense of racial responsibility and in their own individual interest. Permit me to assure you that this combination of motives vouchsafes their sincerity."

All I want is to bury my brother respectfully.

"That is what everybody wants, without a doubt."

"I do not think I can help you," Olga says in German, in a low, fatigued voice.

"I understand that all this might be overwhelming for you. Perhaps you need time to come to terms with the situation. Do be aware, however, that we have no time. The rumor has it that the Goldman woman is coming to town, indubitably to cause trouble, and we need to address the problem before your poor brother has irreversibly metamorphosed into an anarchist martyr."

He gives her his business card and, neatly tucked into the newspaper with Lazarus's picture, a stack of crisp, new dollars. Taube is smart: Olga does not carry a purse. She lays the handkerchief on his desk, takes the money out of the folded paper, and throws it on the desk.

"Please know that at times like this any one of us might be called upon to do their part," Taube continues. "And keep in mind we are at your service, Fräulein Averbuch. I hope to talk to you again very soon, but feel free to put in a phone call at any time, today or tonight. Naturally, we will accept the charges."

She leaves, the newspaper in hand, without saying good-bye. As she walks out through the tavern and the front door, the young detective downs his beer in a hurry and leaps off his stool. She wobbles past the loafers, who watch her in silence. They say nothing, but when the young detective brushes past, one of them drops his cigar to the ground and crushes it, twisting his foot until only crumbles are left.

On the Halsted streetcar a man with thick glasses and curly hair tucked under a cap offers her a seat. Her sight is blurred, her glasses are grimy. She takes them off and cleans them with her dress hem. The young detective moves closer, stands right before her, so that his groin is facing her. He must have called the station to report on her whereabouts; if they had discovered Isador she would have already been arrested. She feels a hurtful urge to look at her brother's face on the front page, but the photo is facedown in her lap. He was so beautiful, such a handsome young man. On the back page, she reads that *the Chief of Police in Birmingham, Alabama, received through the mail a note reading: "Chief Bodeher, we give a you ona weeka to quita a joba. You finda out a knifa if you don'ta."* Several foreigners were arrested today. Chief Bodeher says he will take no chances.

The whole world has gone insane and I with it. Fatigue is pushing her down, she slouches into her pain, clutching the paper's edge like a knife handle.

Dear Mother,
Lazarus's funeral was beautiful. The rebbe spoke of his kindness, and there were hundreds of his friends, mountains of flowers.

The same woman with the fox-fur collar is sitting next to Olga, as though she were biding her widowhood on the streetcar. The fox's eyes are staring at Olga again, the widow dozing off, her gloved fingers intertwined. For a moment Olga thinks that she dreamt Taube and his office. *In Grand Rapids, Michigan,* she reads, *Judge Alfred Wolcott of the circuit bench died of apoplexy this afternoon, five minutes after he was stricken. His wife, a devout Christian Scientist, refuses to admit he is dead. Three different physicians have pronounced his life extinct, but Mrs. Wolcott maintains that they are in error.*

I am running out of life, Olga thinks. What am I going to do? What is there without life?

Lazarus used to work in the corner by the window, next to Greg Heller, packing eggs without a word all day. He worked so hard Heller often had to tell him to slow down. Only at the end of the shift would he sometimes jabber in as much English as he knew, mixed with strange foreign words. He never mentioned anarchism, Heller said, except once: Emma Goldman, the anarchist queen, was coming to Chicago to speak, and Lazarus tried to talk Heller into going with him to hear her—which Heller rejected in disgust. "The rich have all the money. I have none. You have none," Lazarus said, waving his arms, his eyes shining. Heller told him to keep busy and he would earn some. Mr. Eichgreen confirmed that Lazarus was a good worker; he never talked anarchism to him. If he had come to work on Monday, Mr. Eichgreen would have sent Lazarus to Iowa to learn the egg-packing business from the bottom. Young Averbuch, Mr. Eichgreen said, he seemed fond of America.

SOMEONE ONCE ASKED ME how I saw America. I wake up in the morning, I said, and I look to my left. And on my left I would see Mary, her face serene and often frowning. Sometimes I'd watch her sleep, licking her lips or gibbering in the middle of a dream. I seldom dared kiss her, because she was a light sleeper and likely to be tired after a shift of brain-chopping. When I did plant a touch-kiss on her cheek, carefully and slowly, she would break through her slumber and look at me flabbergasted and frightened—she could not recognize me. And when she was in surgery and there was no body on her half of the bed, just the wrinkled indentation and her scent and an occasional long black hair on the pillow, I would rise, fainthearted, for somehow her absence opened up the possibility that my life and all of its traces had vanished, that Mary had left me, took it all with her, and we would never read our book on our chest again. In the kitchen, I would find a bowl with a very small spoon in it, crumbs of organic cereal dissolving in the pool of milk at the bottom. The coffee machine would still be sputtering; the *Chicago Tribune* folded on the table, except for the Metro section—she liked to read obituaries on her way to the hospital. There was often a note for me, signed with a flourishy *M*. Sometimes it said *Love, M.*

Rora and I had breakfast at the hotel restaurant—boiled eggs, butter, pieces of dry rye bread. A businessman in a leather jacket sucking a toothpick wobbled in, his gait suggesting a sore groin. The television set was on, showing *Fashion TV*. A couple of prostitutes, their night shift finished, drank coffee and smoked, savoring the sunny, pimpless morning. They were crumpled and tired, indifferent to anything or anybody outside their own esoteric intimacy. The carmine lipstick; the garish makeup on their pale, creased faces; the formerly puffed-up bangs now sagged—it was as though they had finally forsaken straining themselves to be attractive. They spoke to each other with surprising vigor, something was at stake. I wondered what it was, and I realized that I would never find out.

After he spoke with Karadžić and faxed the interview to New York, Rora said, Miller wanted to celebrate his exclusive and relax a little, for the whole thing had been rather stressful. So Rora took him to Duran's brothel, mainly serving the foreigners—peacekeepers, diplomats, and journalists, who affectionately called the venue Duran Duran—although during a truce you could find people from both sides of the war there. Rambo himself, of course, was a frequent, unpaying guest and brought along many friends. He liked to treat the foreigners he was in business with: there were distinguished diplomats whose happy political lives would be jeopardized if it ever came out what kind of games they played with those girls. Duran's brothel was a place insulated from the war: soft music, fresh flowers, no siege stench, the girls clean and neat, some of them even pretty. They were mainly from Ukraine and Moldova, although there were a couple of Hungarian firebrands for the special clientele, like the president's son—also Rambo's good friend.

Miller got a bottle of Johnnie Walker, and they drank and enjoyed some lap dancing, until Miller started hollering and bragging to other men (a Canadian major, a French colonel, an American spy) that he had just interviewed Karadžić. He was a true reporter, exclusives gave him hard-ons, and the major and the colonel and the American drank to it, and the girls drank to it, and Rora drank to it, with a pebble of disgust in his throat. When it came to doing business with the girls, Rora couldn't do it. He went up with a good-looking Moldovan girl who styled herself after Madonna, complete with the scarves, the belts, and the hoop earrings. She called herself Francesca and was drugged enough to appear genuinely interested, but he just couldn't do it. She passed out on the bed; he sat in the chair, smoking and waiting for Miller to be done. He took some pictures of her; her lips were ajar and one of her incisors was poking her lower lip; she sniffed and rubbed her nose with the back of her hand; her wheeze was on the verge of a snore. How did she end up here? Rora thought. She had family somewhere, a mother or a brother. Everybody comes from somewhere.

. . .

THE YAWNFUL WEIGHT on my shoulders; the literal pain in my neck; the silence after Rora's story; the sense of liberating futility—I carried all that down the dusty streets of Chernivtsi. We were heading for the Jewish Center but allowed ourselves to be sidetracked by an abundant outdoor market: Rora took a photo of a stall with a large heap of crimson cherries, and of a woman with a cabbage leaf on her head in lieu of a sun hat, and of a lamb carcass hacked to pieces with a cleaver. We walked by a schoolyard where there were rows of children exercising to the commands of an instructor in a Communist-red tracksuit, raising their arms up to the sky, then bending to touch their toes. The instructor blew his whistle, and the throng of kids sorted themselves into columns of pairs and started running in circles. We walked by the Viennese Café, where the businessman occupied the same exact position, still barking into his cell phone, as though he had not left since the day before. A fetching young lady, severely miniskirted, sat opposite him, speaking into her cell phone, conducting her business, whatever it was.

Let me tell you a joke, Rora said. Mujo is a refugee in Germany, has no job, but has a lot of time, so he goes to a Turkish bath. The bath is full of German businessmen with towels around their waists, huffing and puffing, but every once in a while a cell phone rings and they pull their phone out from under the towel and say, *Bitte?* Mujo seems to be the only one without a cell phone, so he goes to the bathroom and stuffs toilet paper up his butt. He walks back out, a long trail of toilet paper behind him. So a German says, You have some paper, *Herr,* sticking out behind you. Oh, Mujo says, it looks like I have received a fax.

IT TOOK US a while to find the Jewish Center. Perhaps understandably, there were no signs pointing toward it, tucked in the far corner of a leafy square facing the theater. Nobody was answering when I rang the doorbell of the Center. My lazy heart fluttered with joy, for I was aspiring to a prosaic day at the Viennese Café, hopefully ogling the white-thighed maiden in the businessman's utopian orbit.

But as we were leaving the premises, a man with a pear-shaped torso clad in an unflattering horizontally striped shirt asked us in Russian what it was that we wanted and instead of telling him the truth (idling, coffee, ogling) I told him we wanted to speak with someone from the Center. The man extended his hand to me, but said nothing and unlocked the door.

"So what language would you like to speak?" he asked me once we were inside.

"What do you have?" I asked him, in Ukrainian.

"Russian, Romanian, Ukrainian, Yiddish, German, and a little bit of Hebrew," he said.

The office was boxy and dusty, vacant bookshelves lining the walls. The man's name was Chaim Gruzenberg; he set up two chairs facing each other and I sat across from him. He smelled vaguely of sardines. I hereby admit that it might have been an olfactory hallucination.

"How come you speak so many languages?"

"When I was growing up, there were all kinds of people here. No more. Now everybody is independent, or gone."

At the desk in the far corner a man was writing vigorously; the tip of his pencil kept breaking, he kept sharpening it, volutes of gray hair quivering over his forehead. With occasional help from my Ukranian dictionary, I spoke to Chaim about the murder of Lazarus, about my project, about Lazarus's journey to America in 1907, about his escape to Czernowitz after the pogrom and his time in a refugee camp here.

"Ach," Chaim said, "that was so long ago, a whole horrible century ago. So many things happened since then, so much to remember, and forget."

Rora was taking pictures of framed black-and-white photos on the walls, of the spines of the books on the shelf, of the front page of a brochure with a Star of David. He resembled a ghost in the counterlight. Chaim said he was not an expert in history, for history fed nobody. His job was to provide food and care for the elderly Jews in the town, those who had no family left; he was too busy finding ways to help them; people were getting older and sicker and more helpless. If I would like to help them, he could help me do that, he said.

"Sure," I said. Rora moved out of the counterlight; a swarm of motes whirled where he had just stood.

"All of you foreigners come looking for your ancestors and roots," Chaim said. "You are only interested in the dead. God will take care of the dead. We need to take care of the living."

I promised a donation for the living, but I could not relinquish the dead: I asked him if any of the elderly Jews perhaps remembered stories of the Kishinev refugees, stories their parents or grandparents bequeathed them; maybe some of them were descendants of the refugees who settled here.

"Nobody stayed," Chaim said. "And if they stayed they were quick to forget what happened in Kishinev."

"Perhaps someone remembers."

"They are old, sick people, dying slowly. Their lives are filling up with death, they remember nothing. Why would they want to bring in more death, from before they were born?"

"How many clients do you have?"

"They are not my clients. They are my family. I have known them since before I was born."

The gray-haired man at the desk was listening to us. Rora used the chance to photograph him, and the man peevishly waved him away. There was a framed poster on the wall, announcing something that happened on September 11, 1927.

"I remember my grandmother telling me about the Jews coming

from Kishinev. Some of them were rich. There was one named Mandelbaum," Chaim said. "They came with carriages full of carpets
and chandeliers. He brought a grand piano. He lost it all gambling,
my grandmother said. His daughter married an actor."

"Did your grandmother remember a family named Averbuch?"

"Half of the Jews in these parts were named Averbuch."

"Do you have any clients named Averbuch?"

"They are not clients."

"I apologize."

"There is Roza Averbuch, but she is very old and sick, and she
has lost all her marbles."

"Could I talk to her?"

"Why do you want to talk to her? She doesn't remember anything. She thinks I am her grandfather. She is afraid of strangers."

The writing man said something testy in Yiddish to Chaim, who
responded in like manner; they were having an argument. The
phone rang but they paid no attention whatsoever to it. Rora
trained his Canon on Chaim and the writing man, who wagged a
finger at Chaim and us and returned to sharpening his pencil, hiding his face from Rora's lens. Chaim snorted and said to me:

"There were many pogroms in Russia before the Shoah, and then
there was the Shoah. This town was always full of refugees from
Kishinev or some other place, escaping from the Russians and the
Romanians and the Germans. Those who survived went elsewhere,
few stayed. Not many people are left, and they are dying, too."

I capitulated; I didn't really know what to ask. I convinced myself I didn't really need any testimonies; I had pretty much completed my research; I had sifted through all the books. Just being
in this room, facing Chaim, seemed like an accomplishment. Besides, Rora was shooting a lot of pictures I could look at later on;
we would study them together later. Perhaps it was time for some
caffeinated contemplation. I pulled out my wallet and offered
Chaim a wad of the Susie money, a hundred euros in all.

"No, no, no," he said. "That is plenty but not enough. That money can buy food for a week, but we need clothes and medicine too. I respect your good intentions. But I ask you to go to your synagogue, talk to your congregation, tell them we need help."

He went to the writing man's desk, plucked the pencil out of his hand, ripped a piece of paper out of a notebook, and wrote down the address of the Center. It didn't even cross his mind that I might not be Jewish. I couldn't confess, of course, for that would have converted everything I talked about into deception.

"Is he a Jew, too?" Chaim asked, nodding toward Rora, who was reloading film. He looked up at me and I knew he understood.

"No," I said.

"He has Jewish hair," Chaim said. "A handsome man."

Lazarus's head was shaved for lice on Ellis Island, his eyes checked for trachoma. The guards bayed at him, prodded him with their batons. The first English word he learned was *water* because a woman in a white apron filled up his tin cup with water out of a barrel. On the boat from Trieste, he had slept next to an old Sicilian who kept gabbing unintelligibly to him, pointing at his hair. Even in his sleep, Lazarus clutched the money in his pocket, the money Mother gave him, all of her savings. Just before he left Czernowitz, he had received a letter from Mother telling him Papa had died of apoplexy, he just fell off the chair and was gone. He did not know if Olga had received the news. He envisioned Isador, who had left Czernowitz a month before, at the Chicago train station, waiting for him with Olga. He wondered if there was something going on between her and Isador. He was not there to watch over his sister, so Isador could pour sweet poison into her ear. Or perhaps she met someone else; maybe she would wait for him with her new man, maybe even a real American goy. He worried if he would be able to recognize her. There are a lot of Jews in Chicago, she wrote. I do some sewing for Mr. Eichgreen's wife. He promised me a job for you.

. . .

AFTER THE JEWISH CENTER and a contemplative cup of coffee at the Viennese Café, we—ever the dutiful researchers—decided to visit the Museum of Regional History, right up the street from the café. We wandered through the musty museum, ambling, solemnly as though in the wake of a coffin. Each room we entered was guarded by a menaceful *baba*, her ankles swollen.

The first and the biggest *baba* was in the World War Two room and frowned at us when we stepped in, as though we disturbed her meditation. All around the room there were portraits of the Soviet heroes of the region who died for the freedom of the motherland. Volodya Nezhniy, for example, hurled himself fearlessly at a German machine gun with a cluster of hand grenades attached to his chest. There were red-starred helmets and shell casings and the stretched red flags of various Red Army units. There was a retouched photo of mass executions: a line of people kneeling on the edge of a ditch, their heads bowed to receive the bullets.

In the next room, the *baba* flashed a very brief, but far from inviting, smile. One glass case was full of locally produced screws and metal thingamajigs; another featured single shoes, varying in size, implying a mob of one-shoed people hobbling around like zombies.

The *baba* in the third room stood by a wooden relief featuring Mr. Christ dragging his toy cross and a devout entourage shedding wooden tears. There were various Virgin icons, craftily carved crosses, and ornately painted Easter eggs.

Out of the redemption and resurrection room, into the orientation room: on the wall there was a shirt and a picture of Juri Omeltchenko, the silver medalist at the Finland 2000 World Orienteering Championship. In the picture, Juri was doggedly orienting himself amidst the trees, his determined face and blond hair dappled with the leaf shadows. Here was another fellow human who dedicated his life to not being lost.

Next room: walls plastered with posters and record covers of the children of the region who achieved the local equivalent of stardom. They had pompadoured heads and spectacular sideburns and rouged cheeks; they had names, too: Volodymir Ivasyuk, Nazariy Yeremchuk, Sofia Rotary. A gramophone with a record was on a pedestal, the *baba* standing honor guard next to it. We dutifully examined it and were about to move on when she sternly stopped us in our tracks. She played the record for us; we listened, eschewing eye contact. A mellifluous voice struggled against the cracking, singing, from what I could understand, about going to the well with a hole in her bucket; it seemed she never brought any water home, but she still kept doing it—it rather seemed like a metaphysically demoralizing situation. The *baba* pointed to one of the record covers: the singer's name was Maryusa Flak; she wore a woeful bandana; her mouth was heart-shaped.

All around the next room were head shots of uniformed young men who had served and died in Afghanistan. The region was proud of them for having served their country, a sign said, and they would never be forgotten. Residual trinkets of their lives were laid out in glass cases: here was Andriy's report card (he was a good student); here were Ivan's wool socks and a letter from his mother ("Be brave and work hard and know that your sister and I think of you all the time"); a belt was stretched out like a dead snake, the rim of the penultimate hole thoroughly worn out; a tiny, tinny medal with a frayed red ribbon, and a single leather glove that used to belong to an Oleksandr. Rora took a couple of pictures, whereupon the *baba* darted over to prevent his photographing.

Next we walked through a hallway with glass cabinets full of insects neatly pinned in rows. One of the rows featured progressively bigger cockroaches. For all I knew, they might have all been collected in our hotel. The first one was small and looked like a baby roach, whereas the last one was thumb-sized, so large that one could easily imagine her having mothered all of her row mates.

How come, I asked Rora, how come you have not talked to your sister since we've been on the road?

Who says I haven't?

Have you?

I have. Yes.

How come you never mentioned it?

There are so many things I don't mention, you could write a book about them.

How come you never talk about your sister?

My sister has not had a happy life. Talking about it helps nobody.

What happened to your parents? Did they die in a car accident?

They were in a bus that tumbled into the canyon of the Neretva. Will you stop asking questions now?

How old were you?

Six.

Do you remember them?

Of course I remember them.

What were they like.

They were like all other parents. My mother liked to feed us. My father liked to take pictures. Can you stop asking questions now?

The last room contained allegedly eighteenth-century stuff: hosts of wooden spoons and bowls, cracked; rings and chains and daggers and obscure tools for extinct kinds of labor, resembling torture instruments; a tapestry picturing a secluded meadow at sunset, the darkness arriving over the trees; and, in the corner, a case with stuffed birds. The centerpiece of the installation was an eagle with a rabbit in his talons, spreading his wings over the oblivious ducks and nameless birds, his eyes eternally marble-glassy. Were these creatures stuffed in the eighteenth century? Or did some idle provincial philosopher working as a custodian of regional memory seek to suggest that death was undatable, that it was always the same thing, regardless of the century?

I suppose this is no Louvre, I said.

I bet the old ladies are part of the collection, Rora said. They'll embalm them when they die.

ACROSS THE STREET from the stale disreality of the Museum of Regional History was an Internet café called Chicago. We entered it without thinking, as though going home: there were pictures of the Sears Tower and Wrigley Field and the Buckingham Fountain, and there was a glum attendant whom I addressed in English, which he chose not to understand or respond to. Rora and I took seats at our respective computers and did not look at each other. I would have liked to have seen who Rora was writing to but was too busy with a long e-mail to Mary, at the end of which I wrote:

Very much thinking of you. The hotel we are staying in is a whorehouse, apparently. Rora is taking a lot of pictures. How is your dead?

George, her *dead*, had had his prostate taken out and was currently wearing diapers. Once, I had found him weeping into the open fridge; the tears on his face were emblazed by the fridge light. He shook his head, as if to shake off excess moisture and woe, and took out a salami, snarling: "Do you eat crap like this in your country?" While waiting to die, he invested all his impressive energy in being angry at life, and he no longer regularly talked to Mr. Christ, the light of God extinguished in him by hormonal therapy. I often caught myself hating his retired-businessman gray hair, his popishness, his insistence on my gratefulness to American greatness, and his constant, stupid questions about *my country,* questions like: "Do they have opera in your country?" or "Your country is west of what?" *My country* was this remote, mythical place for him, a remnant of the world from before America, a land of obsolescence whose people could arrive at humanity only in the United States, and belatedly. He feigned concern for the heartening immigrant experiences related in my columns, largely because he wanted to assess how long my journey had been from being a half-ghost in *my country* to being an attempt at an American, the unfortunate husband of his unlucky daughter. I occasionally amused Mary with mock answers to George's imaginary questions. "In my country," I'd say, she giggling already, "candy is the chief currency." Or: "Airflow is illegal in my country."

Mary would sometimes confess to me how she had always felt deprived of his love, how sickening to all of them his Catholic sternness had been, how she had always longed for his unconditional kindness. She never said it, but I knew that she resented him for his condescension and insistence on my foreignness. He believed she had married me because she couldn't marry an American; she desperately wanted him to see that I had succeeded at being American, that the humanizing process had been completed, my extended unemployment notwithstanding. Yet I could recognize George in her: she was prone to self-righteousness; she snapped at me for no obvious reason, for she held a deep, hurtful grudge she repeatedly refused to talk about; after bad fights she took on grueling extra shifts, as though to expiate her sins. I hated the George in her.

The possibility of cancerous demise made him only more awesome and redoubtable to her, his petty patriarchal cruelties now forgivable. At family dinners he would push a pea around his plate ponderously, while we waited in solidary silence for the death thought to pass. Even though the therapy was reportedly successful, the stench of fermented piss reminded us that his dying had accelerated and that he was headed for oblivion. I suppose part of me had wished him dead, and now I gave it away—"How is your dead?"

I may have just done serious damage to my marriage, I said to Rora later on, while we drank the hundredth coffee of the day at the Viennese Café. You've never been married, so you don't know, but it is a fragile thing. Nothing ever goes away, everything stays inside it. It is a different reality.

Rora sipped his coffee. His Canon was in his lap, his left hand on it, his index finger on the shoot button, as if waiting for the right moment to photograph me.

Let me tell you a joke, Rora said. I was about to object, but it seemed that he wanted to cheer me up, so I let him try.

Mujo and his wife, Fata, are in bed. It's late at night. Mujo is falling asleep, and Fata is watching porn: a horny couple, all silicone and tattoos, is sucking and fucking like there is no tomorrow. Mujo says, C'mon, Fata, turn that off, let's go to sleep. And Fata says, Let me just see if these kids are going to get married in the end.

Ah, Rora. He was becoming one of the many people who suffered from a surfeit of good intentions.

Sunday Market
Chicago Ghetto

Stepping off the Halsted streetcar into the ankle-deep mud, Olga loses her other heel. The crowd pushes her forward, their hands and arms brushing against her; there is no way of retrieving it out of the mush. Another loss, she thinks. The more you lose, the more is to be lost, yet it matters less. The shoes have long been caked in mud and filth, the soles long soaked, her feet wet for days. She worked many fifteen-hour days to save money for these shoes, but now they are decrepit already, the seams unraveling, the laces snapping. She could slip out of her shoes and leave them right here, stuck in the muck, and then get rid of her dress and everything else: her mind, her life, her pain. The abandon of having nothing to lose, the freedom of being divested of all earthly burdens, ready for the Messiah, or death. Everything is attracted by its end.

The end of the world might be near, Isador said to her once, but we don't have to rush to reach it. We might as well just stroll over, have some candy on the way. But her legs are too weary and sore; still in her shoes, she keeps walking down 12th Street, turns toward Maxwell. It has warmed up; the sun is out and the rag sellers exude vapor, as though the spirits were deserting them. At their feet, mangy dogs are basking. There seem to be more people here than before, taking up more space. Where did they all come from? The city has become smaller; the sidewalks are dense with bodies squeezing between pushcarts and horse carriages, milling meaninglessly, in no hurry to get anywhere. The men's clothes enfold the winter dampness; they pull their hats down to their eyes, for it has been a long time since they've seen the sun. The women take off their gloves to touch the rags; their cheeks are still red from frostbite; they bargain tenaciously. Every one of them is somebody's brother or sister or child; all of them are alive; they know the good ways of not dying. A horse is neighing; the hawkers are hollering over everybody's heads as though casting a net, offering cheap things: socks, rags, hats, life. A short-haired young woman is handing out leaflets, yelling hoarsely: "No tsar, no king, no president—what we want is freedom!" Here and there a child is squirming through the forest of legs. There is a disorderly, testy line outside Jacob Shapiro's store. A blind man is facing it, singing a plaintive song, his eyes milky, his hand on the shoulder of a boy, who is holding out a cap for nickels. The man's voice is unfaltering in its sorrow, everything is awash with it as in sunlight. A pervasive stench of unfresh fish is advancing from the obscure stalls. In front of Menduk's store a boy is selling the *Hebrew Voice,* shouting alternately in Yiddish and English. As she's passing near him, he shouts out: "Lazarus Averbuch was degenerate assassin, not Jew!" Does he recognize her? Did they put her picture in the papers? Is he yelling after her? She turns around to look at him, at his capacious hat and snotty snout and pointed, nasty chin, but he does not return her blistering gaze. "Jews must join Christians in war against anarchism!" She wants to slap him, to beat some color into his pallid cheeks, to twist his ears until he screams for mercy.

Two policemen in dark uniforms are coming down the street, their shadows stretching before them, the crowd parting, the young woman with leaflets quickly vanishing. One of them is twirling his

baton; his hand is large, his fingers knuckly; a large gun is hol-
stered at his waist. His face is wide and square, the nose flattened
from some fight; he does not glance at the people on the street—he
might as well be walking between tombstones. The other policeman is young; his mustache too kempt, his uniform buttons too
shiny. Yet he shares in the exudation of power; his thumb is stuck
in his belt and he scans the crowd as though from afar, seeing no
single face. Olga has a clear vision of the young *politsyant* falling to
the ground, facing the sky, her foot on his chest while she swings
the baton to smash the bridge of his nose; the stream of blood
parts to run down each cheek, soaking the *vontses*. She would beat
the other *politsyant* across his large, meaty, bovine ears until they
turn to bloody cauliflower. The police walk by her; they are so tall
that their badges blaze at her at eye level. She would hit their knees
until they collapse and then gouge their eyes out. "Deranged
woman mauls policemen to death!" the boy would yell. He would
surely recognize her next time.

She shoulders her way through the crowd, toward a clear patch
where they won't rub against her; they part obligingly before she
even touches them, as though her anger were sending ripples
ahead of her. She wants to howl with rage at their complaisance,
but nobody would hear her; here, noise is like air, everywhere and
necessary.

> *Dear Mother,*
> *You will think me cruel and mad, but I cannot keep this inside*
> *me anymore. Lazarus has been slain like an animal for no reason*
> *at all and yet they call him an assassin. He—an assassin. There is*
> *no end to evil, it reaches us here too.*

Suddenly, the path through the crowd has closed off. In front of
Olga there stands a small woman in a dirty white dress and mush-

roomlike hat, her eyes febrile. The woman's mouth is agape, and it is unclear to Olga whether she is attempting to smile or if it is just that her gums and teeth are too painful, for the cavity looks pustulous, her breath reeking of cadaver. Olga tries to get around her, but the woman steps in front of her, staring through Olga's face. She speaks with a voice between a hiss and a whisper: "He whom you love is ill."

Olga elbows her aside, but the woman clutches her sleeve and pulls her back. "But this illness is not unto death. It is for the glory of God, so that the son of God may be glorified." The hiss has gone beyond whisper and turned into wailing. Olga is pulling forward but the woman is not letting go of her. "Leave me alone," Olga growls. The woman has only lower teeth, her tongue lapping at the upper gums. "Unbind him," the woman caterwauls. "Unbind him and let him go." Olga rips her arm out of the woman's grasp and hurries forward. The crowd has slowed down, some men have stopped and are now watching them, already beginning to form a circle. The woman, now fully gibbering, grabs Olga's hair and tugs it back. With a rapid turn, Olga smacks the woman with the back of her hand; she feels her knuckles bounce off the woman's cheekbone, her skin breaking. The woman stops, lets go of her hair, looks astounded. "Your brother will rise," she says perfectly calmly, as if all misunderstanding has now been resolved. "Lazarus shall rise. Our Lord will be with us."

AT THE TOP OF THE STAIRS, the *politsyant* is rocking on the hind legs of his chair, a grotesquely gigantic cigar in his hand. "Nice to see your pretty face again, Miss Averbuch," he says, grinning. "Happy to report everything is just the way you left it." She walks by him without a word. A white cross is chalked on her door; she wipes it with her hand, puts the key in, but the door is unlocked.

Maybe Isador has left, somehow getting past this *shmegege*. It is a miracle they have not found him yet. Lord, why did you leave me in these woods?

"All kinds of Jews have been visiting your neighbor, Miss Averbuch. Many long beards. For all I know, they were plotting new crimes with the Lubels and such. If it was for me, I would drown you all in the lake, like rats, all of yous. But you Jews have important friends everywhere, don't you, so we have to be nice to you all of a sudden. Don't you worry, though. Do not you worry. The time shall come."

The fury forms a sentence in her head and she turns to deliver it, but it falls apart as the Lubels' door opens and five men in black coats come out. Olga recognizes Rabbi Klopstock, his long beard. He averts his eyes from Olga as they file down the stairs. Nobody has come to see her; nobody wants to be close to her. Rabbi Klopstock hurries past the policeman, followed by the other men, whom she does not recognize. None of the men have beards; they wear American attire, clutching bowler hats much like Taube's.

"See? I told you," cackles the *politsyant*, munching the cigar. He stops rocking; the front legs of the chair hit the floor; he sits up to watch the Jews filing downstairs. "They don't like you much, do they?" She would like to kick this *shvants* off the chair and push those bowler-hatted bastards down the stairs so they can pile up on top of the good *rebbe*. May they never become who they want to be. May they be pickled in pain and humiliation. Her feet are hurting, her legs shaking with fatigue; she would like to sit down or stretch in bed. Instead, she goes to the Lubels.

The small room smells of camphor; a pot is steaming on the stove. Pinya is weeping over it, as though she were boiling her tears. Isaac is in bed; his swollen, bluish feet are sticking out from under the blanket, at the other end of which his sallow face is flinching in pain, blood bubbling up on his lips. Zosya and Avram are sitting on the bed by his side. They are sucking on candy, the paper bag in Avram's hand, Zosya staring at it voraciously. Isaac does not seem to be aware of them; his eyes widen, now and then, as he grunts. It has been a long time since Olga was here; everything seems to be different. The *politsey* ransacked the Lubels' home, but their few possessions are all in the same place: the shelf with plates and cups; the rack for the pots and pans; a little stack of books in the corner; the uncovered mirror. Olga's previous life was a hallucination, everything before Lazarus's death was *khaloymes*. Here now is a true reality.

There is just enough space between the bed and the stove for Pinya and Olga to stand awkwardly close to each other. Pinya's eyes are at the center of dark stains, as though they were leaking ink.

They broke his ribs, Pinya says, whimpering. And something else inside. They beat him and beat him. They took him away last night, beat him through the morning, returned him unconscious. They beat him all night. I think they simply like beating him. They asked him about Isador. They claim he knew something about anarchists and Lazarus. I don't know what. I don't know what I am going to do if he goes. Who is going to feed these children? They are always hungry.

She wipes her nose with a piece of undergarment, whereupon she drops it in the pot; she is boiling laundry in it. Her nostrils are thick and red; a bead of sweat is rolling down from her temple.

Dr. Gruzenberg thinks his kidney has been detached, Pinya says. Rebbe Klopstock is going to send a letter to the authorities.

Olga snorts with contempt, and Pinya nods in agreement. Isaac is not aware of anyone in the room: his eyes dart in different directions, as though he were following his kidney shuttling between different areas of his body. He seems to be surprised by every one of his short breaths. Lord, Olga thinks. That's me.

It never ends, Pinya says. Every time, you think maybe this here is a different world, but it's all the same: they live, we die. So here it is again.

Olga embraces her. But Pinya is even taller now, so Olga has to press her cheek against her chest. She hears the heart booming steadily, indifferent to their shared sobs, to Isaac gasping for life.

Naturally, the ten-o'clock bus to Chisinau did not show up. Nobody said or knew anything; Rora and I just waited with everyone else for a couple of flaccid hours, and then the twelve-o'clock bus showed up. If you wait long enough, something will happen—there has never been a time when nothing happened.

At one o'clock, the twelve o'clock bus was still in the station, and I was blaming the wait and the heat on my fellow travelers: they stank, they were ugly, they were pissed and passive, I hated them. Rora, on the other hand, wandered around, photographing. He seemed at home in the uncertainty of the moment, in the mayhem of waiting for something to happen. Every once in a while he would come back and ask if I needed anything, the main purpose being, I suspect, to display his superiority in the situation. I needed everything—a shower, water, to shit, comfort, love, to reach the end of this lousy journey, to write a book. I need nothing, I snapped. He snapped back at me, a close close-up.

The birch branches beyond the bus lot slumped down forlorn; against the revving of the engines, birds twittered chokingly; the garbage container was bubbling up with moist plastic bags. How the fuck did I get here, to southwestern Ukraine, to the land of the pissed and passive, so far from everything—anything—I loved?

Lazarus, on the train from Vienna to Trieste: third class was full of emigrants, whole families sitting on their valises, imagining an incomprehensible future; men slept on luggage racks. In Lazarus's compartment, three Bohemians played cards for money; one of them seemed to be losing a lot—it didn't look like he would ever make it to the ship. Lazarus was sweating but did not want to take his coat off; he kept his arms crossed to protect the money in his inside pocket. Landscapes blurred by; the windows were smudged with the yolk of the setting sun. Everybody knew the name of their crossing ship. Lazarus's was *Francesca;* he imagined her long and wide and graceful, smelling of salt, sun, and gulls. Francesca was a beautiful name. He did not know anybody named Francesca.

It was horribly hot: my shoe soles stuck to the pavement; I had new life-forms developing in my armpits. My Samsonite suitcase looked ridiculously out of place amidst buckets and boxes and checkered-nylon tote bags turgid with cheap stuff. Apparently everyone in Eastern Europe, including *my country,* received one of those bags in compensation for the abolition of social infrastructure. I was as conspicuous as an iceberg in a pool. I had no doubt that gangs of thieves had already congregated to plan the filching of my possessions. And where was Rora?

Well, he was right there, snapping pictures of me when I was not looking. Stay here, I growled, and watch my suitcase. Stay he did, lighting up a cigarette, smiling at the bucket *baba,* then photographing her as she crumpled her face in a spectacular scowl. I pushed through the crowd, they pushed in return; I bought a Bounty chocolate bar, then threw it away because it was liquid; I was wary of these people, these foreigners; I pushed through the crowd on my way back.

Everybody imagines that they have a center, the seat of their soul, if you believe in that kind of thing. I've asked around, and most of the people told me that the soul is somewhere in the abdominal area—a foot or so above the asshole. But even if the center is elsewhere in the body—the head, the throat, the heart—it is fixed there, it does not move around. When you move, the center moves with you, following your trajectory. You protect that center, your body is a sheath; and if your body is damaged, the center is exposed and weak. Moving through the crowd at the bus station in Chernivtsi, I realized that my center had shifted—it used to be in my stomach, but now it was in my breast pocket, where I kept my American passport and a wad of cash. I pushed this bounty of American life through space; I was presently assembled around it and needed to protect it from the people around me.

It was well past one o'clock; we had no idea when the bus would leave, but I thought it would be prudent for us to take our seats, given that ticketless people were swarming around the door and arguing with the driver. The bus was at least thirty years old, built before the advent of airflow, hot as a furnace; Rora took the seat by the window so he could take more pictures, forcing me into the olfactory inspection of every passing armpit. I would not have minded abandoning him here; I could go alone now; I was alone anyway. I could laugh at myself (ha-ha, ha ha ha ha!) for being stupid enough to ever embark upon a journey with this two-bit gambler and ex-gigolo, this wannabe war veteran, this Bosnian nobody. I watched him raise his Canon to point it through the window at some helpless tote-bag carrier. The seat of his fucking soul was that camera.

The driver looked like he hadn't slept in weeks; he smoked as though possessed, his hands trembled. A teenage boy who clearly had not yet experienced the manly pleasure of shaving appeared to be his copilot: he checked the tickets and helped the advancing peasants with their buckets and baskets. He had the calm demeanor of a man in charge, of someone enjoying his own exertions of power. He yelled at an old man carrying a sack bulging with what turned out to be shoes, for the man took out a black high-heel shoe and shoved it in the boy's face to prove some point.

When the bus finally left the station, I was unsettled by the feeling that we could not return now. Where can you go from nowhere, except deeper into nowhere? Before we even left Chernivtsi, my head was dipping into the well of bad dreams, following the rhythm of obstreperous, incomprehensible banter between a sleeveless lad and the young woman he was flirting with. Rora never slept in motion; the moment the wheels started rolling, he was wide awake and ready to talk.

When you went into the Tunnel under the tarmac, Rora said, you entered darkness and immediately slammed your forehead against the first beam. Your eyes adjusted, you bent your neck, and went on, deeper and deeper. It was like descending into hell, and it smelled just like it: clay, sweat, fear, farts, aftershave. You stumbled and touched the cold, earthen walls; you were in a grave and a corpse could grab you and pull you deeper into the earth. There were no markers, you didn't know how far into the Tunnel you might be; you just had a sense of the person ahead of you. You lost all sense of time, you lost air—older people regularly passed out—and just as your breathing was about to cease you felt the slightest of breezes, barely a wisp, and the tiniest modulation of light, and then you were out into what looked like all the lights of the world ablaze at once. I've read about the people who died but then came back. They described it as passing through a tunnel. Well, the tunnel they passed through was under the tarmac of the Sarajevo airport.

Death must be pleasant, the pain and shock of its infliction notwithstanding. A bullet tearing through your lungs, a knife slitting your windpipe, your forehead smashed in by a steel rod—I concede those would be rather unpleasant. But that pain belonged to life, the body had to be alive to feel it. I wondered if George's living body and its pain would be undone when he died, as he was going to, if he would experience the bliss of release and relief, the joy of completion and transformation, of dumping the garbage of existence. Never mind Mr. Christ's eschatological circus—there must be the postorgasmic moment of absolute peace, of coming home, the moment when the fog of life floats away like gun smoke and everything is finally nothing.

Perhaps that was what Mr. Christ deprived Lazarus of. He may have been okay dead; it was all over, he was home. Maybe Mr. Christ was showing off in order to lay—spiritually speaking, of course— Lazarus's sisters; maybe he wanted to show that he was the boss of death, as he was the boss of life. Either way, he couldn't just leave Lazarus alone. Once Lazarus was thrown out of the comfy bed of eternity, he wandered the world, forever homeless, forever afraid to fall asleep, dreaming of dreaming. It all made me so goddamn angry. I said nothing to Rora, however.

Instead I said, Moldova is a weird place. When it was part of the U.S.S.R., it produced wine sold all over the Motherland. There are endless cellars, tunnels upon tunnels, where they used to store wine and champagne. Now they have nobody to sell it to. I had read up on this: there are parts of Moldova where people use dung for heating, because Russia cut off coal and gas supplies. Everybody wants to leave it; one-quarter of the population is missing. The rest are trying to think up ways to use wine as fuel.

Do you know the story of the Moldovan underwater hockey team? Rora asked.

What the hell is underwater hockey?

Two teams push the puck on the bottom of the pool.

Why?

They just do. Anyway, there was a women's underwater hockey world championship in Calgary, and the Moldovan team was supposed to compete, but at the opening ceremony not one of them showed up. The moment they landed in Canada they all dispersed and vanished without a trace. It turned out that some clever Moldovan businessman heard about this idiotic sport, charged the ladies fifteen hundred dollars to join the national underwater hockey team so they could get visas to escape Moldova and get to Canada. Some of the ladies could not even swim, let alone push the puck.

How do you come up with stories like that?

I knew someone who knew the businessman, Rora said. It's all about knowing the right people.

IT TOOK US FOREVER to cross the Ukrainian-Moldovan border. First, we had to get out of Ukraine, which was not all that easy. We had to step out of the bus and give our papers to Ukrainian border guards. After they cursorily checked everybody else's local IDs, they devoted all their attention to our passports, reading them like books. It must have been a while since any Americans crossed this border—neither of us cared to brandish our patriotic but useless Bosnian passport. Rora's weary American passport was an absolute page-turner: the border guards passed it from one to the other, reverently, paying particular attention to the smudged stamps. They pointed at a couple of pages with runny smears and I translated Rora's answer: he had once been caught in the rain. Even I knew it was an old trick: washing your passport to cover up for the missing entry stamps. But the Ukrainians were happy enough with it to let us leave and become a Moldovan problem.

As Rora and I walked across the no-man's-land toward Moldova, I worried we could be thrown into a Moldovan dungeon—formerly a wine cellar, no doubt—and then taken away, hooded, by our American compatriots. Our fellow travelers, already cleared by the Moldovans, stood by the bus like a choir, smoking and sweating, arguing as to the degree of our unquestionable international criminality. The sleeveless guy left the group and strolled over to the ramp that marked the entrance to Moldova. He looked suspicious;

he probably didn't even have a passport, but he was fearlessly talking up the guard at the ramp.

The Moldovans were impressed with our passports as well. They took them inside a shack at the far end of the no-man's-land and got on the phone. The choir was antsy; they reentered the bus and pressed their melting faces against the grimy window, watching us. I saw the boy conductor climb into the bus, shrug his scrawny shoulders, and say, "*Amerikantsy,*" by way of explanation.

The sleeveless guy was now squatting under the ramp, below the sight line of the guard in the booth; everyone else was looking toward the guards in the shack, where they were relating the gripping story of our passports to distant authorities.

Can you take a picture of that guy? I asked Rora, who looked over with a bit of disinterest and said, Borders cannot be photographed. They would take away my camera.

When Lazarus was crossing the border between the Russian and the Austro-Hungarian empires, a long column of refugees stretched down the road for miles. He carried the leather bag Papa had given him; inside it, a scarf Chaia knitted for him, a shaving kit (a present from Olga), socks and underwear, and a few books he would not be allowed to import into the good empire. Once he crossed, he looked back and recognized, without sorrow or excitement, that he would never return. He could only go forward, deeper into the tunnel of the future.

The sleeveless guy frog-walked under the ramp, the top of his head actually touching it. He stayed low enough so that the guard could not see him, then stood up and ambled calmly for a few dozen yards down the road. He lit a cigarette, pulled out a comb from his back pocket and dragged it through his recalcitrant hair, as though erasing the traces of his self-smuggling.

It was most fascinating and encouraging, his disrespect for international—indeed, all—law, his absence of fear of armed, uniformed power. I couldn't even begin to contemplate such an operation, because I had places to go and get back to. There was home and away-from-home in my life, and the space between the two was rife with borders. And if I violated the laws governing the home/away-from-home transitions, they would keep me away from home. It was that simple.

Once upon a time, when I was going through a heavy-drinking phase after I lost my teaching job, I came back home at dawn and found, to my inebriated surprise, that there was a door chain barring access to our nuptial bed. Naturally, I kicked the door a few times to break it down, but only left black marks I would later have to scrub off. I kept kicking until Mary's furious eyes burnt holes in my forehead through the door ajar. Wordlessly, she shut the door and locked it, leaving the key in. I kicked the door an additional couple of times and then walked away, determined never to return. Outside, an angry spring storm had started—I broke through the sheets of it, getting soaked within a befuddled thought. I had nowhere to go: I walked up and down the streets of Ukrainian Village, where we lived then. Chestnut trees were coming into leaf, the dawn was redolent of tree bark. I was never going back home, I kept swearing, kept walking, until I was overwhelmed by fatigue and sat down on a playground bench piebalded with tiny puddles. If I had a job, I would have gone straight to work and from there to a hotel. But, as my cold underwear crawled up my crack and rivulets of rain ran down my forehead, I understood a simple fact: if you can't go home, there is nowhere to go, and nowhere is the biggest place in the world—indeed, nowhere is the world. I returned home, remorsefully, rang the bell, contritely, and begged to be let in.

Finally, the Moldovan border officer returned our passports and we boarded the bus. I dispatched a few futile apologetic American smiles to our bus mates, but they were uniformly ignored. The guard lifted the ramp and we entered, stopping shortly thereafter to pick up the sleeveless, passportless guy, who inexplicably winked at me before he reinstalled his armpit over my head.

RAMBO LIKED TO BE in the pictures, Rora had to take pictures of him all the time. I suppose he imagined himself a hero, someone who would always be remembered. He provided film to Rora, his headquarters had a darkroom for him; he looted a camera shop just for his photographer. He liked to look at the photos of himself: here was Rambo bare-chested, pointing his silver gun at the camera; here he was with an automatic rifle in hand, its butt resting on his thigh; here he was clutching in jest the hair of a young woman smiling, painfully, next to him; here he was sitting on top of a corpse of one of our soldiers, some poor sap who stood up to him in front of the wrong audience—the boy's eyes were glassy and wide open in surprise, Rambo on his chest with a cigarette in his mouth, as if he were in a commercial for a vacation in Iraq.

Rambo thought that the war would never end because it could never end; he thought he could forever be the guy with the biggest dick in town. But he became an inconvenience to his political friends. See, he did business with the Serbs on the other side; he would recover the bodies of the Serbs killed in the besieged Sarajevo and then transport them across the river to his Chetnik partners; they would be paid by the families of the dead and split the money with Rambo. Rambo's men would collect the bodies from the morgue, or off the street, smuggle them through the Rat Tunnel, which was a huge sewage pipe by the Field Museum, then carry them across the river. Business was brisk, and for an exorbitant price he would smuggle out even some living Serbs. During a truce, business slowed down, and Rambo deployed Beno in search of more profitable Serb corpses, so people started disappearing. A few wrong ones got killed, however, and people started talking, journalists started asking questions. Rambo had to dress down a curious French TV crew—he took away their bulletproof vests and their cameras and cars, and slapped them around to boot. Even Miller was showing impertinent interest and had to be taken by Rora to Mostar to report from there, which left his nose out of shit.

But Miller slipped Rora in Mostar and returned to Sarajevo. Explaining that careless inattention to Rambo would have been a big problem, a huge problem—Rambo had his crazy moods, he could enter a fog of rage, and you did not want to be around him then. No friend, no brother, nobody was safe from Rambo's fury; and he never forgot: those who did wrong by him were never forgotten or forgiven. Rora had a choice: if he were to go to Sarajevo, Rambo might kill him; he could try to escape from Mostar via Medjugorje, go to Germany or somewhere, but he had no money, knew nobody there. But then he heard that Rambo had almost got assassinated. Someone waited in ambush near the Chinese restaurant; Rambo's car was blown up by a handheld missile launcher. He was in the backseat for some reason, had let someone else drive, and only the driver got killed. The official version was that it was a Chetnik attack, but Rambo knew better. He knew it was someone close. If I didn't go back, Rora said, Rambo would have thought that I was involved in that and he would have tracked me down to the ends of the earth.

Were you involved? I asked.

Are you out of your fucking mind?

Who was it, then? I asked.

Why do you want to know? You know nothing about these people, Brik. Nothing about the war. You are a nice, bookish man. Just enjoy the story.

Who was it? You can't tell me a story like this and not tell me who it was.

He looked at me for a long time, as though deciding whether to initiate me, whether I was ready to enter the parallel universe of iniquity and murder.

Tell me, I said. Come on.

Well, it was Beno, obviously. Somebody high up in the government promised him he would he boss if he took Rambo out, and so he sincerely tried. And fucked up.

Why did the government want Rambo out?

He was crazy. They couldn't control him. They thought they were using him, until it dawned on them he was using them. They thought Beno would be more pliant, promised him friendship and steady business, and he went for it.

What happened to Beno?

What's with the questions? You are not going to write about this, will you?

No, of course not. I've got another book to write.

Rambo caught him. He beat him for days, then stuck his gun up his ass and fired. He bragged all over town that the bullet came out through Beno's forehead.

Good God.

He was going to catch whoever put Beno up to it. He was going to kill him, and no government could stop him. He was crazy. Rambo's own men hid from him, because they knew that if he came upon them he might accuse them of being in cahoots with Beno.

What about you?

I had to come back from Mostar. No point in running away, he would have found me. I had to find Miller before Rambo ran into him and make him give me an alibi, tell Rambo we were together the whole time. I had to be very careful not to end up face-to-face with Rambo. He was avoiding the government liquidators, hunting down his enemy; he was crazy. Those were crazy days. In the beginning, every war has a neat logic: they want to kill us, we want not to die. But with time it becomes something else, the war becomes this space where anybody can kill anybody at any time, where everybody wants everybody dead, because the only way you are sure to stay alive is if everybody else is dead.

And did you find Miller?

Eventually.

Ah, Moldova! (How did I get to Moldova?) The rolling hills overgrown with sunflowers; the deserted villages, the driveways between the houses overtaken by grass and weed; the peasants huddling together to mark a bus stop; the city called Balta, fit to be used as a postcataclysmic movie set; a mob of people trying to board our overcrowded bus. Moldova now had nothing but independence, its entire population dying to join their underwater hockey team.

I was never so afraid for my life, Rora said, ever stimulated by motion. I couldn't find Miller. I felt that everybody was after me—the Serbs in the hills, the Bosnian government, Rambo himself. He went completely insane: the government sent, stupidly, a couple of young policemen to arrest him, and he killed them on the spot and sent their balls back in an envelope addressed to their bosses. He wanted Beno's government protector, and he was going to get him.

Did he get him?

No. Rambo got shot by a sniper. The sniper must have waited for days before Rambo came by Djul-bašta. He got a bullet an inch away from his heart. He needed an urgent surgery, but he knew that if he went to the government-controlled hospital, he would surely expire on the surgical table, to everyone's relief. He forced a surgeon at gunpoint to operate secretly. He was smuggled into the hospital under a different name; the bullet was taken out, and he was removed from the hospital immediately afterward. He was then smuggled out of the city and driven to Vienna.

Who was the doctor?

Another useless question, Brik. Nobody you know.

And how did he slip out of Sarajevo?

Will you lay off? Isn't this enough?

You're full of shit. You start telling me the story, you tickle me and titillate me, and then you pretend to be surprised when I want to hear the end of it.

Rora said nothing, of course. I had a point. He looked out the window; I nearly dozed off while he was contemplating whether to answer.

Well, the corpse-smuggling business with the Serbs never stopped, not for a moment—it was too lucrative and there were people in the government who were ready to take over. Rambo got out through the Rat Tunnel, pretending to be a Serb corpse. They wrapped him in a shroud, they put an amputated, rotten limb in with him to make him stink; two policemen carried him across the river to the other side. His Chetnik friends arranged everything else; once he got across the river he was resurrected, and they drove him straight to Vienna.

Every once in a while the police stopped our bus and the teenager copilot talked to the policemen in Russian or Romanian; they would appear stern and determined, they would flip through the papers and shake their heads. Then the kid would announce that we had been fined for some traffic violation or other and that we needed to collect some money; to pay for it or we couldn't go on. We delivered our money; we had no choice: I forked out a few uncrisp Susie dollars. The teenager would then give the money to the police, they would count it and give him back some, which he would pocket in plain sight. Rora would stop talking during that racketeering routine and watch the transaction with disinterest. For him it was but low-level graft, motivated by the survival instinct; it was like watching children quaintly playing. For me, however, it was nauseating, as everything merged into one foul whole: the armpits, the rolling hills, the gun up the ass, the empty villages, the bullet an inch away from the heart, Rambo sitting on a dead Bosnian soldier, my dry mouth, Rora's world-weariness, the precociously nefarious teenager, the heartbreaking stench of it all.

I recalled Mary, her strained, half-assed Catholic innocence, her belief that people were evil due to errors in their upbringing and a shortage of love in their lives. She just could not comprehend evil, the way I could not comprehend the way the washing machine worked or the reason the universe expanded into infinity. For her, the prime mover of every action was a good intention, and evil occurred only if the good intention was inadvertently betrayed or forgotten. Humans could not be essentially evil, because they were always infused by God's infinite goodness and love. We had conducted long, unerotic discussions about all this. I also heard it from the high horse's mouth, from George the Dead himself, who once upon a time contemplated becoming a priest. I deigned to suggest to him that it was also the American thing—America was nothing if not good intentions. Damn right it was, George said. For a while, I had believed her; it was gratifying to understand everything around me—Chicago, my American life, the politeness of our neighbors, Mary's kindness—as a result of generally intended goodness. I had believed her that our good intentions would bear fruit, that we could reach the far horizon of immaculate marriage.

It's a funny thing, marriage, what keeps it together, what rents it asunder. Mary and I had a desultory, hurtful fight over the Abu Ghraib pictures, for example. All the random insults and unsupportable accusations aside, the gist of it was that what she saw was essentially decent American kids acting upon a misguided belief they were protecting freedom, their good intentions going astray. What I saw was young Americans expressing their unlimited joy of the unlimited power over someone else's life and death. They loved being alive and righteous by virtue of having good American intentions; indeed, it turned them on; they liked looking at the pictures of themselves sticking a baton up some Arab ass. Eventually, I flipped and turned crazy; I smashed the family china set we inherited from George and Rachel—what set me off was Mary saying that I would understand America better if I went to work every day and met normal people. I told her I hated the normal people and the land of the fucking free and the home of the asshole brave, and I hated God and George and all and everything. I told her that to be American you have to know nothing and understand even less, and that I did not want to be American. Never, I said. She screamed that once I got a job I would feel free to be whatever I wished to be. I told her she was no different from any of those angelic American kids who plug curly-haired people into an electric current after a relaxing waterboarding session. It took us weeks to make up, but our marriage was harder thereafter. The baggage I dragged around the eastern lands contained the tortured corpses of our good intentions.

Rambo particularly liked me to take pictures with the dead and then look at them later, Rora said. It turned him on—that was his big dick, his absolute power: being alive in the middle of death. That was all that it boiled down to: the dead were wrong, the living were right. The thing is, everybody who has ever been photographed is either dead or will die. That's why nobody photographs me. I want to stay on this side of the picture.

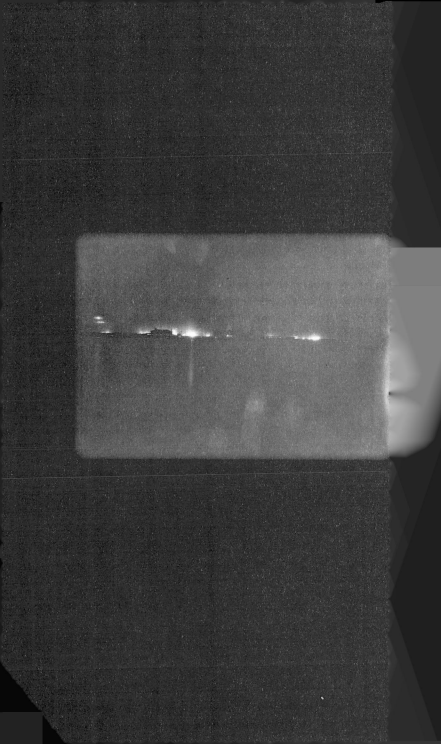

Isador, Olga whispers. Isador, are you there?

Isador is under a pile of rags, in the airless wardrobe, his limbs benumbed and aching. He listened to her restlessness all night: the creaking of the bed frame, the cracking of the mattress, the crinkling of her writhing body, the music of her nightmare. He had been in the wardrobe all day yesterday while Olga was away: he was looking forward to the sounds of her presence. He cannot feel his own body; he has been afraid to move and his body is as rigid as a corpse. After something had scurried across his feet, he considered getting out, or at least pushing the rags and the valise aside, cracking the door ajar to let some light in, but then the *politsyant* sneaked into the flat and crept around, snooping. Isador felt his weight shifting along the floor, moving toward the wardrobe to open it and pick through Olga's things on the shelves, chuckling and mumbling to himself. Isador was afraid to breathe or even think about moving a muscle. The *politsyant* stole something and left, failing to close the door completely. When Olga returned, Isador could see her small heels and frail ankles as she took off her shoes, sitting on the bed.

Isador, say something. Are you there?

She can still smell the shit he was coated in. The room absorbs his presence; there is another breath touching things in here, another life, as when Lazarus was alive—being alone is hearing yourself breathe and then not. It is incomprehensible how the *politsyant* managed not to sense Isador; perhaps he was too busy rummaging through her undergarments, stealing a pair of her drawers. You can always count on the slimy stupidity of the law and order, and for once she is thankful for it. The *politsey,* like time, exists indifferent to the world and its suffering. Here comes another day marked by her brother's mortal absence, another day when everything will be the same for everybody else, for nobody else can notice his absence. Outside, the gray dawn is breaking.

I am dying, Olga, Isador whispers. What do you want me to say? I love your wardrobe?

Talk to me about Lazarus. Tell me something I don't know. What he loved, what he hated, what made him laugh. You knew him better than I did.

He groans; she can sense him move. He must be in pain, he must be desperate and hungry. His voice is muffled, disembodied, the voice of a ghost. He says:

We used to walk by the lake. It was like wilderness to us, its vastness. We could turn our backs to the filth and the grime and the slums. We looked at the waves and the horizon, sometimes we could see the other shore. He wanted to write a poem about what he saw.

What did he see?

He saw a lot of water, maybe Indiana, maybe nothing. How do I know? Can I come out?

Did you read the poem?

He never showed it to me, if he ever wrote it. He never showed me any of his writing. Let me come out. I cannot feel my body, and I am cold.

You have to tell me what he was doing at Shippy's door. Why

was he there? Why wasn't he with me? Why did you get him involved in that anarchist madness?

I did nothing of the kind. I did nothing. We went to hear Ben
Reitman once. We went to one or two Edelstadt lectures on literature, but it was because we wanted to write. And they also talked
about, you know, unemployment, injustice, and poverty. Look at
where we live, for God's sake. Can I come out?

You are lying to me, Isador. You must tell me the truth. I have
to know. I can accept it. I am aware I did not know everything about
him. But I cannot understand what he was doing with George
Shippy.

I don't know. Maybe he was looking for a letter of recommenda-
tion. He was talking about going to Valparaiso University. Maybe
he wanted to get an exclusive interview with Shippy so he could get
into the reporting business. Or maybe he wanted to discuss injustice with him. How in the world can I know? I was not there. Either
let me come out or turn me in.

Where were you that morning? Olga asks.

I was with a friend.

What friend?

A friend of mine.

What friend?

Can I come out, Olga? I beg you.

What friend?

I have friends.

What friend?

I was playing cards at Stadlwelser's, all night, through the morning. Can I come out?

Stadlwelser. I know him. I know who he is.

He is a friend.

Good friends you have.

A good friend is a treasure in your chest.

You fool, Olga says. Come out.

He wiggles through the rags, as if hatching out: she sees his head first, then his scrawny torso in a long-sleeved undershirt; he stretches out of the wardrobe. On his knees, he crosses to the bed, moaning; she lifts the blanket and he slides in with her. She is still in her dress and wool stockings, having slept in them, but she can feel how cold his feet are. He is wearing Lazarus's undershirt, with holes on the elbows. She cried as she went through pair after pair of threadbare socks: Lazarus died with his feet cold; the *politsey* exhibited him, and everybody saw him with his socks torn. Mother would never forgive her that, if she ever found out. Isador is shivering next to her and she draws closer.

What are we going to do, Olga? They are going to catch me. I will never see the light of day again. Even my own people want me apprehended. You are everything I have.

We will think of something, Olga says and strokes his cheek. Something will happen. There was never a time when nothing happened.

She does not believe in what she is saying. He puts his hand on her thigh and presses his pelvis against hers.

Stop that, she says, or I will turn you in.

Ever a doltish scoundrel. He retracts his groin, but leaves his hand on her thigh; she feels the cold through the cloth.

I have to ask, Olga says. Was he a true anarchist? Did you turn him into an anarchist?

God, Olga, will you stop asking questions? You know as much as I do. He could be angry just like any of us. Packing eggs was not his life's dream, you know.

What did he want?

He wanted to write. He wanted to meet girls, have some fun. He wanted to be liked. He wanted to be like everybody else. He wanted to buy you new shoes. I thought you could use a little hat.

Why a hat?

I like hats.

You are a fool, Isador.

They hear a scraping sound in the wall. The rats are up and running. May they feast on the *politsyant* for breakfast, Olga thinks.

It kills me, she says, that I don't know what he was doing there, at Shippy's doorstep. The newspapers say he had a knife and a gun. I used to protect him from other boys; he didn't even know how to use a stick to beat them off. Where did he get a knife and a gun? Did you get him a gun?

I did nothing of the kind, Olga. They are lying. Shippy killed him because he was there. Now they are going to arrest whoever they don't like. They are going to clean up what they see as filth. Those they don't arrest will be grateful and grovel and slobber at their feet.

When you went to Edelstadt meetings, to those lectures, did you talk to others there, to some real anarchists? Did they talk to you?

What do you mean, a real anarchist? The rich are sucking our blood. The *politsyant* came in and went through your things as if they belonged to him. The only way they know how to talk to us is by force. People are angry. Everybody is an anarchist.

I am not an anarchist. People who have a job and work, they don't get so angry. Normal people have no time to be anarchists.

I was normal, too, not so long ago. It was not my fault I got fired. I stole no eggs. I don't need their eggs. Heller lied about me to Eichgreen. I was as good at packing eggs as anyone, but it is a stupid, demeaning job. Who could expect me to be happy about it?

Who are these people? Do I know any anarchists? Is Mr. Eichgreen an anarchist? Is Kaplan an anarchist?

Who's Kaplan? Your lover?

No.

I don't know any Kaplans. Who is he? Is he your lover?

Never mind Kaplan. Is Isaac Lubel an anarchist?

Isaac would be an anarchist only if Pinya were the Red Queen.

Did you talk to anybody from Edelstadt? Did Emma Goldman talk to you?

Handsome though I may be, Olga, Emma Goldman would never talk to me. And the Edelstadt boys are haughty and windy because they think they are so smart.

I thought he was going to work that morning. He said he was going to work. He kissed me good-bye. He lied to me. Are you lying to me, Isador?

About what?

About anything.

No.

Everything just crumbled. I know nothing now. I feel dead.

You cannot feel dead. If you can feel anything, you are not dead. I can feel you are alive. You are too warm to be dead.

I am dead, Isador. I am dead. And you are not telling me the truth. You played cards at Stadlwelser's all night. You want me to believe that?

Isador says nothing. He snuggles up to wedge his face into the curve of her shoulder. His breath whirs up and down her neck.

Isador, she says. What are we going to do?

I don't know, Isador says. Let's just sleep now, we'll dream something up.

I cannot sleep.

You have to sleep.

Isaac Lubel is dying, she says.

I know, he says. I heard Pinya cursing him.

What are we going to do?

He says nothing, just sighs and smacks his lips. His stench is turning sour. She squeezes him closer to her bosom. If you want me, he says, why don't you just say so?

What a fool you are, Isador, Olga says.

· · ·

LAZARUS WALKS TOWARD Olga swaddled in cloth, grinning shame-lessly as though wearing smart new clothes on his way to a rendez-vous. Through the holes in his socks she sees eggs instead of toes. Walking by, he tips his brow in greeting, as though flirting with her, and says, No tsar, no king, no president, no police, no landlord, but I love you. Then he is swimming the backstroke through a field of sunflowers in bloom, as vast as a lake, the way he used to in the Dniester. Isador is on the shore, naked and aroused, about to jump in, Lazarus is beckoning him from below. A moment later Isador is falling, and he keeps falling; she is watching his fall from high above, and he is just about to hit the sandy bottom, for the sun-flowers have disappeared, when she is startled out of sleep by the banging on the door.

The day has long broken, but she has no idea what time it is. For an instant she wonders why she is not at work but cannot recall what her job is; she looks around and cannot recognize anything: the extinguished lamp, the disheveled dresser, a pair of heelless, mud-coated shoes, side by side. But Isador fidgets in his sleep and she knows who he is—he is the not-Lazarus, just like everybody else.

The thudding at the door is stronger and faster.

"Miss Averbuch, open the door."

Barefoot, her feet sticking to the chilly floor, she rushes to the door before it is taken down, but then rushes back to wake up Isador—she now fully recalls his body and presence. Isador, dim as ever, has sat up in bed, his hair somehow still unruffled and parted, and is presently pressing knuckles into his eye sockets. She waves absurdly, wordlessly, at him, so as to implore him to hide under the bed, but he just sits there, his face ablaze with idiotic innocence.

"Miss Averbuch, this is William P. Miller, of the *Tribune*," a deep voice calls out. Isador finally slides out of sight, under the bed, and she returns to the door to unlock it. She opens it slowly, as though to impede the flow of time. William P. Miller steps in with a broad grin, followed by Hammond the photographer and the unshaven *politsyant*.

"Good morning, Miss Averbuch," Miller says. "You will forgive me the impertinence." The photographer strides toward the window and immediately begins to set up his camera. The *politsyant* circles around the table, picks up a fork, and drops it into a tin bowl to hear it clang. He goes to the bedroom (Olga's heart stops), opens the wardrobe and leaves it open, lifts the veil covering the mirror to look into it, touching his chin.

"There is nothing there," Olga says. "You already dug through that."

The *politsyant* returns to stand by her side. She embraces her shoulders; a strain of uncoiled hair is curling around her neck. She is squinting at Miller, because her glasses are on the floor by the bed, next to Isador. The *politsyant* is panting like a hound dog, knocking on the table a couple of times, as though to see it if is real. William P. Miller is neatly dressed in a dark suit, an impeccably starched white shirt, and a navy-blue tie with a tiny-star pattern. The photographer is wrestling with the tripod, cursing under his breath.

Miller looks at the *politsyant* with a warm smile and says: "Would you kindly excuse us, Mr. Patterson?"

"As you wish, sir," says the *politsyant*. "I'll be in the hallway if you need me."

He does not close the door as he leaves, so they can hear his heavy, graceless footfalls in the hallway, then the chair screeching under his weight.

"May I presume that you are not hiding your brother's body here?" Miller says, taking off his bowler hat.

"My brother's body? They take my brother's body and throw him in hole. Why can I have my brother's body?"

"I'm ready," the photographer says, his left hand petting the camera.

"Last night I received a tip suggesting that your brother's body was not where it ought to be," Miller says. "So I checked the burial location and indeed the body is absent. I came to you before I divulged this to anyone else, for I believe you ought to know first."

Olga's knees give way and she slumps into the chair.

"It is obviously a flagrant desecration, a grievous sin. Perhaps your brother's anarchist friends, led by the fugitive Maron, stole him from the grave."

Olga is out of breath, gasping. A throe climbs from her heels to her spine to lodge itself in her skull. The camera flash goes off, a cloudlet of acrid smoke drifts toward the bedroom.

"Goddamn it," Hammond says. "This one is messed up. Can we move her closer to the window?"

"Or perhaps agents employed by the Red Queen, Emma Goldman herself, have spirited it away," Miller goes on. "What is your opinion, Miss Averbuch?"

The pain is burrowing deeper into her head, but in the middle of it all, she recalls Isador sitting up in bed, rubbing his eyes. William P. Miller drops his chin on his tie's knot and is looking at her avuncularly. She closes her eyes, as though to make Miller disappear.

"You wouldn't happen to know where Maron is?"

"Below my bed," she snaps. "And my brother in my dresser. Ask your man in the hall."

Miller chortles and pulls a pen and notebook out of his pocket. *Her indomitable spirit was not intimidated by the presence of the law*, he writes.

"There is another thing," Miller says. "Are you aware that there are some devout Christians for whom your brother's resurrection is an uplifting possibility? Have any of them talked to you? They are praying for your soul, too."

"You have pity?" Olga whimpers.

"I wish eternal peace for your brother as much as you do, Miss Averbuch. I would like you to understand that we have a common purpose in the present circumstances. We both want to know what happened. If you help me get the truth about your brother out to the people, I will help you get what you want."

"What I want from you? What you want from me? I have nothing. I want my brother, that I can bury him like man."

"Have you been approached by any of your distinguished coreligionists? Have they discussed any funeral arrangements with you?"

"No," Olga says. "They stay away from me. Maybe they think I have some disease."

She regards offers of help and support from others with utmost disdain, Miller writes.

"Excuse me, Mr. Miller," Hammond says. "I have some damn good light here. Could she move closer to the window?"

The floor in the bedroom creaks and Olga resists an impulse to turn and look. Hammond looks toward the bedroom, but Miller does not seem to have noticed, or does not care.

"Did any of your anarchist comrades come by?"

"Go away, Mr. Miller. Leave me."

Upon hearing the news, the Jewess wept: "Leave me alone to die with my grief. All I had in the world was my brother Lazarus and now he is lost forever—I cannot even talk to his grave. I am alone for eternity."

"I can't do nothing from this far," Hammond says. "And the light here is perfect. Can you come over here, Miss Averbuch?"

Our room in the hotel—unimaginatively called Chisinau—overlooked a humongous square with a couple of bronze Soviet soldiers cast in victorious eternity. A twenty-four-hour supermarket flashed its lights from across the square. Attracted by the neon blaze like a moth, I ventured in that direction to get us some food and drinks as soon as we arrived. There was everything there, *everything* being the brand whatchamacallits you could find in American and Western European supermarkets: Bounty candy bars and nutritious Tropicana juices, Johnnie Walker and Duracell, whitening Vademecum toothpaste and liquid Dial soap, Wrigley and Marlboro. I bought plenty of toilet paper and some Moldovan wine with the word *blood* in its name. Behind the young cashier, there stood a stately bruiser with a large pendant ID pouch on his chest and a black piece of gun on his hip. He glared at me, while the cashier, all in virgin white, like an angel, avoided my gaze, said nothing, and just pointed at the total on the cash register screen—she had identified me as a foreigner. If I had walked out of that store in Chisinau and into oblivion, loaded with toilet paper and a bottle of blood wine, if I had been subsequently swallowed by the ubiquitous, ever-looming nothingness, neither the virgin nor the bruiser would ever have devoted another thought to me, their lives would have stayed exactly the same. Home is where someone might notice your absence.

Back in the hotel room, we found out that we had no glasses for the wine, so I called the reception desk and made the dumb mistake of speaking in English. "Could we have some glasses?" I asked. "What?" the lady said. Her voice was surprisingly pleasant.

"Glasses, for drinking," I said.

"Girls, yes. Want girls?"

"No, not girls. Glasses."

"What number of girls?"

"I want glasses. Two glasses."

"Want blonde?"

Finally, I came to my senses and retrieved the Russian word for glass—*stakan*—from my dictionary, whereupon she informed me there were no *stakani,* but we could get *dyevushki.* I hung up.

Did you want some girls? I asked Rora. All aspiring members of the national underwater hockey team.

Not right now, he said. Did you get any glasses?

THE FOLLOWING MORNING we set out to explore the landscapes of Chisinau, rather strikingly different from the depopulated country-side. We walked down Stefan Cel Mare, the wide main boulevard lined with ancient chestnut trees and store windows promising glittery cell phones and Kodak instant memories. There were stores selling bonbons, chocolate, and Moldovan wine, formerly the most popular wine in the U.S.S.R., which now nobody in the world would drink—not even the two of us after the previous night's bottle of acrid blood. There were, naturally, currency-exchange booths, each stuffed with a clod-headed money-laundering thug in an Italian tracksuit. People strolled on their way to the rest of the day, the birds in the trees collaborated with the reasonably good morning:

sun, warmth, quietude. I experienced a sneeze of profound joy at the sight of a young couple holding hands, sprightly and supple in garish red tracksuits. For some reason I thought they might be on their way to play table tennis with each other; what elated me was the thought that their souls were Ping-Pong balls levitating at their respective centers. O the levity of young love! Mary and I had gone bowling every once in a while, with her hospital friends; the young doctors rolled the balls as though they were Ping-Pong balls, while I dropped them on my toes.

At the far end of Stefan Cel Mare, within sight of an atrociously Soviet-looking building, there arose an unreal McDonald's, shiny and sovereign and structurally optimistic. It was a fantastically recognizable sight, therefore exceedingly heartening.

What I like about America, I said, is that there is no space left for useless metaphysical questions. There are no parallel universes there. Everything is what it is, it's easy to see and understand everything.

What? It's not a river? Rora said.

Fuck you, I said.

I am not your wife. I don't have to listen to you, Rora said. It was rather uncalled for, his mean attitude. Perhaps it was the blood-wine hangover.

I seldom talked to Mary (or anyone else, for that matter) about such things, about the metaphysics, the existential loneliness, the ways of being. She was a lifesaver; she worked on life, the way people work on their cars—she was a life mechanic. I would embark upon ponderous monologues about, say, the ineluctable finitude of existence and her eyes would acquire a sheen of remoteness; she had no philosophical bone in her body, so I avoided boring her.

But she liked it when I read to her. Often, before sleep, I would read aloud from our book on our chest or, rarely, from one of my immigrant columns. Tired from opening up skulls and digging through the gray matter, she would pass out, but when I tried to quit reading, she would wake up and implore me to read more. I enjoyed the calm on her face, the revolving ceiling fan, the hum of the distant traffic, our neighbor's malamute howling, the serene logic of it all, completing my universe for a moment. Yet when I turned off the light and listened to her breathing, a coven of tormentful thoughts and doubts would descend upon my heart. I could not embark upon my recollections; I could not count on my dreams to erase the pain. And she would be elsewhere, beyond my reach, leagues upon leagues of distance between us I could never tell her about. For if I did, it would have belied all that we had together and called love.

Let's go and eat, Rora said. That is the only existential problem I am interested in right now.

I used to have a blind uncle called Mikhal. Whenever we took group photos at family gatherings, he was in the central position—he sat or stood in the middle, the kids in the front row, his brother and sisters and their spouses standing behind him or flanking him—as though his blindness made him the head of the family. When we passed those photos around, he would always say, Let me see. He would flip through the photos, while someone described them to him: And here is Aunt Olga, smiling . . . And that's you . . . And there is me. He always looked at the photos, nobody ever found it strange. Once I abruptly realized that we could give him any batch of photos and describe whatever it was he was willing to see.

Sometimes I read to Uncle Mikhal; he enjoyed stories about explorers and great scientific discoveries, about great naval battles and failed invasions. I would occasionally simply add things: there would be a new ship sinking in the Battle of Guadalcanal; there would be a fourth explorer trudging through the Arctic ice and snow; there would be newly discovered subatomic particles that changed our thinking about the universe. I would experience a beautiful high because I was constructing a particular, custom-made world for him, because he was in my power for as long as he listened to me. I thought I could always claim misunderstanding if he busted me changing history or dissembling false scientific facts. I dreaded that possibility, however, for I understood that had I been caught in a single lie—if he found out that there was no subatomic particle named *pronek*, or that the 375 sailors of the U.S.S. *Chicago* had never died—the whole edifice of the reality I had built would have crumbled and nothing I had ever read to him would have been true. It had never crossed my mind that my uncle might have been aware of my deception, that he might have been complicit in my edifice-building, until I found myself confessing it all to Rora in line at the Chisinau McDonald's. It presented itself as the clearest of possibilities. Had I been able to imagine Uncle Mikhal as complicit in my fabrications, we would have arranged more gigantic battles, explored more nonexistent continents, and built stranger universes from the strangest particles. That had taken place a long time ago, when I was a boy.

Could you possibly shut up while we eat? Rora said.

I was having a Big Mac, large fries, and a large Coke. Rora got McEggs and a milk shake. We sat outside and ate quickly, greedily. This was no comfort food; it was food that implied that there had never been and would never be any need for comfort. Passersby looked at us with undue interest: an elderly couple, each carrying a checkered tote bag, actually stopped and watched us eat. It wasn't clear to me whether they were hoping we would offer them some or they had recognized us as foreigners. What may have revealed our foreignness was Rora's camera at the center of our table: large and black and shapely. I slowed down the chewing and had trouble swallowing until the elderly couple moved on.

I imagined Lazarus eating eggs all the time, every day—he hated eggs. He had to buy from Mr. Eichgreen all the eggs he cracked in packing; the first few weeks at work, Olga and he ate nothing but eggs: fried eggs, boiled eggs, raw eggs, beaten eggs with sugar.

Isador did not have to buy eggs, because he was good at packing them, but he stole and sold them, until he was caught and fired.

An unshaven portly father watched over two girls blowing their straws—all they seemed to be having were Cokes. A professorial-looking middle-aged woman munched her fries. A very un–Eastern European blond man with Lennon spectacles held the hand of a gorgeous, definitely local, brunette, who looked around, oblivious to his loving touch. By the time we were drinking our McCoffees, I could not keep my mouth shut any longer.

When I went to Sarajevo a couple of years ago, I said, I found out that if I looked into the faces of the people, I saw what they used to look like—I saw their old faces, not their new faces. And when I walked among the prettied-up ruins and bullet-riddled façades, I saw what they used to be, not what they were now. I X-rayed through the visible and what I saw was the original past version. I couldn't see the now, only the before. And I had the feeling that if I could see what it really looked like now, I would forget what it was before.

Goddamn it, Brik, you like to listen to yourself. How does your wife put up with it?

I went to Sarajevo without Mary last time, I continued, unfazed. So I had a crazy, liberating feeling that my life was neatly divided: all of my now in America, all of my past in Sarajevo. Because there is no now in Sarajevo, no McDonald's.

But that's not true, Rora said.

What's not true? I asked. I was expecting his silence at the end of my discourse.

What you're saying is not true. If you can't see it, it does not mean it is not there.

What is not there? Mary? I asked. I have to confess that I could not exactly remember what my argument was.

What you see is what you see, but that is never everything. Sarajevo is Sarajevo whatever you see or don't see. America is America. The past and the future exist without you. And what you don't know about me is still my life. What I don't know about you is your life. Nothing at all depends on you seeing it or not seeing it. I mean, who are you? You don't have to see or know everything.

But what do I get to see, then? How do I get to know? I need to know some things.

Know what? Everybody knows some things. You don't need to know everything. What you need to do is shut up and stop asking so many questions. You need to relax.

Whereupon a gigantic Toyota Cherokee, or Toyota Apache, or Toyota Some Other Exterminated People, drove up on the pavement, the tinted windows throbbing with concussive fuck-music. The rear doors flew open and there emerged a pair of legs stretched long between the high heels and the flashing groin, over which a pair of bejeweled hands pulled an insufficient skirt. Somewhere up above the legs there appeared a pair of bulbous silicone protuberances, and then a head with a lot of dark, shampoo-commercial hair. The little girls stared at her, their mouths lasciviously tight around their straws; the middle-aged lady shimmied in her plastic chair; only the blond man paid no attention. A businessman came out of the Toyota, with the body and the mien of a porn star, complete with pointy boots, a tenderloin breaking out of his tight jeans, and a triangular torso partially covered with an unbuttoned shirt. The businessman paraded with the bimbo through the outdoor seating area and entered the McDonald's. The driver stepped out of the Toyota and looked, predictably, like a second-rate version of the boss. They must have all been made in the same factory, in a converted wine cellar where they line-assembled independent individuals designed for the challenges of the free market and democracy. Maybe I could take some Susie money and buy myself a cheap Moldovan bodyguard; his duties would include listening to my metaphysical abuse. The bodyguard stood with his legs apart—a smaller pubic bulge—and scanned the crowd, his hands wedged in his armpits: should we decide to fuck with the king or disrespect the courtesan, blasts of death should come from his sweaty corners. These people were all about now, no traces of the past, no interest in it. Rora, perhaps making his point, took a picture of the two little girls and their father.

So, how did you find Miller? I asked him.

Good motherfucking God, Rora said. Will you shut up and let me eat?

I just need to know, what is the problem?

Let me tell you what the problem is, Brik. Even if you knew what you want to know, you would still know nothing. You ask questions, you want to know more, but no matter how much more I tell you, you will never know anything. That's the problem.

He stood up and left, disappearing rapidly down the street. I angrily chalked it up to his war trauma, this kind of erratic behavior, clearly another symptom of his PTSD, on top of an inability to communicate emotion (never talking about his relationship with his sister); insomnia (whenever I woke up he was always already awake); compulsive behavior (his constant photographing); anger with others because they had not gone through the same trauma (me). Conclusion: his head problems were not my problem.

I finished my McMeal and subsequently wandered lonely as a cloud through a street market, abundant with ugly underwear and plastic guns and clothes hangers, Chinese screwdrivers, pliers, and backscratchers, crockery and deodorants and soaps and wedding gowns, caged birds which did not sing and rabbits and T-rags picturing Michael Jordan and the Terminator, mysterious liquids in small bottles and myriad nameless flowers. One person's garbage is another person's commodity. Stray dogs slept on their sides under the stalls. Men loitered at the street corners, offering sotto voce to sell me something very cheaply, which I refused even though I had no idea what it was. I walked through it all as through a dream, ending up on a leafy street with lace curtains and icons in the windows of the houses.

Eventually, I sat down on a bench in a park domed with high tree crowns reaching for one another. Beyond the unkempt lawn, on a paved, cracked, sunlit tennis court, there was a group of people in what looked like nineteenth-century costumes; the women wore long, conical dresses and bonnets; the men were in long coats, with wide-brimmed tall hats and ribbon ties. It looked like they were rehearsing a play: while others watched, two of the men moved erratically around the court only to face each other, deliver their lines, then part again. They argued and ranted; their high voices rang around the park; they spoke Russian. The shorter man delivered a long, incensed speech; though I could not hear what he was saying, it was clear that this was an important moment in the play, for he flung his hands and wagged his finger while the other listened, motionless and passive. When the taller man finished, everyone applauded. It seemed that the argument was won.

Lazarus and Isador sat in the back of the room, listening to the incalescent Edelstadt speaker, flinging his arms, shaking his curly red hair in increasing fury, pointing his finger at the innocent ceiling. "The exteriors of prisons, churches, homes," he ranted in Russian, "show that that is where the body and soul are subdued. Family and marriage prepare man for them. They deliver him up to the State handcuffed and blindfolded, yet his cuff links are sparkling. Force, force—that is all that is. The writer does not dare dream of giving the best of his individuality. No, he must never express his anger. The vacillating demands of mediocrity must be satisfied. Amuse the people, be their clown, give them platitudes about which they can laugh, shadows of truth which they can hold as truths."

Suddenly I noticed Rora shooting the actors, leaning on a tree beyond the court, his white shirt glinting in the sunlight. The two men performing paid no attention, but the three bonneted women were looking at him with flirtatious interest. They walked over to him, said something, and laughed; a moment later they assumed their graceful poses and he pointed his Canon at them. The two men finally quit their playacting to observe Rora circling around the women. I imagined them jealous and angry; I hoped they would assail Rora, punch him in the face, so I would have to run and save him and he would owe me and never be an asshole to me again. But they stepped up to him and shook his hand. I watched the dumb show with no desire to cross over and be part of the mutual amusement and negotiations that seemed to be taking place among the new friends. The two men threw their arms across each other's shoulders and faced Rora smiling. Rora was a whore, nobody mattered to him, not me, not his sister; he never mentioned any friends, no family; he seemed to need nobody. I itched to get up and leave, to go on without him—I needed him no longer. Far from all and everything, I no longer needed anybody. Rora took a series of photos, stepping away from the two men. I did not want to be seen sitting here, yet I could not get up.

Lazarus speedily wrote down notes, as though the speech were a dictation, while Isador daydreamed, hardly listening, ogling the bespectacled stenographer. "But what about the lives that we could live, the lives that cease to be an endless, mad drudgery, repugnant struggles?" the speaker went on. "What about the lives worth living? We need new stories, friends, we need better storytellers. We are tired of the preponderance of lies." Afterward, Lazarus remained in his seat, as the hall was emptying, still struck by the intensity of the speech, by the thoughts that raced through his head as he took notes. I want to write a book, he said to Isador. Don't we all, Isador said. But I am going to write it, Lazarus said. Just watch me. I am going to write it.

Rora finally saw me; he shook all of the hands and bid good-bye to the actors; he walked toward me, across the grass, tinkering with his camera so as not to look at me. He sat down next to me without a word. The men were now dancing with the women, the third woman watching with her arms crossed on her chest. The couples mirthfully waltzed, occasionally stumbling on the cracks, but kept circling around the court.

Rora reloaded the film in the camera and said, I have no idea what they were just saying to me.

I kept quiet. The men bowed to the ladies and walked to their imaginary seats.

Rambo killed Miller, Rora said.

Fuck you, I said.

Miller got a bullet in the back of his head. He was an idiot, he thought he could get out of his debt to Rambo by allying with Beno. And New York wanted the story about the power struggle between Rambo and the Government Guy.

I really don't care, I said, though I was lying.

So Miller had been asking questions, and, worse, he had placed the wrong bet that Beno could be the new boss. He had been seen following and sucking up to Beno, had been reported to have interviewed the Government Guy more than once. Rambo saw through it all, he was not stupid. He ran into Miller looking for Beno at Duran Duran. He pistol-whipped him, kicked him unconscious. He wanted Miller to talk, yet he was out of his mind, blind with fury, so he shot Miller in the head. Pop! In the back of the head. When I arrived, Rambo was gone, Miller was dead, leaking brain onto the floor. Duran told me what had happened. He, too, was crazy with fear. Duran had spent decades in prison, but he was shaking. Later on, he forgot what had happened; later on, he remembered that a sniper shot Miller.

I find that hard to believe, I said.

Rambo could take on the Government Guy, Rora went on, let

alone Beno. But he knew that the Government Guy was going to use his killing an American reporter against him. He knew that he was going to whip up the fear among the government people, try to convince them that it was time to take Rambo out. He was racing all over the city, looking for the Government Guy to kill him. And that's when he took a bullet near the heart, a sniper working, without a doubt, for the government.

What happened to the Government Guy?

He would eventually disappear; they would find his head in a ditch, but never his body. People thought that was Rambo's signature, for he had promised he would rip his head off. The Americans asked a lot of questions about Miller's death, but then let it all go. I think they were led to believe that the Government Guy had put a contract out on Miller because he had sniffed something out. Rambo returned to Sarajevo after the war. Rambo's friends in the government protected him. He owed them now; it was a way to control him. He still has a bullet an inch away from his heart, so he avoids excitement. He discovered Islam and now has prayer beads in his hand all the time. He runs the racketeering business all over the city, drugs as well for his friends in the government. Duran was killed, too.

Did you take a picture of Miller at Duran's? I asked.

Yes.

Aren't you afraid to go back to Sarajevo?

Rambo won. He cannot be touched these days, so he does not care. And I don't care. Nobody cares. Rambo is pretty much part of the government now; the business is running smoothly: he gets them the money, does not misbehave, they treat him as a war hero. It doesn't matter what I could say. That still doesn't mean I should be talking about him.

Who else knows about this?

Nobody. You, now.

The actors stood in a circle and smoked. The men took off their tall hats and wiped their foreheads with their sleeves, perfectly simultaneously, as though they had rehearsed that, too.

Fuck *me*, I said.

See what happens, Brik? See where we are now? Do you ever think of anyone other than yourself?

Assistant Chief Schuettler flings the door of his office open and the Fitzes carry Olga in, holding her biceps. William P. Miller follows behind them, his suit begrimed by his night adventures. The Fitzes sit Olga down in a corner chair and when she tries to stand up, they push her back into it.

"If you would be so kind as to be quiet, Miss Averbuch, perhaps we can have a civilized conversation," Assistant Chief says.

"Damn you."

"Now, now. Those are not the words that should come out of a lady's mouth."

Olga is hissing with fury. Fitzgerald puts his hand on top of her head. Fitzpatrick's hand is on her shoulder, his hairy fingers digging into her flesh.

"That is much better," Schuettler says.

"Damn you," Olga mumbles, but Schuettler ignores her.

"Mr. Miller, would you kindly step out with me? You, too, Mr. Fitzgerald."

Assistant Chief holds the door open for Miller and Fitzgerald. Before he follows them out, he says: "Things are not what they seem to be, Miss Averbuch. They are never what they seem to be."

As the door closes, Fitzpatrick takes his hand off of her, but somehow that just increases the weight on her shoulders. She is coated in sweat and filth, the thick film of anger and humiliation, of Lazarus's absence. The nightmare has assumed its own random direction, like a frightened horse. She cannot remember her life before Lazarus's death; that life took place in a different world.

"Things are a wee bit crazy today, don't you think?" Fitzpatrick says. He lights a cigar and sits in a chair next to her, putting his hand on her knee. "Now is the time for all to stick together."

Olga pushes his hand away and stands up.

"Do sit down, lassie. Don't make me get up."

She walks to the door and before she can grab the handle, Fitzpatrick is twisting her arm, bending her over. He leads her back toward the chair; she produces no sound.

"Sit down now," he says, turns her around, and shoves her into the chair. "Sit still. We don't want no pain here, no pain."

Her pain has solidified in her head, where her living love for her living brother—her soul—used to reside; tears are running down her cheeks. The door abruptly opens, and, walking in with Taube, Schuettler says:

"Perhaps you will be able to break through her anger and defiance and calm her down, Herr Taube," Schuettler says. "Perhaps you can make clear to her the seriousness of the situation at hand."

"*Natürlich,*" Taube says and clicks his heels. "Do give me a few moments with Fräulein Averbuch."

Assistant Chief nods sternly and leaves. Before he closes the door, he yells into the hallway: "Fitzgerald, get me Stadlwelser! And I want to see him get up and walk."

Hat in hand, Taube pulls a chair to face Olga; she refuses to look at him. He says nothing for a while, waiting for her to raise her eyes. When she does not, he says, speaking German:

"I thought you might want to know that the apparent reason for your brother's visit to Chief Shippy was to deliver a message. According to the assistant chief, Mr. Eichgreen was letting Chief Shippy know that Emma Goldman was coming to town, planning to stay in the ghetto with her anarchist friends."

Olga looks up at Taube. For a moment, she considers the possibility that what he's saying is true. Lazarus was a good boy, he wanted to get ahead in life. Mr. Eichgreen liked him.

"Mr. Eichgreen is a loyal American," Taube goes on, his face tubercularly calm, "as unlikely to condone anarchism as anyone. I am convinced he was trying to help your brother."

There is an excess of sincerity in his words and grimaces, Olga thinks. He is working too hard to tell the truth.

"I don't know you well, Herr Taube," she says, "but you are getting worse at lying, you and your *politsey* friends. How can you lie so? And maybe Lazarus shot himself seven times after he delivered the message? What else you want me to believe?"

"Allow me to advise you that you ought to recognize we have a bit of advantage in this situation. They owe us."

"We have advantage? They owe us? Us? Since when are we the same people? I don't know who you are. You are mocking me and my pain. Damn you."

"You might also already know," he continues, unperturbed by her hostility, playing with his bowler hat, "that your brother's body disappeared. We have reason to believe that it was stolen by enthusiastic medical students interested in the particularities of his anatomy. There are young men—alas, our future surgeons—who believe they serve science by violating the sanctity of death."

She presses her hands against her face and wails into her palms.

"Fortunately, Assistant Chief Schuettler deployed his best men to seek young Lazarus's body," he goes on. "Finding it was a matter of utmost urgency for them, and there was little doubt that his men would succeed. And indeed they did. They found Lazarus's body."

Olga has reached a point beyond disbelief—she suppresses a giggle. He is torturing her at Schuettler's behest. Taube leans over and touches her arm.

"Unfortunately, it is not complete."

"Not complete? What do you mean it is not complete?"

"Some organs are missing, I am afraid. I regret I have to be the one to tell you this."

"What organs? Are you mad?"

"The spleen. The kidneys. The heart. And it appears they could not be retrieved."

Olga swallows her breath and faints, sliding off the chair. Taube kneels over her, touches her cheek, as though to see if she is still alive. Waggling his hat in front of her face, he calls for help. Fitzgerald peeks inside: "Yes?"

"Could you fetch some water and sugar for Miss Averbuch, please?"

"What is she, fainted?" Fitzgerald says, amused.

"Could you hurry, please?" Taube says with testy urgency. He goes on flapping his hat before her face until Olga comes to. She opens her eyes and looks at him with such intense hatred that he retreats back into his chair.

"You are a monster, Herr Taube. You are just like them," Olga growls, sitting up. "What do you want from me?"

Taube caresses the brim of his hat, as though the answer is inside it. She sits back into the chair, brushing off the hems of her dress. Biting his lip, he goes on:

"Your brother's body was missing for almost two days. It seems he was disinterred shortly after the burial. Perhaps they should have told you sooner, but the assistant chief did not wish to add to your agony. The word was out quickly that they could not find the corpse. The anarchists and other fanatics were conducting special meetings, waving their black flags. Emma Goldman has now arrived, but she was pulling her maleficent strings even before. They are preparing something big, and the ghetto is angry. The reds are claiming that Chief Shippy killed Averbuch just because he was an immigrant and a Jew. They think your brother has the makings of a martyr tormented as much in death as he was in life. Revolution is a religion, and like any religion it fabricates saints and martyrs. And martyrdom is contagious. At any moment some hotheaded, half-literate anarchist might spring upon a policeman with a knife, or hurl a bomb into a crowd of innocent, law-abiding citizens. If something like that happens, we have a choice between revolution and riots."

"Would you please stop talking, Herr Taube? How can you lie so much so early in the morning?"

Fitzgerald comes in carrying a glass of water and a couple of sugar cubes on a saucer. He offers them to Olga, who pays no attention to him.

"Leave it on the desk, Mr. Fitzgerald, please," Taube says.

Fitzgerald puts the glass and the saucer on the desk, but one of the sugar cubes slips off the saucer and falls to the floor. He picks it up, drops it in the water, and leaves without a word. Taube drops the hat on the desk, then lifts it immediately as though to see if there was something under it. Nothing is there. Nothing is everywhere.

"Moreover, Fräulein Averbuch," Taube continues, "there are some among the Christian population who give exaggerated significance to the coincidence of your brother's undue absence from his grave and his name being Lazarus, if you know what I mean."

"I do not know what you mean. What do you mean? What are you talking about? My brother was stolen from his grave and cut up. Stop talking, I beg you."

"There are Christians who would believe that their Bible story is about to be repeated; some of them are ready for the arrival of their Messiah in the shape of Mr. Christ. Such people look forward to the Apocalypse. And I do not need to tell you what a crowd of excited Christians is capable of doing. You lived through that. Everything is ready to burn, all that's needed is a spark. And when the fire starts, we will be the first ones to turn to ashes. Even Mr. Miller is willing to help us."

"What do you want from me?"

"This might be very hard for you to hear. Very hard." He retrieves the glass from the desk and shoves it under Olga's face. Bubbles are streaming upward from the sugar cube. She turns her face away from the glass. Taube sighs. "Please listen. We must quell the rumors that your brother's body is missing as quickly as possible."

"It is missing. My brother's body is missing."

"Please listen. We need to rebury him according to our customs, in the full view of the public, before it is too late. We have to put it all away and go on with our lives."

"You want to bury him without his heart? How could you even begin to say something like that?"

"There are Hebrew religious leaders who will be glad to approve of the funeral; indeed, even to be present at it. And the assistant chief will now be glad to allow your brother's proper burial. He is basically a decent man, if too beholden to power. He has realized that disorder and mayhem will not help him in his further pursuits."

He leans back in his chair, looks to the left and to the right, nodding. She shakes her head, first slowly, then fast, until the pins loosen and her hair unfurls and now it just whips around. The glass escapes Taube's grip and rolls under the chair, but he pays no heed to it.

"We have no choice, Fräulein Averbuch. It is a question of life and death."

"What makes you think I want to live? You killed my brother. You have been lying to me. You put him away without a *shivah*, without Kaddish. None of you brought me a meal. And now you want me to bury parts of my brother as my brother? Have you no shame, Herr Taube? Have you no soul?"

"I can understand your pain, I truly can. I have recently lost a close relative myself. I know as well as anybody how hard it is to live after a grave loss. But life needs to go on, it must never stop. It is our duty to keep life going."

"You are mad. What do you want me to do? He will never have peace. His soul will wander for eternity. My God!"

She places her face on her palms and sobs into her hands. Taube can see teardrops squeezing between her fingers.

"Please bear with me, we have no choice." He inhales deeply and closes his eyes as though about to sink in deep water. His cheeks are flaming, ruddy. Exhaling, he says:

"The Messiah would know what we have to do. We will afford all the necessary respect, all according to our ancient customs. We will bury both the anarchist hatred and the Christian superstitions. We will have all the proper rituals performed, the Kaddish recited, death will be tamed. We will sit *shivah* together, in peace, finally."

"You are a monster, Herr Taube. Do you think I would be able to live with myself if I did that?"

"I spoke to Rabbi Klopstock," Taube says. "He says that Lazarus's spiritual body will be fully present. Our love in God will complete him. Rabbi Klopstock is willing to give you a special dispensation and to stand by your side, to offer solace."

"You are a *monkalb,* and so is your good rabbi. This goes against everything we ought to believe in. I don't want a dispensation. It was bad enough that I could not bury him after he was killed. Now you want me to do it with chunks of his flesh, cut up by insane surgeons? And you are a fool if you think that the anarchists and the Christians and the assistant chief will return to their wives and eat their dinner in peace because I lied to myself and to God."

"God knows our despair. God wants His chosen people to live in peace. God loves life, cares less about death. We need to live. I want to live, I want my children to live. Everyone I know wants to live. You have to ask yourself what is more important to you, life or death. What is this world about—life or death?"

Olga stares at him as he peers down at the glass under the chair, then back up at her. She lowers her voice and speaks slowly, to ensure he will understand every word:

"May your dismembered body rot in a ditch, Herr Taube. May worms nest in your eye sockets. May you never have peace, not in life, not in death. May your ashes be scattered in fallow fields."

She wants to get up and leave, but her legs are dead, the weight on her shoulders is immense, her head is pure solid pain. I am nothing, she thinks. I am gone.

"Why don't you and your rich friends stand up to Schuettler and the anarchists and the Christians and whoever wants to take your *gilden* life away from you? Why do I have to spit on my brother's grave because you and your *negidim* friends are scared of death? Tell me, Herr Taube."

"I understand your dismay, Fräulein Averbuch. I truly do. I am not certain I would be able to make the decision I am asking you to make. I would be just as tormented, just as anguished. I would be angry at those who asked me to decide. But I cannot be you; we cannot be someone else. We are within our life and we stay there for as long as possible, that's our home. We need life. There is too much death already, and there is probably more coming our way."

"What is life? This is no life. Who wants this life?"

"The dead leave it to us to struggle in this world. They go else-where, wherever it is, and wait for God to sort it all out. But we have to stay here, to be here, no matter how hard it is. Nobody can be alone. Life is the life of others. My life, your life, that is nothing."

"Curse upon your head, Herr Taube. May you reach the bottom of my suffering and die there."

"Think of life, I beg you. Let's live. We have to live."

Mary and I, we used to look at our pictures together; it was one of our marital rituals. But we could only go so deep into the common past: its rock bottom was a picture taken by a photographer at the Art Institute the night we met. We stood side by side, grinning at the camera, close enough to imply our mutual attraction, far enough to protect ourselves from it, glancing sideways at each other. We would look at that picture, we would measure the distance we traveled from the beginning, each step of the journey marked by another image: here we were on our Paris honeymoon, beaming in front of Notre Dame; here we were at Christmas dinner, my mouth stuffed with turkey; here we were in Vienna, on our anniversary trip, our cheeks touching; here we were happy, laughing it up, our eyes fiendishly red; here we were not looking sideways but straight at the camera, as though oblivious to the presence of the other. In my wallet, I had Mary's passport picture. I had not looked at it once on this trip.

And I no longer noticed when Rora took pictures. The presence of his Canon used to turn everything into a possible image for me; I looked at things and faces before us and tried to imagine what they would look like in the photos. Andriy's profile; the wrinkled *baba* in the Bukovina Business Center; Chaim's swollen hands; the grimy passengers on the bus to Chisinau—I imagined them as I would see them at some future moment, when the photos were developed. At some point, I was curious enough to suggest sheepishly that he have his pictures done at one of those Kodak, Fuji, or Agfa shops, ubiquitous in every town we passed through, promising photos in one hour. (What was the rush? I wondered. Was it the fear that everything could vanish in the future looming beyond the one hour?) Rora had refused to consider having the pictures done by anyone other than himself, though he did get some rolls developed and showed me the negatives, from which I could discern next to nothing.

Now I didn't care about the future in which I would be looking at Rora's photos. The pictures would offer no revelations; I would have seen all that mattered already, because I was present at the moment of their creation—Andriy smirked at me; the *baba* gave me a roll of pink toilet paper; Chaim put his hand on my shoulder; our fellow passengers offered me their armpits. I didn't think that in the future I would know anything I didn't know before it. I didn't care what would happen, what had happened, because I was present as it was happening. Perhaps this was the consequence of our rapid eastward movement: we moved mindlessly from one place to another; we didn't even know where exactly we might be going. All I could see was just what was right there in front of me, before I moved on to the next thing.

The yeshiva in Chisinau, for example, was right there in front of me. Having been bombed and burned in the Second World War, much like the rest of the city, the yeshiva was nothing but the tall walls and the hollow yard; here and there on the walls I could see a fading Star of David. It was there, the yeshiva, but I had nothing to do with it; it stood the way it had for sixty years, and I simply was as I had been the moment before I saw it, unrelated to it and its reality. It was liberating to look at it with such profound indifference—in a moment or two we were going to leave and never come back, and the yeshiva and everything around it would stay exactly the same. I felt as though I had achieved the freedom of being comfortable with the constant vanishing of the world; I had finally become the Indian on a horse with a branch tied to its tail. Still, we had to go on; therefore, the two of us who could never have experienced the pogrom went to the Chisinau Jewish Community Center to find someone who had never experienced it and would tell us about it.

IULIANA HAD A pale face with deep, mournful eyes and dark eyebrow dashes. Her hair seemed to be ponytailed to the point of pain. She greeted us in English and firmly shook our respective hands, yet she frowned at us sorrowfully as though our presence made her want to weep. I had called her from the hotel, told her we were from Chicago, that I was researching for my book. I had not told her that we were Bosnian, or that neither of us was Jewish. When we met her at the Center, she did not ask any further questions about us, but I did about her: she was twenty-five; she studied history; she volunteered at the Center; she was married. She was beautiful.

I was rapt listening to her sleep-talking through the history of the Jewish community in her country: the long presence, the restrictive laws of the Russian Empire, the many pogroms, the Romanian occupation, the Holocaust, the Soviet occupation, one fucking thing after another—and here we were now. She rested her hands over her groin, as people do at funerals. Occasionally she would lick her lips between sentences, and they shimmered under the strong ceiling lights. Rora wandered off ahead, but I followed her through an exhibit of restored black-and-white photographs documenting the presence and the suffering and the distinguished individuals.

"I am particularly interested in the pogrom of 1903," I said to her back. She had brushed her hair that morning; the end of her ponytail was neat and unfrayed.

"Let us go to another room," Iuliana said.

The other room was all about the pogrom; Rora was there already, examining the photographs on the wall: bearded, mauled corpses lined up on the hospital floor, the glassy eyes facing the ceiling stiffly; a pile of battered bodies; a child with its mouth agape; a throng of bandaged, terrified survivors; Krushevan the rabid anti-Semite, with his pointy beard and curled mustache and the calm, confident demeanor of someone wielding the power of life and death. In the glass case below the photos there was a facsimile of the front page from Krushevan's newspaper, *Bessarabets,* and next to it a threadbare prayer shawl.

"The hundred years since the pogrom that devastated Kishinev have done little to heal our wounds or assuage our grief," Iuliana said. "The Kishinev pogrom, far from the first or the last attack on a helpless community, is indelibly stamped upon our consciousness."

She clearly knew these lines by heart; she seemed to be indifferent to Rora taking pictures of her or browsing through the photos. At the curve of her jaw, there was a birthmark, a slight spot whose color rhymed with her eyes. She went on:

"Was it an outburst of bestial anti-Semitism or a carefully planned attack? How could those who only the day before were on respectful and peaceable terms with their neighbors forget their humanity and slaughter them? Why did those who considered themselves enlightened turn their faces away and the police remain idle?"

She paused and touched the hollow above her lip with her index finger. She did not seem to expect any answers from us, or indeed from anybody—it was too late for answers. I wondered how often she delivered this speech, in her nearly fluent English. How many

English-speaking visitors came by? How did she learn the language so well? She was in the midst of a life I could not imagine.

"The rioters assembled on Chuflinskiy Square on Easter Sunday, April 6. They were incited by the false news published in the *Bessarabets* that a Christian boy was ritually murdered by Jews in Dubassary—the age-old blood libel. But there are indications that the rioters were accompanied by people, many of them teenage boys, who urged them on and had in their hands lists of Jewish establishments and houses. Many local Christians, anxious to protect their homes and shops from violence, had chalked large crosses on their doors or had prominently displayed holy icons in their windows."

Rora was in the back of the room now—I could hear his camera snapping—which meant that I could not leave the reciting Iuliana alone. I did want to watch her; I wanted to enter deep into the history she was telling, even though I had already read plenty about it. But the room was overlit; her face was too pale; the photos too perfectly restored. I nodded occasionally, to suggest that I understood what she was talking about and that she could therefore stop, but she was fixated on a midair point, obviously committed to completing her lecture. The sorrow in her eyes never wavered.

"When a group of Jewish men assembled on Monday morning in the New Marketplace, armed with stakes, canes, and a few firearms, and determined to prevent a repetition of the previous day's vandalism, the police dispersed them, arresting a few in the process."

Rora was in an alcove behind a panel with the list of the victims' names; I moved a few steps to the side to see what he was shooting: there were a couple of dummies in Orthodox Jewish attire, positioned around an empty table, their eyes wide open, their hands resting on the table's edge. They could not bend enough to be sitting, so they seemed to be sliding under the table. Everything in this museum seemed solidified, like those plastic brain models Mary kept around the house and sometimes played with absent-mindedly while watching television.

"That is a Jewish family from the time of the pogrom," Iuliana said by way of explaining the dummies, then continued: "Before the violence ended, a total of forty-three persons had lost their lives. The dead represented a broad cross section of Kishinev's Jewish population"—she respired poignantly—"and included an apartment owner, a poultry dealer, a cattle dealer, a baker, a bread dealer, a glazier, a joiner, a blacksmith, a former bookkeeper, a bootmaker, a carpenter, a student, a wine shop proprietor, and several other shopkeepers, as well as a number of wives and mothers, and even a few children."

Finally I interrupted her.

"Was any of them named Averbuch?" I asked. Her body abandoned her recitative posture; she flinched.

"Why?"

"Well, I am writing . . ." I said and realized the verb was far too optimistic. "I am doing research on someone named Lazarus Averbuch. He survived the pogrom, escaped from Kishinev, and ended up in Chicago. And then the Chicago chief of police killed him."

Iuliana's eyes teared up; she covered her mouth with her hand, as though shocked by the news of a 1908 murder. She smelled of warm cleanliness; her tight hair shone; I wanted to embrace her and comfort her, the way I embraced and comforted Mary when she cried after our fights.

"This was a few years after the pogrom, in 1908. Lazarus had a sister, Olga. She left Chicago a few years after his death and settled in Vienna."

"My grandmother's maiden name was Averbuch," Iuliana said. I very much wanted Rora to take a picture of Iuliana in her permanent, indelible grief, not so I could remember this particular moment—for I could never forget it—but because she was heartbreakingly beautiful. Rora stood afar, changing film in his camera.

"Olga disappeared from history altogether upon her return to Europe," I said. "She may have perished in the Holocaust."

"My grandmother was shot by the Romanians in 1942," Iuliana said. "She was in her thirties when she died."

"Have you ever heard of Lazarus Averbuch? Have you ever heard a family story about someone with that name?"

"No. My father was still a little boy when his mother was killed. And his grandparents were killed, too. We have few family stories."

"Are there other Averbuchs here? Do you know any?"

"No," she said. "There are no living Averbuchs here."

"Are you sure?"

"We are a small community. Everybody knows everybody. There are no Averbuchs. But you could go to the cemetery. There must be a lot of Averbuchs there."

THE CEMETERY WAS behind a nondescript, crumbling wall; we had a hard time finding the gate, rusted and heavy. In front of it, an ancient Dacia was carelessly parked; a man sat smoking in it, watching the gate intently, as though he were a getaway-car driver. Iuliana had to ring a bell, and a man in tall rubber boots unlocked it, then restretched himself on a bench from which he had obviously just arisen. It was a beautiful sunny day; there was a pleasant whiff of summer abundance in the bright air; birds were deliriously atwitter. We walked down a narrow path into a vault of greenness and quietude, the light diffused by overleafed trees. The path forked and dead-ended and widened; we wandered inward, deeper and deeper. Some of the gravestones were swallowed by the baroque bushes and ivy; some of them were ruins; many were desecrated—a chunk missing, clearly beaten off with a hammer; the photos of the dead smashed or cracked. Some tombstones were clean and kempt, which made them appear unreal, as though they were inferior replicas of the original, unviolated, ones. There were tombstones with something in Russian written on them, which I could not decode.

"What does this mean?" I asked Iuliana.

"It means: 'Do not destroy. There is still family,'" she said.

The birds were suddenly quiet; there were no sounds whatso-ever coming from the outside; indeed, there was no outside. The leaves did not move as we brushed past them; the twigs did not break under our feet; there was no sun, though there was light, heavy and viscous. This was all, the world of the dead: Rozenberg, Mandelbaum, Berger, Mandelstam, Rosenfeld, Spivak, Urrman, Weinstein. I could not remember how long I had been away, how I had gotten to this point. Hoydee-ho, haydee-hi, all I ever do is die. Rora was falling behind, getting ahead, photographing without pause. I could not understand what he saw, what there was to pho-tograph, how he could not feel helpless and hopeless.

"Is your family buried here?" I asked Iuliana.

"Some of them are," she said. "But most of this cemetery was dug up by the Soviets to build a park."

Rora shouted from somewhere deep in the woods and called us over. Iuliana and I got lost looking for him, then she got lost too, and I was suddenly surrounded by a herd of mausoleums, their little portals ajar, falling off their hinges, the cavernous darkness gaping through a broken wall. The voices of Iuliana and Rora were distant, and then were gone. Everything I had been was now very far away; I reached elsewhere. I could not remember how long ago I had left Chicago and Mary. I could not recall her face, what our house looked like, what it was that we called our life.

Why did you leave me lost in these woods, Mary? I loved you because there was no other place for me to go. We were married because we did not know what else to do with each other. You never knew me, nothing about me, what died inside me, what lived invisibly.

Some part of my life ended there, among those empty graves; it was then that I started mourning. I can tell you that now, now that there is little but mourning.

Iuliana shouted, in a high-pitched voice that suggested a touch of panic; and then Rora did, too, and then I did. I was afraid that shouting might wake up the dead; I stepped lightly on the path. We found each other by a large monument on which all the Hebraic letters had been viciously scraped off, but below them in Russian it read: *Averbuch Isaac 1901–1913*. Here was someone I would never know anything about; here was a life entirely absorbed in death. Here it was. Iuliana was flustered, blushing, a globule of sweat sliding down past her ear, then curving at the jawline. She smiled at me—I could have kissed her right there, those living lips, those gloaming eyes, that pale face. That's me, I thought. That woman is me. Somewhere beyond the roof of tree crowns the sky grumbled, gearing up for a storm. Rora took a picture of her, then of me, then of us.

It took a while to find a way out. Rora's hair was sweat-pasted to his skull and neck, a gray oval of perspiration growing on his back—the closer we got to the exit, the bigger it was. And again I thought: That's me. The thought bounced in my head deliriously, I couldn't get to the end of it, could not fold it up into meaning. Iuliana walked behind; I heard her gentle panting. She was me, Rora was me, and then we came upon the man on the bench, drooling asleep, his mouth open enough for us to see a graveyard of teeth, his hand wedged inside his pants' waist—and he was me, too. The only one who was not me was myself.

I practically broke out of the cemetery; outside, the car was still parked, now empty, revealing faux-leather seats bespeckled with cigarette burns. We walked downhill, past the houses I had not noticed before, the dogs now barking at us angrily, past the park where children who had not been there before now swung on the swings and slid down the slides.

"Tell me, Iuliana," I said, envisioning her hand in my hand. "Tell me, what is this world about—life or death?"

Rora looked at me with a knowing smile, but what it was that he knew I did not know.

"That is a very strange question," she said. "What do you mean?"

"Is this world for the dead or for the living? Do you think there are more dead than living people?"

"Why do you worry about that?" She looked at Rora, who shook his head. They were concerned about me, I realized; they found solidarity in worrying about my sanity. In my country, death is on the national flag.

"If there are more dead than living, then the world is about death, and the question is: What are we to do with all the death? Who is going to remember all the dead?"

She was thinking about it, scratching the parting in her hair. She would one day die, and so would Rora, and so would I. They were me. We lived the same life: we would vanish into the same death. We were like everybody else, because there was nobody like us.

"I think it is about life. I think there is always more life than death," Iuliana said. "Those who lived are always alive for someone. Those who are alive remember life, not death. And when you are dead nothing happens. Death is nothing."

Mary always thought I was grave; I was getting even heavier on this trip. The weight could keep me here forever. Iuliana and I, we could keep each other sad and live off sardines for the rest of our lives and through the nothingness beyond. I would stroke her hair with my heavy hand; I would write my book and read it for her, very slowly; I would kiss her dimple before heavy sleep.

It thundered above, the growling stomach of the void. As we reached the foot of the hill, the oily, isolated drops hit us painfully, then multiplied into a deluge. Rora and Iuliana charged toward a restaurant veranda across the square, while I philosophically kept my slow pace. They leapt over the fast-forming puddles, sprinted across the street, avoiding a bus and a streetcar; as they found cover under the eaves of the veranda, it appeared to me they were holding hands. I reached the cover soaked to the brain; Iuliana was in the bathroom; Rora was painstakingly wiping his lens, drying his camera. There was nobody at the restaurant, no waitstaff or patrons in sight. The sky opened up; rivers poured off the roof; the eaves burst with waves, the street gray with the heaving water. Iuliana walked out and stood on the veranda, watching the deluge, pensively, calmly, as though she had always known it was coming. I could see myself standing next to her, my hand touching the nape of her neck. But of course I did not move. I remembered the joke Rora had told me:

Mujo left Sarajevo and went to America, to Chicago. He wrote regularly to Suljo, trying to convince him to come, but Suljo did not want to, reluctant to leave his friends and his *kafana*. Finally, after a few years, Mujo convinces him and Suljo flies over the ocean and Mujo waits for him at the airport with a huge Cadillac. They drive downtown from the airport and Mujo says, See that building, a hundred stories high?

I see it, Suljo says.

Well, that's my building.

Nice, Suljo says.

And see that bank at the bottom floor?

I see it.

That's my bank. And see that silver Rolls-Royce parked in front?

I see it.

That's my Rolls-Royce.

Congratulations, Suljo says. You've done well for yourself.

They drive to the suburbs and Mujo points at the house, as big and white as a hospital.

See that house? That's my house, Mujo says. And see the pool, Olympic size, by the house? That's my pool.

There is a gorgeous, curvaceous woman sunbathing by the pool, and there are three healthy children happily swimming in it.

See that woman? That's my wife. And those children are my children.

Very nice, Suljo says. But who is that brawny, suntanned young man massaging your wife?

Well, Mujo says, that's me.

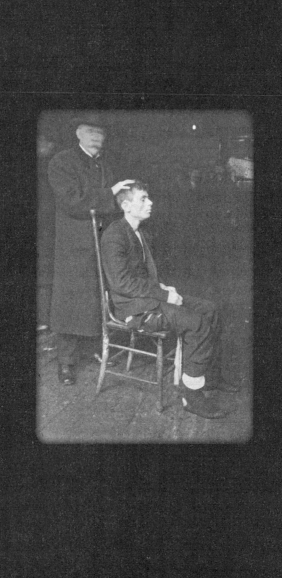

They ripped out Mr. Mandelbaum's beard, tore all of it out, Lazarus said, mewling and trembling in my arms. Seryozhka Shipkin held up a blood-dripping tuft of Mr. Mandelbaum's beard in his hand. They beat Mr. Mandelbaum with canes and crowbars. He begged them for mercy. I heard his bones breaking. Seryozhka stepped on his face with a boot, cracked Mr. Mandelbaum's skull. I heard the sound, Lazarus said. Mr. Mandelbaum's left foot flapped around like a carp the whole time, his shoe fell off. He had a hole in his sock. He is dead. I saw it.

Chaia was biting her knuckles as she listened, tears abseiling down her cheeks to gather at her chin.

Roza sat at the table, apparently waiting for her lunch, an empty plate before her. Always hungry, she was.

Mother was busying herself at the stove, banging the pots, stir-ring the kasha, boiling the eggs, but we could see that she did not know what she was doing.

We were all thinking, Maybe they will pass our house. But we knew they would not. Fear leavened in my stomach.

They ransacked Mr. Mandelbaum's store, Lazarus said. They stole everything. They turned over the barrels with potatoes. They smashed the jars of sardines. There was candy all over the floor, potatoes, too. They carried off the scale and the ladder. They nearly caught me. Two *politsyanten* were watching everything. One of them took a cookie box. I was hiding behind the counter, then I darted out. There was a lot of blood, all over the floor. A pogromchik ran after me but slipped on a puddle of blood and fell. I was very scared. I ran straight here.

Papa was stroking his beard, soughing heavily. Nobody said anything.

His sobs dying down, Lazarus pulled a little paper bag out of his pocket and put a piece of candy in his mouth, rewarding himself for telling the story. Sniffling, he sucked on it, as though everything had happened to someone else. Such a boy he always was. He had skidded across a puddle of blood for his life.

They are coming this way, Papa said. They shall come, no doubt.

And as if on a cue, a brick crashed through the garden window. Then another one from the street. It landed on Roza's plate, smashing it. She yelped but did not move. The rest of us were on the floor already, shrieking. That sound, shrieking. You wanted to talk, you wanted to hear others talk, but all that came out of your mouth was shrieking. We shrieked.

The pogromchiks pounded at the door, screaming our names, blood thirst in their hoarse voices. How did they know our names?

I thought, This is our home. They cannot come in. This is not their home. They are outside.

Chaia was blubbering.

Mother sat down on the floor with her back to the stove. I was afraid that her dress would catch fire.

Papa was stretching on the floor to reach his yarmulke, as though something depended on it.

I held Lazarus tightly, his face in my bosom. I could not feel his breathing. Oh, don't go, I thought. Please don't go. But then he sniffled again. Such a boy he was.

Roza was still sitting at the table, now holding her fork and knife, looking furious. She must be very hungry. She was at that age. Always hungry.

The pogromchiks burst in, abruptly filling up the room. They set out to break everything: the lamps, the vases, the vitrine with the china. They swept the books off the shelf. Our life was blowing up, the shrapnel flying around the room.

With his sleeves rolled up for hard work, one pogromchik grabbed Roza's hair and pulled her off the chair. She held on to the table edges, dragging, as she fell, the tablecloth, all the cups and the plates and the fruit and the flowers cascading down, smashing against the floor.

I saw his face. A young, feverish face, with whisker shades, his ears ruddy. He had a glass eye that stayed unexcited as he threw Roza down on the floor. He pressed himself against Roza on her back. She was shielding her face with her hands.

Papa leapt off the floor like a frog, grabbed the man's neck. He started choking the man, the redness spreading from the ears to the cheeks. A *politsyant* came out of nowhere and punched Papa behind the ear, blood spurting forward out of his mouth. The *politsyant* pulled the man off Roza and slapped his face. I wanted him to kill him. I wanted to see blood.

Someone plucked Lazarus out of my arms and threw himself on top of me. The swine pulled up my dress all the way to cover my face. He was groping for my undergarments. His breath stank of kvass and garlic.

Lazarus jumped on his back and dug his nails into his cheeks. The swine stood up and screamed, thrashing. Lazarus clung on to the swine's face, his feet flying around. The swine grasped Lazarus's hands. He turned around and punched him, once, then twice. Blood streamed out of Lazarus's nose. He held Lazarus by the throat, bashing his face with the other hand, over and over again.

I shrieked. Lazarus went limp, but the swine kept punching

him. He stopped only after he hurt his hand. He let Lazarus drop to the floor, kicked him in the stomach in fury. He was about to step on his face, when the *politsyant* pushed him aside and away from Lazarus. The swine recoiled. He glared at the *politsyant*, deliberating whether to assault him. But then he thrust Lazarus, unconscious, off the carpet, rolled it up with one hand, and took it under his arm.

Lazarus used to pretend that was a magic carpet; he sat on it in the middle of the room and imagined flying to far-off places: Moscow, Paris, Greece, America. Such a boy he was.

The *politsyant* kicked Lazarus in the head to show the swine panting with bloodlust and rage that they were on the same side. The swine spat on the floor and took off.

Someone sat on my chest. I blacked out. When I came to, all the pogromchiks were gone. The *politsyant* was carrying out the red velvet–upholstered armchair. He had difficulty getting it through the door, making two steps back until he found the right angle. He said to someone outside: "The job is finished here. They are all dead. Go over to Rozenberg's house."

Then there was silence. The electricity of violence and fear in the room. The down from torn pillows floating, like souls, through the fog of what had just happened. The air reeking of sweat and blood, of smashed furniture and shards of glass, of spilled food and fear. There was a black leather glove in the puddle of kasha on the floor.

Mother hiccupped and started sobbing; Papa moaned.

Manicheyev was the *politsyant*'s name. He used to patrol the New Marketplace, took bribes from the vendors, always smiled and tipped his hat to greet the ladies.

A horse whinnied outside. The wind came in through the windows, but nothing inside moved.

No one moved: Papa's face pressed against the floor in a puddle of blood; Mother lying on her side, facing the wall next to the kitchen door; Chaia curled up, her knees to her chest, the hem of her dress touching her ear; Roza on her back still; rivulets of blood spreading away from Lazarus's nose and eye sockets, across his cheeks and mouth, down to his neck.

He is dead; they are all dead, I thought. The horrible fear rushed from my stomach to my head. They killed them all. Here it is, then.

But then Roza rose, brushed off strands of hair from her cheeks, pulled her skirt down, and, still sitting, started picking up the forks and knives and unbroken cups and saucers. She set the table with what she had collected, straightened up her chair to seat herself at the empty table.

I could not comprehend what Roza was doing. Why was she doing it? Why was she moving at all? It was like a dream, everything taking place outside any sense, and slowly.

Roza looked toward the kitchen, as though to see whether the breakfast was coming.

Nothing would ever be the way it used to be. It was impossible to remember what it used to be like at all.

On the stove, the kasha pot lay on its side, the kasha steadily, determinedly dripping on the hot plate, burning, the smoke spreading across the room.

Thus we were winnowed.

"OLGA," TAUBE SAYS. "Say something."

She looks at him as though surprised that she can hear him at all, that he can speak.

"Allow me to get you another glass of water," Taube says and stands up. "You look pale."

You don't talk to me about pogroms, Herr Taube, Olga says in Yiddish. You have your Viennese diploma, your rich friends, your good intentions, your perfect German, your charming English. What can you ever know about what a pogrom is? What do you know about life and death?

"Indeed," Taube says, "I don't wish to learn about death." His cheeks are radiating consumption. Olga can see he is going to die.

You know nothing, Olga says.

"I do not wish to learn, Olga. I assure you."

Taube sits back down to face her and grabs her hands. She pulls them back, but not far enough to get out of his grip.

"Please. I beg you. We would do anything you ask us to do."

Would you?

"We would," Taube says. "Anything within our power."

Iuliana helped me find a driver to take us from Chisinau to Bucharest, where we could get a train to Belgrade, from where we could reach Sarajevo. At the bus station, we picked through a mob of taxi drivers loitering, smoking, drinking, sleeping in their cars, wishing for an odd ride. I selected the most honest-looking one: a hoary, fat little man he was, with thick glasses suggesting that, before he regained his freedom and Moldova her independence, he might have been a respected literary critic. He asked for a hundred euros and I would have brutally bargained if Iuliana had not been there. The fat little man's name was Vasiliy; he seemed sufficiently grateful and was going to pick us up at six a.m.

It was early evening; the sun was sunk below the treetops; the smell of linden managed to override the reek of dust and diesel; Chisinau appeared a pleasant place to be. The cemetery-roaming had created an odd intimacy between Iuliana and me, so we went to a coffee shop, in front of which the same gangstermobile as in front of the McDonald's was parked, but no businessman in sight. I told Iuliana about the businessman-and-bimbo spectacle I had witnessed; she seemed to be listening with interest but said nothing. I liked the way she was comfortable and confident in nothing

being said. She was like Rora in that regard—his statements were
completed, his sentences did not spill into each other. Like Rora,
she was sovereign when silent; her silence was not an absence of
words, it was a thing unto itself, shaped by her. How did they do
that? Silence terrified me—whenever I stopped talking, the possibility of never saying anything again was horribly present. Therefore,
I asked:

"Do you like Chisinau?"

"It is okay."

"Have you ever thought of leaving?"

"Yes."

"Why don't you leave?"

"Where would I go?"

"America."

"I need a visa for that."

"Maybe I can help you get a visa."

"My family is here, all of them. My husband has a job."

She sipped her coffee; she had a husband; she bent the tiny
plastic spoon in and out of shape. I strived to complete myself with
words; it was a hopeless project.

"How do you feel about the pogrom?" I asked.

"How do I feel about the pogrom?"

"Yes. How do you feel about the pogrom?"

Silence. Then she said:

"That outburst of bestial anti-Semitism is indelibly stamped
upon our national consciousness."

I chortled, but she was not kidding. I said:

"No, really. How do you—you, Iuliana—feel about it? What do
you feel when you think about it? Anger? Despair? Hatred?"

She wagged her head to show she did not like the question.

"See, I am actually Bosnian," I said. She did not react to the
news. "And when I think about what happened in Bosnia, I feel this
filthy fury, this rage at the world. Sometimes, I fantasize about

breaking the kneecaps of Karadžić, the war criminal. Or I see my-self smashing someone's jaw with a hammer."

I had no idea whether she knew what happened in Bosnia. Mary did not like to listen about the war and genocide and mass graves or about my accumulated sense of guilt in relation to all that. Iuli-ana stopped shaking her head, though, and was listening to me. In retrospect, I can see I may have frightened her.

"I imagine him writhing in pain, on the floor, then I hammer his elbows, too," I said. "Do you ever want to break someone's jaw?"

"You are strange," she said. "I thought you are from America."

"Yeah, I am now from America, too. There are a lot of jaws there I would like to break."

The businessman walked out of the next-door mobile-phone store; he strode, throwing his shoulders back. This time I could see his eyes: they were washed-out blue. If I had a hammer, I could smack him between his porn eyes, crack his forehead, disfigure his nose. And then, in the same moment, I thought: *That's me.* I could be him. I could smash in my own forehead. That would be fun.

"My grandfather," Iuliana said, "was in the Red Army. He was in the platoon that raised the Soviet flag on the Reichstag. He was the only Jew in his battalion."

She said nothing else—apparently that was a fully completed statement. The gangster leapt into the driver's seat of his gangster-mobile and sped away. There go I but for the grace of God.

"When I think about the pogrom," Iuliana said, "I feel love for those people. When I think about my grandfather, I think about how hard it must have been for him, how lonely and happy he was on top of the Reichstag. When I think about those things, I love him."

"I see," I said.

Once Mary lost a patient on the surgical table. He was a gang member taken down in a drive-by shooting. The bullet was lodged in his frontal lobe; somehow he was conscious when they brought him in. He talked to her; he asked her for her name; he told her his—it was, unbelievably, Lincoln. But there was nothing she could do; he died under the knife. That night she sat in the living-room armchair as on a throne, staring at the same page of a *People* magazine for fifteen minutes before she passed out, her cheek on her shoulder, only to wake up and confront my relentless questions: "How did you feel after he died? What were your thoughts?" Whereupon Mary got up, dragged her blanket to the bedroom like a gown train, and pushed the door in my inquisitorial face. I was enraged; I banged at the door and eventually slammed it open, as though I was breaking in, to find her in bed, turned to the wall, the blanket pulled up to her temple. "Don't you ever get angry?" I shouted. "You must get angry. You must hate somebody. What makes you so goddamn different?" Later on I apologized halfheartedly, and so did she. "When a patient dies," she explained, rather unhelpfully, "I feel that he is dead."

As IULIANA AND I parted for good, I kissed her cheek; it was as soft as an inside of a thigh. Afterward, in the Chisinau Hotel room, Rora asked me, Did you bang her? She has a husband, I said. You have a wife, Rora said. I ignored his remark and reported on tomorrow's transportation arrangements. I turned and faced the wall, stared at the cracks before I tried to sleep, but couldn't. Rora was flipping through the silent channels. I could hear a rare car circling the bronze heroes in the square.

Aren't you worried that Rambo might come after you in Sarajevo? I finally asked.

Rora kept flipping the channels.

Do you have pictures of Miller dead stashed away somewhere? Is that your insurance?

Don't you worry about me, he said. I'll be all right. Nobody cares anymore. I just want to see Azra and then I'll be gone.

How old is Azra?

Fucking questions again, Rora said.

Was she in Sarajevo during the siege?

Yes.

What did she do?

She amputated limbs. She is a surgeon.

Mary is a surgeon, too, but she cuts the brain.

Rora said nothing.

Is she married? I went on.

Not anymore.

Why not?

Do you ever stop?

No.

She was married before the war, for seven years. But when the war started her Serb husband loyally went up in the hills to shoot at her with his Chetnik brothers. He sent a letter from up there demanding her to join him. He said it was her duty as his wife.

What did she say?

What kind of question is that? She told him that it was his duty as her husband to go and fuck himself.

ALL WE HAD LEFT to do together, Rora and I, was get back to Sarajevo. We stayed up and talked all night. I could not stop listening, and after I listened I had to speak, and so it went on. We spoke slowly, whispering, acknowledging the necessity of slumber.

Once when I was on the front line, Rora said, I saw a magic carpet flying across the river. It was a blue-and-white piece of UNPROFOR nylon, but still I could not stop seeing it as a magic carpet. It looked sinister, coming to taunt us from a different world, where people still told fairy tales. It came down on the river's surface, it bobbed and undulated going downstream until it sank. The Chetniks kept shooting at it, they had a lot of ammunition.

I told him how much Mary wanted children and how opposed

to the idea I was—I told her that I didn't want them to live in the world as it was, but in truth I was afraid they would become too American for me. I was afraid I would not understand them, I would hate what they became; they would live in the land of the free, and I would live in fear of being deserted. The thought of Mary leaving me was ever present in my mind, particularly after I lost my teaching job, after I started needing her even more. This trip was good because I was the one gone, she was the one left behind.

When my sister and I were kids, Rora said, we adopted a stray, mangy dog; we called him Lux, after Tito's dog. It followed us everywhere. We trained him to obey and showed him off to other kids. Lux would carry our schoolbags. He would sit outside waiting for us, while we were in class, afraid he might be gone before school was out. And once we found him terrified and stuck up in a tree—someone had put him up there. Lux was whining, afraid to move, his paws clinging to the bark. Azra called him to jump into her arms; she was bigger and stronger than me. The dog jumped, he trusted her. She caught him and fell, he was really scared. She carried him home in her arms. But one day he was gone and never came back.

I knew Mary would one day leave me because she liked being apart from me: she turned away from me sleeping; she was always willing to swap shifts or work two shifts in a row—her work kept her away from me. When we talked, she often looked off to the side of my face. When she went out of town to conferences she called me only after she had arrived and just before she would return. Our children would be miserable mongrels undoing their foreign dead-beat father in themselves, that was my fear.

Once in Paris, Rora said, I was doing a married woman who locked her little son up in a closet while we were in bed. Her husband came back home abruptly and I hid with the kid in the closet, full of mink coats and silk dresses. The funny thing is, the kid seemed to be used to the situation. We played a mute game with our fingers, odds and evens, that sort of thing; the kid kept winning. The husband never asked or looked for the kid.

Mary carried a picture of her seven-year-old nephew in her wallet, talked about him all the time: how he thought that the point of a lacrosse game was to catch a butterfly; how he drew God having many big eyes; how at the age of five he could dance those Irish dances. He was Mary's little lamb: when we baby-sat him, she told him fairy tales.

Once, in the war, Rora said, I was caught up in a burning skyscraper. I had to keep running upstairs from the fire climbing up. On the top floor I burst into someone's apartment. Whoever lived there was gone, but on the table was a *džezva* of coffee and a demitasse and a stack of photos. The coffee was still hot; the person had just left. So I poured myself some coffee and looked through the photos. Most of them were of a teenage boy: pimpled and scrawny, smiling cutely, looking at the camera with red eyes. There were a few pictures of the parents with the boy—they clearly lived somewhere abroad. You could see the neatness of the rooms where the photos were taken. Wherever they were, Sweden or some such place, they did not have to burn their own furniture to survive a winter. In one picture, there was a television set showing a soccer game, but the boy in the picture had no interest in it. The boy's life was big, everything was ahead of him. He was going to watch a lot of soccer games, so he didn't have to watch this one.

You know, Rora went on, Miller once demanded from me that I keep taking pictures of children running away from snipers, ducking and hiding behind garbage containers, even though there was heavy sniper fire. He paid some of the kids to run back and forth under fire so I could take a perfect picture. Still, I felt bad when Rambo clipped Miller. He deserved a good beating, but not death. Nobody deserves death, yet everybody gets it.

. . .

WE WERE OUTSIDE the hotel as the dawn was breaking, having slept for only a couple of dreamless hours. The literary critic was there, but not alone—there was a younger, slimmer man, named Seryozha, leaning on a Lada, smoking, his tracksuit pants tucked into pointed cowboy boots; his sweatshirt read *New York*. He was going to drive us to Bucharest, the literary critic said, in a feeble voice; it was plain that he'd been bullied into this concession. Seryozha grinned at us and offered to shake our hands. I was on the verge of canceling the whole trip, but Rora grabbed his hand and shook it, so I thought, What the hell, let's go.

I sat in front, ever the captain, Rora in the back. Seryozha had pictures of saints stuck above the rearview mirror, and a pine tree–shaped air freshener which entirely failed at freshening. The car smelled of sweat, cigarettes, and sperm—intercourse must have taken place in it not so long before. I did not buckle up, lest I insult him.

We drove in heavy, tense silence, speeding as though pursued by the demons of police. Seryozha swerved jerkily around the potholes; he zoomed over the corrugated patches of the carless road. I convinced myself that he knew what he was doing, that, being native, he had a special connection with the aboriginal roads, that he could, passing a snaky truck, sense a car behind the ninety-degree uphill curve. In his country, cars were as smart as horses and people never died in road accidents.

Fields of coy sunflowers, hills reticulated with untended vineyards, hutlike houses huddled in shallow misty valleys—they all passed by us as in a dream, accompanied by jumpy Russian disco Seryozha found on his radio. We flew by oxen carts and peasants walking alongside them who seemed to be standing still. The trance of moving forward, the pasty sleepiness of the morning—I passed out. I dreamt.

I normally remembered only fragments of my dreams; I forgot a lot of them, too, though I could often abstractly recall their intensity. Usually, they had something to do with the war: Milošević, Mladić, Karadžić, and, lately, Bush, Rumsfeld, and Rambo figured in them. There were knives and severed limbs and rape with random, sharp-edged objects. Sometimes, I would have communal dreams: we—and *we* included Mary (always Mary) and family and friends and complete strangers who felt familiar and close—we would do something together, say, play hide-and-seek, or spit-roast a lamb, or pose for a photo. We did it in Chicago, though once or twice we got together in Sarajevo, too; everything was always taking place before the war, though we always knew it was coming. From such dreams I woke up bereaved, for the *we*—whoever *we* were—the *we* could never be assembled but in a dream.

But in the dream in Seryozha's car, the only *we* were Mary and me: we were in a dark forest, walking a duck on a leash; George was playing golf with an umbrella among the trees and the ball kept bouncing off the trunks. Then we were on a ship, and it seemed we were crossing a lake as big as an ocean, except it was not water but sunflowers. There was a boy swimming in the lake, his little curly-haired head bobbing among the sunflowers. Mary said: "We can get him when he's ripe." But then the captain of the ship shot at him with a sniper rifle and the kid burst like a balloon and, in my dream, I thought: That kid, that's me. That's not Mary. That's me.

In Seryozha's car I woke up with a brick-thick chill of despair in my chest. It didn't help that the Lada was nearly tumbling down a dirt road, along which dilapidated houses lined up obediently. There were apple trees among the houses, their fruit-heavy branches bending and breaking—everything seemed forsaken. I didn't know where I was, nor who the driver was. I snapped out of oblivion when Rora lazily said from behind, I think he is planning to murder us. I looked at Seryozha's stolid, scruffy face—he could in fact easily be a murderer. In Ukrainian, I asked him: "Where are we?" He appeared to understand, but ignored me, until I asked him again. Whereupon he said in Russian what I deciphered as: "We are picking up my girlfriend."

The girlfriend was a comely young woman in a short, glittery skirt utterly unbefitting the idyllic catastrophe of the village. Seryozha escorted her, gripping her biceps, out of a tiny, filth-roofed house, a thin ribbon of smoke rising from the chimney. He opened the rear door and shoved her inside; Rora scooted over to the other side. "Elena," Seryozha said. Elena was redolent of fresh milk and glycerin soap; her cheeks were rurally flushed, partially covered with long, straight black hair. Seryozha drove uphill now; Elena looked out the window. A rabbit ran out in panic from one of the overgrown hedges; there were no human beings in sight. Maybe they all lived underground, in hiding from some peril invisible to me. By the time we reached the top of the hill and the asphalt, the car was hot: the smell of Elena's skin turned slightly manure-sour. Controlling—if that is the word—the steering wheel with his knee, Seryozha took off his sweatshirt and cobwebs of hair sprung from his onionesque armpits. Nice girlfriend, Rora said. Elena closed her eyes and leaned her head back, pretending to be sleeping. Apparently, she was going to Bucharest with us.

The roads were narrow and serpentine, curving against any logic between gently sloping hills. Seryozha lit cigarette upon cigarette, letting go of the steering wheel every time; he passed the rare truck and rarer car without regard for what might be coming at us; once we nearly pulverized a pack of dogs. I should have asked him to slow down, but I didn't. The velocity paralyzed me; fear stirred at the bottom of my mind, but was very far from the surface. As a matter of fact, the passivity was exhilarating: it seemed this madness could very well go unpunished. But I did buckle myself up quietly. I felt Elena's hand grabbing the back of my seat every time Seryozha cut across a bend; we shared the liberty of perfect helplessness.

Lazarus bent over with his arm twisted behind his back by Shippy, who was calling for his wife. For a moment Lazarus did nothing, did not squirm, did not try to writhe out of the grip; Shippy kept pressing him down, clearly trying to snap his arm. Lazarus felt his shoulder straining toward a break, the pain fast arriving. "Mother! Mother!" Shippy shouted.

We reached the Romanian border alive; the line of cars was short, the border guards were idle. The familiar fear of borders overcame me, but I disregarded it, as though it were a cold, and obediently gave my passport—my soul—to Seryozha. Rora glanced at me with what I read as contempt, but he delivered his passport just as passively. Seryozha seemed to have already been in possession of Elena's so he handed the passports to the guard. While he was chatting him up, the guard flipped through them, then picked up the phone and, avoiding looking at any of us, called somebody. Seryozha turned to Elena and glared at her with a hissing gaze.

I understood at that moment that the young Elena was not traveling to Bucharest of her own volition; Rora and I and our American passports were there to provide plausibility, a respectable cover—Seryozha probably told the border guard that we were all great friends, if not family. Rora must have figured it out too; Elena seemed to be terrified. And for all we knew, our illustrious, insane driver could have been in cahoots with the border guard, who was putting up a show for those who might be watching. We were in a bind; even if the border guard were honest and we could communicate with him, Seryozha could tell him that we were the ones who brought the girl along; we could be stuck in the nowhere land between Moldova and Romania, possibly accused of human trafficking. The border guard—and here it might be useful to give him some kind of a face: pale, mustached, squeezed between two large ears—the border guard asked me something in Romanian. The only thing I understood was "America," so, leaning forward over Seryozha's lap, I said, "Chicago." He pointed at the girl and gibbered again. "Elena," I said. "Bucharest." Seryozha looked ahead, as though none of this was his business; I envisioned shattering his jaw with a sledgehammer. The guard gave Seryozha back our passports—he was definitely in cahoots with him—and he contemptuously passed ours to Rora rather than to me. Elena was probably going to end up as a prostitute in a Koševo brothel, or in a Bosnian hotel, or on a Milan street. Seryozha was going to pass her on to someone in Bucharest. We had no choice but to go with him.

Romania was flat, the road dreadfully straight. Seryozha quickly hit 190 kph, put his left boot up on the dashboard, and leaned his head back. Elena was sleeping; I was passing in and out of guilty slumber, coming up with excuses for being in this situation. There was nothing we could do; Seryozha was packing at least a knife, probably a gun, and I did not want to get stabbed or take a bullet in the head; we had no other way of getting to Bucharest; it was better not to get involved; perhaps Elena knew where she was headed; perhaps that was her way out of the shithole; perhaps that was how she would put herself through college; it was probably her choice. Who was I to judge Elena? Each life is legitimized by its rightful owner.

I was on the El once, on my way home from work, when one of my fellow passengers, a lady with a fox-fur collar and thick red lips, went into a seizure: she foamed at the mouth, her face gripped by a hideous grimace, her left foot flapping like a dorsal fin. Everybody on the car was stupefied; a couple of teenagers giggled; I could not think of anything to do, as I was not a doctor; I waited for someone else to do something. But nobody did; nobody was a doctor; the woman kept foaming and twitching and someone mercifully dragged her out of the El car. As we were leaving the station, I could see someone leaning knowingly over her, pulling her tongue out, stroking her cheek, showing the onlookers what to do. If Mary had been there, she would have known what to do, and it would not have taken her long to get around to it. And so I told her nothing about the seizure incident when she got home from her shift.

I knew, of course, that if Mary had been in Seryozha's car, she would have demanded that he slow down; she would have said something about Elena to the guard; she would have found a different way to get to Bucharest; she would have set everything right. I was glad that she wasn't there, for her presence would have shamed me, as it often did. The Lada was trembling with lullabying speed.

He's falling asleep, Rora said, startling me. I looked in the rearview mirror and saw that Seryozha's eyelids were drooping, his chin occasionally touching his hirsute chest, the car swerving every so often. He was going to kill us; I could not think of a way of not dying; Mary wasn't here. Elena exuded the musty sweat of mortal anxiety; she coughed and whimpered. She said nothing; Rora said nothing. It appeared I was in charge, except Seryozha was the one who held our lives in his hands. Perhaps, I thought, a quick death would resolve this uncomfortable situation.

I had drunk and driven, of course, in my drinking days. And sometimes, late at night, driving away from whatever bar was feeling like home at the time, I would step on the accelerator and speed down the empty street, daring myself to see how long I could keep the accelerator floored before I chickened out. Once I had managed to pass through every light—a few of them red—without stopping. The danger, the disregard for death, would clear my mind. I would park in front of our house and feel intensely alive, shivering with an adrenaline high. I felt as though I had earned more life credit, which I would spend in the better future. I would lie down next to Mary, overwhelmed with a sense that I was worthy of her love. She never knew how close she was to losing me.

Seryozha was hitting the accelerator like there was no tomorrow. What's to be done, I said, in Bosnian; I think I was saying it to Elena. Seryozha kept shaking his head like a rattle, slapping himself a few times—he did want to live, the idiot, he was just entranced with the speed and his power over us. The Russian disco was pumping; I was afraid of dying, but not afraid enough; perhaps I could survive this without exerting any effort. That was what life ought to be about, living without regard for death; this was a test. I looked at Seryozha's drowsy face and thought: That's me. And everybody was me, and I was everybody, and in the end it didn't matter if I died.

But Rora was himself; he tapped the hell-bent driver on the shoulder and said: *Polako, jarane, polako.* Miraculously, Seryozha slowed down, then pulled over at the gas station to splash his face and torso with water in the bathroom. Rora stepped out after him; I could tell he was tempted to slap him, but he lit up a cigarette instead. I watched the smoke emerge from his mouth and curl up into his nostrils. I did not feel intensely alive; I felt intensely nothing.

WE REACHED BUCHAREST by the afternoon. We crept through the messy, unintelligible city, through the narrow streets that opened into vast boulevards that climbed up toward an insanely enormous building. Seryozha circled around an oval building that was plastered with billboards: Sony, Toshiba, Adidas, McDonald's, Dolce & Gabbana. The young, beautiful, white-faced supermodels looked down on the streets from their unimaginable worlds, implying blatantly better lives to the riffraff presently pushed around by Seryozha's fearless vehicle.

We came upon the train station unexpectedly. Seryozha tried to hustle us, claiming that the charge was a hundred euros per person—a cheeky, brazen bastard he was—but I just ignored the demand, while Rora audibly scoffed; we survived the drive and he could scare us no longer. We took our luggage from the trunk: Elena was still in her seat, forlorn, not moving or looking up at us, let alone bidding us good-bye. What are we going to do? I asked Rora. Relax, Rora said, and be quiet.

We walked away, but before we entered the ramshackle station, Rora lit a cigarette and assumed a position behind a pillar from which he could monitor Seryozha. Our friend was rummaging through the car, digging through the glove compartment, raking under the seat, barking at Elena. He got out and climbed waist deep into the trunk; he slammed it down and had her move to the front, pushing her head down as she crouched to get into the seat. She sat there, looking ahead. The way her body slumped, the way her hair hung like a veil over her cheek apples, her visible despair—it was all making me angry, I wanted to disappear. Seryozha locked the car door and, leaving Elena in the car, headed toward the other end of the station.

Come with me, Rora said. We followed Seryozha at a distance.

The bathroom walls were daubed over with various venereal diseases; the lines between the tiles brimmed with unspeakable ecosystems. The moment we entered the bathroom, Rora dropped his duffel bag and zeroed in on the stall where Seryozha was—to this day, I do not know how he knew which one it was. He kicked open the foolishly unlocked door and there was our chauffeur with his pantaloons halfway down. Rora socked him instantly, stepped in, and closed the door. I remained outside like an experienced accomplice and bodyguard (except for my Samsonite on wheels) and listened, with acute, indecent pleasure, to the sounds of smacking and whimpering and toilet flushing. There was no one in the bathroom; it lasted but a minute, for Rora was good at such things. He stepped out; Seryozha was sitting on the toilet seat, wheezing, his forehead against the wall. Rora was washing his hands as I stepped in and slugged Seryozha in the jaw; he flinched, and I pummeled him again, gashing his cheek. I felt the bones cracking under my knuckles, but I kept punching until his jaw was crushed, until my hand was finally and thoroughly broken. I wished Mary could have seen me at that moment, the lethal combination of wrath and good intentions. I wished she could have held my crushed hand in hers, put it in a splint of unconditional love. Seryozha slid off the toilet seat; blood gushed down his sweatshirt front, soaking into *New York*. One of his eyes was glass, for it slid out of the socket and tumbled to the gory floor. Life is full of surprises.

I hope you didn't kill him, Rora said, as we strode through the station hall. I think I broke my hand, I said. Put it in your pocket, he said. And stop grimacing. I had no idea where we were going, I just limped behind him and we emerged from the station right in front of Seryozha's car. As Elena watched him in disbelief, Rora unlocked her door, whisked her out without a word. She retracted her head, cowering from anticipated slaps, but Rora shoved her passport and a bundle of money in her hand, while I watched nervously for Seryozha, implausibly running toward us with a broken-up bloody face, dropped pants, and a piece of gun in his hand. My hand was throbbing with beastly, thrilling pain. Rora shook her, gripping her forearms. *Idi*, he said. *Bježi*. She understood, but was hesitating. What if she wanted to come with us? What if we took her along? There were so many lives she could live.

But then she slipped out of Rora's grasp, slowly, and grabbed her purse out of the car, stuffed the passport and the money in it, and, much too slowly, strode away. As she was crossing the street without looking back, I saw that she wore silvery soccer shoes and white tube socks. Rora took a picture of her walking away.

LAZARUS STEPPED OFF the New York train into the crowd, enveloped in a cloud of steam; he pushed his way through it; they pulled and pushed him and thrust him aside. This was America; this passion of the mob; this struggle to protect your soul from the voracious mass. Someone tried to rip his suitcase out of his hand and he swung it forward, slammed himself in the knee as it swung back. He rose on the tip of his toes to look for Olga over the sea of heads. She stood under a large moonlike clock, pale and small, his big sister. He picked up his pace, scurrying forward, but tripped and nearly fell flat on his nose. Olga was scanning the crowd for him when she saw him coming—tall, scrawny, hair unruly—but did not fully recognize him until he stumbled. The fear that he might get hurt gave him the shape of her little brother, love fluttering up her bosom. Lazarus, she called him, Lazarus, I am over here. Lazarus.

Unsettling dreams have been swarming in Isador's head, but when he snaps out of slumber he cannot remember them. The suitcase corner is poking his kidney; rags are covering his face and even when he uncovers it, the wardrobe is airless and lightless. His body is too uncomfortable to allow him to reenter his dream. He has run out of things to think about: he has thought about Olga, contemplated Lazarus's death, dwelt on the game at Stadlwelser's, when he should have waited for Stadlwelser to bet, about the debt he would have to pay back. He ought to leave Chicago without a trace. He refuses to think about the possibility of being arrested. If he does not imagine the *politsey*, the *politsey* don't exist. He has gone back and forth through reveries about Olga's slim body and the book he used to think he would write, a novel about the adventures of a clever immigrant called *The Adventures of a Clever Immigrant*. He envisions himself as rich; throwing parties, riding in a car driven by his own chauffeur. He twists his body, looking for a comfortable position, presses his ribs against the suitcase corner. The seats would be made of soft leather, you would be able to hear the sighs of slaughtered calves when you leaned back. He would sit in the back and tell the driver through the horn where to go. "Hippo-drome," he would say. "And fast."

The wardrobe door is flung open, the rags are pulled apart, and before Isador can think or say anything, a hand grabs him by the scruff of his neck, another quickly covers his mouth, and he is whisked out. The light blinds him; two men hoist him by the arm-pits and drag him toward the door, his toes dragging across the floor. Their hands are big; the palm on his face spreads from ear to ear. Isador is terrified; he wants to scream, writhe out of their grip, but everything is happening fast. Nothing is said; they lift him higher so his feet are in the air now. One of the men tells him in German:

"Be quiet. We are going to get you out of here."

Isador wiggles and the other man knees him in the thigh.

"Keep still or we'll knock you out."

There is a large casket before him in the center of the room; out of mortal fear Isador stops fidgeting.

"We'll let go of you. But if you make a sound, we'll knock you out cold."

Isador relaxes his body to signal he will obey them. The hand is removed from his face—it nearly tore out his jaw. They release their grip and put him down on the floor, but his knees tremble and they have to hold him up. The men are large, wearing suits and bowler hats. One of them has a neatly trimmed mustache. They are speak-ing without excitement or urgency.

"Get in," he says and points at the casket.

"You go first," Isador whimpers. The men exchange quick glances, whereupon the mustached one socks Isador in the jaw, knocking him out.

When he comes to, his jaw is pulsing with pain; he knows he is in the casket: it smells like pinewood and cadaver. There is some-thing on top of him, heavy and hefty. The casket is being carried; when it dips every now and then, Isador tightens, frightened to the point of thinking that this might all be a dream. His heart is beating fast; he can hear it; he can feel it throbbing inside him. The weight on him is clothed; his cheek is chafed by felt. There is a dead body on top of him, he realizes, a corpse. He recognizes its rigid coldness, its stiffening joints cracking; what is pressing his cheek is someone's ankle. They are going to bury him alive. Alive. He is going to die in airless darkness. And his skin tingles with the pricks of fear, his head empties; he is breathless and paralyzed. Maybe he is dead already; perhaps this is it. Yet the pain in his hips, the strain of his ribs under the weight—it still feels like life.

The casket stops undulating, then dips abruptly one more time, before he senses it being slid onto a surface—scraping, a car engine starting, indistinct words. They are taking him to a cemetery to bury him alive. He fidgets but there is no space; he screams but there is no sound. The car moves and keeps going. Death just comes and takes you away and there is nothing you can do.

WHAT STRENGTH IT takes not to break down, not to rave and wail, not to claw out Schuettler's serpentine eyes, not to push the rabbi into the grave, Rabbi Klopstock, who knows perfectly well what is in the coffin. It takes strength; she stands there at the edge, Olga Averbuch, the bereaved sister, because without her the whole edifice of closure and unity would collapse and crumble into Lazarus's grave, much like the sods on which Rabbi Klopstock slips and nearly tumbles into the hole. The pain is grinding inside her head; perhaps grief causes brain inflammation.

The day before his bar mitzvah they went for a walk, Lazarus and Olga. He wanted to talk about life, he said. Things always weighed heavily on him. He wanted to discuss the mysteries of the Torah, his studies, the theme of his address to the congregation: "Why Does the Jewish Day Begin at Sunset?" But they strolled together, talking about nothing; it was the last day of his childhood.

They stopped by Mr. Mandelbaum's store so she could buy him sweets, but Mr. Mandelbaum gave him a swirling-candy stick for free. They sat outside on the bench, and he licked it seriously and strenuously, as if disposing of it quickly was the first task of his manhood.

Tears burst into her eyes, down her cheeks, a sob heaves out of her body. She drops to her left knee for a moment; it leaves an indentation in the clay. Taube holds her up; she feels his hands on her shoulder and back and nothing is real anymore. All she can see is Lazarus licking the swirling-candy stick, the faint mustache over his lip, and she begins ululating incessantly: Lazarus . . . as though the word could recall him into existence. Still, he is not rising.

With her head bowed, the bereaved Jewess wept over her brother's grave. Finally, he was coming into peace. Finally, he has reached the land beyond the malignant reaches of anarchism and the inflammatory ideas of remedying so-called social injustices. And to bid him good-bye with her, there were many distinguished Jews of Chicago: here was the good Rabbi Klopstock; there the wealthy merchant Mendel; tall stood Eichgreen and Liss, leaders among their tribesmen. And there were scores of their anonymous co-religionists, who nevertheless chose the way of patriotism and loyalty over the blood-soaked paths of anarchism and lawlessness. They were there to bid farewell not only to the misguided Lazarus but just as surely to the troubles that threatened to separate them from their American co-citizens. But behind their backs, as though to remind them of the insidious permanence of peril, there stood the dark-faced mourners of black discontent, those who have not given up on the hope that the young Lazarus could become a martyr for their murderous causes. There was Ben Reitman, the dean of the College of Hobos and the notorious consort of the

Red Queen, Emma Goldman; there were the young anarchists of Edel-stadt, their Semitic eyes murked by ire. And alongside the infamous there was many an unsavory character, bristling with devious schemes.

After the Kaddish is said, after the sods of earth start crumbling and falling on the coffin, after more condolences are offered, after Olga's knees buckle again with anger and exhaustion, Taube protectively walks her to the car. Schuettler, catching up so as to appear friendly and caring, walks on her other side. William P. Miller scurries up behind them, red in the face, notebook in hand, his new cuff links sparkling.

The very presence of Assistant Chief Schuettler at the recondite, solemn Jewish ritual vouchsafed the dominion of law and order. Because he was there, dispensing necessary orders by a mere shifting of his gaze, the interment of the unfortunate Lazarus was a dignified affair, devoid of outrageous anarchist excesses. Be it loudly said that the assistant chief's merciless struggle against the evil of foreign anarchism did not deprive him of compassion nor did it inure him to the suffering of others. Ever a gentleman, he offered his arm to the bereaved Jewess, and she, doubtless in need of fatherly strength, walked with him back into her life, away from her younger brother's eternal home. "Thank you, Assistant Chief Schuettler, for your kindness and your help," she said to him, her tenebrous eyes deluged with tears. "Let us return to peace now," he said to her, though the words could well have been said to all the citizens of Chicago.

THE CASKET LID is pried open; the corpse is lifted off Isador. The light blinds him again, but when his eyes get used to it, he can see the two men and a few more, standing around, staring into the casket in silence, as though contemplating their own mortal existence. He sits up, looks around. "Am I dead?" he asks in German. The men laugh at him, then help him hatch out. He cannot feel his legs, so they carry him to the table and sit him on the chair. It is some kind of a cellar; it smells of clay and mold; it is hard to see into the dark corners. The corpse is on the floor by the casket; his face is white as flour, splattered with dark spots, bloated like a bladder; his eyes are black patches—it takes a while for Isador to recognize Isaac Lubel. The two men lift Isaac—he is straight and solid as a board—and put him back in the casket.

"Isaac," he says to the choir of men. "That is Isaac Lubel."

"That was Isaac Lubel," the mustached man says. "Now he is dead."

TAUBE OPENS THE car door for her and she steps in, the driver stirring out of sleep and sitting up erect, fixing his hands on the wheel. She ignores Schuettler and Miller, who are not leaving, pretending to be talking to her for the sake of the crowd. Schuettler raises his hat to her, the *shvants*. Miller is brandishing an idiotic, optimistic smile. Taube speaks into the horn to give the order and off they drive, Miller actually waving good-bye. Vines of hair are creeping up the driver's neck toward a bowler hat. The acceleration presses Olga's vacuous stomach in and she grabs the seat in horror. The speed frightens her; the world is pasted against the window as a terrible blur; everything is disappearing.

Dear Mother,
You must forgive me for what I have done, but I chose life over death. God will take care of the dead. We have to take care of the living.

"Thank you, Fräulein Averbuch," Taube says and sighs. "That was eminently heroic. We will be eternally grateful for your sacrifice."

For Assistant Chief Schuettler knows that this city has suffered enough. It has endured the contaminating presence of the foreign elements who landed on these welcoming shores with no intention to contribute to the commonwealth but to hate and violate. See they not the greatness of our country? Can they not feed their families with the bread, crusty though it may be, earned in the workshops and foundries of Chicago? Have they not come here to escape the madness of murder, the persistence of persecution in their old lands? Have they not found here previously unimaginable freedoms, not least the freedom to go back to wherever they came from if they so desired? Can they not share in our noble intentions? See they not that they have a singular opportunity to be a part of a people who naturally strive toward liberty and excellence, toward the greatness that would dwarf all the sanguine accomplishments of the past empires?

This welcoming city has suffered much, but all lives lost will have been lost in vain if we do not redeem them and find value in their demise. From the bones of the dead, magnificence will rise. Sleep now, beloved Chicago, for your enemies are at bay and your citizens can now thrive in the garden of law and order.

Olga's stomach is churning and she would vomit if there were anything in it to disgorge. The car is skidding over the mud puddles, never too far from the cemetery wall. Taube's hat is bouncing on the seat between them, as though there were a rabbit inside. She lifts it, but there is nothing there.

"As per our agreement, your friend Maron is well protected in a safe house. We hope we can get him to disappear without a trace in Canada, in a day or two, after things calm down. He is probably eating and bathing right now. My men will take good care of him. You'll never see him again. To tell you the truth, I would have liked to have seen him imprisoned, or at least taught a punitive lesson. He is one of those young men who could never see the great future this country offers us. All he could see was now, nothing but now. In their blindness, such young men are incapable of imagining a communal future."

"Herr Taube," Olga whimpers. "Please stop talking. You make me sick. Please be silent."

Taube falls silent. His cheeks are aflame, his knee is hopping in excitement—yet another job well done. He looks out at the small patch of prairie, the dispirited weeds enclosed in meaningless fences; a flock of birds is flapping in disarray across the sky toward the vacant horizon.

The car will take her all the way to the ghetto, but she will ask Taube to let her out a block away from her home, so she can inconspicuously find her way back. The sun will be setting and she will notice for the first time that dusk obscures the shapes of things for her. The *politsyant* will be gone. The Lubel residence will be deserted. Her home will be cold and empty. Night will be falling, dense and boundless. She will not light the lantern, blind to the shadows. She will sit at the table, say nothing to no one, let nothing settle all around her like falling snow.

Before we reached Sarajevo, I had to pass through a world of pain: all night long my hand had been throbbing, and I could feel it getting doughier until it felt like it belonged to someone else. Most of the train ride to Belgrade, Rora smoked outside the sleeping compartment we were sharing. Then he slept on the bus to Sarajevo. It was as though he had said to me everything that could have been said, all of his statements completed. Only as the bus was descending into the gray Sarajevo valley, the city tucked under thick morning fog, did I dare ask him:

Are you worried?

About what? he said.

About Rambo.

No, he said.

About anything?

Everything will sort itself out.

By the time we arrived at the bus station, my hand was shades of indigo and swollen, as though it belonged to a corpse. Rora would not let me take a cab from the bus station to the hotel. Instead, he insisted I walk with him to the City Hospital, where his sister was working, but a few painful minutes away. Rora insisted strenuously that Azra must look at my hand—perhaps he was feeling that the whole Seryozha affair was somehow his fault—while I, deranged by steady pain, kept saying everything would be all right. I could not forget the sweet sounds of Seryozha's face cracking; my pain was well worth it.

Rora carried my bag, as I cradled my broken hand. Walking with him down a Sarajevo street named after a dead poet was a wholly uncanny experience. Everything was as I remembered it, yet entirely different; I felt like a ghost. People passed by without glancing at me; I was fully unexceptional and insignificant, if not perfectly invisible. I recalled my previous life, the life in which I had ridden a bike down this very street, and where the kids on their way to school pelted me with rocks; the life in which I had written some politically charged obscenities on the school wall; the life in which I had effortlessly stolen candy from a store minded by a blind old man who had stubbornly denied his blindness to himself and to others. Nobody seemed to remember me. Home is where somebody notices your absence.

We walked past the hospital security guard watching a Latin American soap opera, went up the staircase (the elevator was out of order) teeming with patients smoking in washed-out pajamas, and found Azra's office at the end of a long, tunnel-like corridor. Rora walked in without knocking and I followed him in, closing the door behind me with my foot, like a proper thug.

I always wanted to watch Mary operate, to see her deft hands saw open a skull, cut through bone and brains. I fantasized about witnessing her absolute absorption, her hands up to their wrists in somebody else's mind, her quiet power exuding through her blood-stained surgical gown. But she never allowed me into the operating room. It was against the rules, and she had a hard time violating any rules. She did let me ask a lot of questions about her surgeries, but her answers were reluctant, vague, amnesic. There were whole worlds of her I had no access to, and she would never allow me to imagine them.

I did get to see her office every now and then, mostly unexpected, ever tormented by the fantastic possibility of a handsome anesthesiologist frolicking with her between surgeries. Once, I came by to get the house keys, as I had misplaced mine after a drink too many, and I brought along a sappy rose. She did not approve of me showing up drunk in her office; she put the rose on her desk and did not look at it. I violated the cleanliness of her sovereignty; I disturbed the order she had established. She avoided eye contact and kept herself busy with rearranging stuff on her desk around the rose. While she was on the phone, I impertinently browsed through the cabinet drawers. I opened one and there was nothing in it except a box—a single sealed box—of ampoules, positioned exactly at its center. The drawer was neither empty nor disorderly: it was full of what it was supposed to be full of. Now I understand that was the seat of her soul. She did not like me looking into it, so I closed it.

There were heaps of things and papers on Azra's desk; her glasses lay supine on top of one of the piles. On the wall, a faded prewar poster warned of the comparatively silly dangers of not washing your fruit and vegetables. Next to it there was a small mirror, which surprisingly did not seem out of place. On the windowsill there was a rotund cactus the size of a clementine. Under the desk, a pair of low-heel shoes, one of them on its side, like a slumberous dog. Azra wore white hospital slippers; her feet were long and narrow, her heels small, her ankles frail. She raised herself on her toes to kiss Rora's cheek; he pressed her temple on his chin and squeezed her shoulders. I offered her my left hand for shaking and the awkwardness of the contact established momentary intimacy. The seat of her soul was in her deep, sea-green eyes. Somehow, she reminded me of Olga Averbuch.

Olga and Lazarus sat outside Mr. Mandelbaum's store, the day before his bar mitzvah. He was licking a candy stick seriously and strenuously, as if disposing of it quickly were the first task of his manhood. He was unable to be still, swung his feet and fidgeted, loaded with life and spirit. People walked by and greeted them: Mr. Abramowitz and Mr. Runic and the Golder girl. He smiled at her, she averted her gaze; Olga saw it could be a beginning of a courtship. A bright day it was, everybody seemed to be enjoying the fact they were alive. Even the ugly Israel Shalistal bid them good day.

Azra touched my broken hand; her fingers were pleasantly cool. She slowly twisted it upward—for her eyes, I winced in pain—and slid her fingertips along the edge of my palm. She asked me to wiggle my fingers and I couldn't. The morning sun was coddling the window, the mists were crawling up the slopes of Trebević. I could see Marin-dvor spreading toward the invisible river, and in an absurd flash I fully perceived it as the neighborhood I had been born and had grown up in. I was somewhere; I had finally landed in Sarajevo. Azra sandwiched my hand between hers; her palms were warm. I did not want her to let go.

It is broken, she said.

I know, I said. It's been broken for a while.

She sent me two floors below for an X-ray. I got lost on the way; I entered a room with a family gathered around a man who was clearly on his deathbed, gazing up out of his pallor at their grim, shamelessly pink faces. I went all the way down and climbed all the way up again, past the same patients smoking newly lit cigarettes. I finally found the X-ray room, manned by a single skinny nurse with a loud radio playing wailful folk songs. She put out her cigarette, and brought out a stack of X-ray plates. She looked at my hand and said, with some delight, It is broken; she seemed to be excited by our common radiological prospects. Her hair was scraggly; she had no earrings, but there was a large hole in each of her earlobes; she kept licking her lips; her voice was hoarse from smoking and therefore affectionate. I put my hand on a plate and while I adjusted and placed it in different positions, she fired a cannonade of questions. I confessed everything under fire; I disclosed how I ended up in America, what my writerly life there was like; I told her about my trip with Rora, Dr. Azra Halilbašić's brother, about my return to Sarajevo. I did not mention Mary. By the time she was done X-raying, she felt entirely entitled to give me advice. Stay here, she said. This is your home. You should marry one of our women. There is no life for you in America. This is where your heart is. They hate Muslims there. They don't like anybody but themselves. I could not tell her I was not Muslim, but I appreciated her kind thought and promised I would seriously consider her proposition. The pictures will be up in the doctor's office in half an hour, she said.

Once the X-rays were in, Azra showed me on the light box where my hand was broken: the zigzagging crack interrupted the steady whiteness of the bone; it was all rather abstract and elegant. That's me, I thought, those fragile, bleached bones. Rora looked at the X-rays closely, as though he were another doctor, nodding as though he were seeing what he had expected to see. Perhaps he had told Azra how I broke it, for she asked me nothing. Still, I longed for an opportunity to describe my heroic punishment of a Moldovan pimp; I wanted to brandish my strength and self-righteousness, my vigilant manhood. Her perfume was Magie Noire; at the same time, the office smelled of troubling disinfectants, implying a lot of blood having been spilled in it. As she was putting on a splint and wrapping my hand with an armpit-smelling bandage, Rora photographed me flinching in discomfort; he seemed to have a penchant for taking pictures of me in embarrassing situations. I did not ask him to stop; being in the same picture

with Azra somehow brought me close to her. She had a gold necklace, the lily pendant resting in the dimple below her throat. I
imagined her standing tall in a purple velvet skirt, her hair held
high by a pin.

Next time you want to rough somebody up, she said wryly, use
your elbow or your forehead. Maybe a table leg or a tire iron. Hands
are fragile, very fragile, and you have only two. I was to come back
once the swelling was down so she could put on a cast.

They saw me out to the hospital gate. I no longer had a home in
Sarajevo—my parents had sold our apartment to finance their exile
in America. Hence I had booked a room at the Hotel Sarajevo for
my homecoming. I had planned to be on my own for a few days, I
said, maybe just walk around and run into people, recollect our
travels and travails in pill-induced tranquillity. Had this been a pil-
grimage, this would have been the time to contemplate my life and
my place in the big metaphysical picture. Good luck, they said.
Rora and I set up a coffee-drinking date in a couple of days. Azra
urged me to stay with them; it was wrong for me to come home to
Sarajevo and stay at a lousy hotel. I said I would think about it and
got into a cab. Call if you need anything, she said. We'll talk, I
said.

The cabbie—who had no front teeth apart from a pair of incisor
goalposts—demanded that I buckle up, but I didn't bother. He
openly detested me and kept insisting and insulting me (he didn't
want to have the blood of an asshole on his hands), until I defiantly
buckled up just before we stopped in front of Hotel Sarajevo. I
handed my American passport to the receptionist but spoke to him
in Bosnian. He said, Welcome home, sir. Breakfast is served between seven and ten.

The following morning, I stared at the ceiling for a while; I immersed myself in the newspaper reports on petty crime and mo-
ronic celebrities over coffee; I went for a stroll. I relished the
Sarajevo pavements under my feet, the asphalt felt softer than on

any other street in the world. I walked up to Jekovac to behold the city spreading out of the valley toward the caliginous mass of the Igman mountain. I gorged on myriad sweet pastry all over Baš Čaršija. I quaffed the cold water from the fountain in front of Gazi-husrevbegova Mosque. I greeted acquaintances, saluted random fellow strollers. Nobody asked me where I was from nor expressed their admiration for my exotic accent and alien culture. I reposed on the benches by the Miljacka, watching soccer balls bobbing desperately in its whirlpools. I ran into Aida, and she said, I haven't seen you for a while, where have you been? and I teared up and hugged her. We had dated in high school; I hadn't seen her for twenty years or so.

Later on that day, I called Mary halfheartedly and was fully relieved when I could not reach her. When I finally did, she told me that George had been taken to the hospital; it seems the cancer had spread to his stomach and brain. It did not look good. I offered her my strength and asserted I would always be there for her. But in saying that, it occurred to me that I would in fact never be there for her, that I would always be here, where my heart was.

Mary could hold a cockroach in her hand, but was spooked by sparrows. Mary loved broccoli and bloody steaks and carrots, but she disliked ice cream and chocolate. Her favorite books were *Sense and Sensibility* and *To Kill a Mockingbird*. When she listened to music, she would sometimes tap her fingers on her knee, but denied it vehemently if I pointed it out to her. She was prone to wearing commodious frumpy clothes, but had an impeccable, fetishistic taste in shoes. Orchids and green onions made her sneeze. Thick eyebrows turned her on. She put two spoons of sugar in her tea, one in her coffee. She preferred bourbon to wine. She could never remember the name of her all-time favorite film. (It was *All That Heaven Allows*.) She had no interest in sports, except for figure skating and boxing—George used to take her to boxing matches. Her frequent karaoke choice was "Hungry Like the Wolf." Her most cherished memory was of a vacation in Florida when she learned to swim: she was nine; her stomach on George's palm, she splashed around haphazardly until she realized he had taken her into the deep and released her. When she was a girl she wanted to become, respectively, a ballerina, an explorer, a vet, a shoe designer, a congresswoman. After her grandmother died, she wept for months and gouged out the eyes of all of her dolls. She lost her virginity at the age of twenty, while in med school; he went on to be the chief anesthesiologist at the Columbia University Medical Center. Buried somewhere in my luggage was a photo of her mincing onions in the kitchen, donning her water-lilies apron, tears running down her cheeks: she wiped them with her forearm, smiling sunnily, a machete-sized knife in her hand. When she was eleven, her puppy dog died and she wanted it stuffed, but George had a sage conversation with her, explaining that the doggie's soul was now elsewhere, that the body without the soul was empty, that it was natural that flesh should rot and turn to dust. She was like everybody else because there was nobody like her.

A COUPLE OF DAYS LATER, Rora was sitting in the sunny garden café down the street from the cathedral, sipping his morning coffee, plodding through the sludge of local news, flirting with scantily dressed young women by way of taking their photos, basking in being home again, waiting for me, when a buff young man with a barbed-wire tattoo wreathing around his right biceps and stud earrings in both of his ears (so he was described by the few witnesses before they forgot what they had seen)—when a buff young man squeezed his buff ass between flimsy plastic chairs and frail tables to step up to Rora and empty his gun, seven bullets in gratuitous succession, to empty his gun into Rora, who was absurdly trying to stand up. Whereupon Rora collapsed, and the young man grabbed Rora's camera and calmly walked away, as the café disintegrated into panicked particles. By the time I belatedly arrived, everybody had cleared out, Rora was alone, bleeding out a venous ocean amidst the strewn chairs and tables, amidst the purses and sandals and burning cigarettes left behind in retreat. Somebody's cell phone kept cynically blaring its "Staying Alive" ring tone.

He was gone before I got to him. The rubbernecked waitstaff lined up against the wall to smoke simultaneously; passersby slowed down to gawk. I wished I had held him in my arms as he expired; I would have liked to have heard his last words, to have said something uncomforting and senseless to him. I merely leaned over him to look: his nose was blasted away, he had brains in his curls, there were no eyes to be seen, the ocean of blood expanding well beyond my shoes. His camera was not there; he was not there; I was there.

So then the police came. Before I was even asked, I eagerly informed the young assistant inspector, who wore a Kappa sweatshirt and sported an elaborate facial-hair contour in lieu of a beard, that Rora's sister, Azra Halilbašić, worked at the City Hospital, that they should notify her immediately. And who are you? he asked me. A friend. Where do you live? Hotel Sarajevo. What is your name? Vladimir Brik. Vladimir what? Brik. What kind of a name is that? It's complicated, I said. When he finally asked me if I had seen anything, I told him I had seen nothing.

It turned out that the waitstaff had also seen nothing; the young women returning to retrieve their fake-brand-name purses had seen nothing; the buff young men who came back for their cigarettes and cell phones had seen nothing; the few who had at first seen something eventually saw nothing. I repeated it all to the *Dnevni Avaz* reporter, a woman so young and dazed that she might as well have been a teenager on a school assignment. She noted down my

name and wrote *ništa* (nothing) next to it. The assistant inspector
came back to tell me, as in a bad detective novel, not to leave the
city. Where would I go? I said. Nobody seemed particularly upset
by the murder, as though Rora had been a victim of a car accident.
Who do you think did it? I asked the assistant inspector. He actually
chuckled. Did you do it? he asked. No, I said. Of course not. Why
do you care, then? he asked.

LOYALLY AND DUTIFULLY I went to the funeral the next day; Azra was
the only woman among the small, silent crowd of men. I looked
for the killer in the crowd, perhaps even Rambo himself. There
were a few men with their heads shaved and faces sufficiently
weathered to suggest criminality, but their eyes bespoke genuine
sadness. On the far edge of the crowd, I recognized the assistant
inspector, still in his tracksuit. Nobody gave a speech, there was
no pomp; squatting over the grave, men mumbled the prayers
with their hands upturned, then touched their faces with their
palms; the dug-up dirt had dried in the sun and kept tumbling
down into the hole. I did not know what to do exactly, so I watched
Azra, did what she did. I folded my hands over my groin, remained
standing when the men squatted; I dropped a clod of earth on the
coffin after she did. Fortunately, she did not wail or faint; her ex-
pression stayed firm, except for the trembling chin. It was quickly
over; nobody indulged in bogus ruminations upon mortality,
ashes, and eternity. I approached Azra to express my condolences,
and she looked through me as though she didn't recognize me.
Perhaps she didn't; she had seen me but once, before her reality
was forever transformed.

I returned to my hotel room, stuffed myself with sleeping pills,
and called Mary. I incoherently told her about the murder and the
funeral and then sobbed into the earpiece, while she maintained

her silence at the other end. Finally, she had a surgery to perform and quietly hung up, but I went on weeping, until I wiped off my tears and tried to write a letter with my unbroken left hand. I wanted to tell her so many things, but I could write nothing.

There is no good way to say this, Mary, I wanted to write to her. Rora was killed in cold blood, I have broken my hand. Otherwise, I'm fine and think of you a lot. I cannot remember what my life used to be, how I got to this point. I don't know where everything disappeared. I think I might stay in Sarajevo for a while, use up the Susie money, until my hand heals, until I sort myself out. I am sorry about George. I hope he gets better soon. I'll be fine and think of you a lot. Why did you leave me in these woods?

And when I woke up I continued imagining the future letter, with a mind so slow it seemed somebody else was tabulating all the losses, pains, and grievances, describing all those nights when I had listened to her unsteady breathing, trying to talk myself out of the pain in my head, imagining a different life for myself, the life of a good man, and a better writer. I told her breathlessly about the can of sadness I had found in our kitchen and how afraid I was of having children and how on this trip I realized that I never wanted to go back to America. I told her that I could never find peace in Chicago and that I could not watch George die. I could have written page after demented page of what would have been a testament to our marriage. *I will never know you, nothing about you, what has died inside you, what has lived invisibly,* I could have written. *I am elsewhere now.*

I DIDN'T EVEN know where in the labyrinth of Baš Čaršija Azra lived. The local custom—*our* custom—demanded that I go and visit her house of sorrow, which would certainly be full of friends and family and acquaintances. And who was I? I wanted to go and see her;

Rora had bonded us. But I could not find her home. I randomly inquired around Baš Čaršija for the house of Azra Halilbašić: most of the people said they did not know; some knew but did not want to tell me, taking it upon themselves to shield her from strangers. Finally, I called her at home and had to get through a series of protective aunts and anonymous men before I could offer my deepest condolences and remind her that I had been Rora's co-traveler, that she had kindly attended to my broken hand. She asked me how it was. It was even more swollen than last week, and quite a bit bluer, too. She said I must come to the hospital's emergency room tomorrow; she would be on duty. Thank you. I know it must be hard for you, I said. I'll see you tomorrow, she said.

In the emergency waiting room I waited to be called upon along with a broken-limbed biker, a battered wife, a skull-cracked drunk, and a boy who sliced his cheeks open attempting to swallow a razor; we sat in collective pain, occasionally expressed by an individual grunt. From somewhere beyond the many doors there came horrible screams. A miserable body was thrust fast through the swinging doors, a blood bag dangling above it like a wet flag.

Between the licks of his swirling-candy stick, Lazarus asks Olga if she loves someone. Yes, she says. He asks her if she is going to marry him. Probably not, she says.

Why not?

Because sometimes you have no control over life and it keeps you far away from who you love.

Do you ever imagine a life different from this one?

Yes, all the time.

A better life?

Yes, a better life.

I imagine my life to be big, so big that I cannot see the end of it. Big enough for everyone to fit into it. You will be in it, Mother and Father will be in it, people I have never met or known will be

in it. I will be in it. I can see it. I have a picture of it in my head. It's
a field in bloom so deep you can swim in it. I can see it now, and I
cannot see its end.

A NIMBLE young nurse called "Brik!" and I hurried after her into
an unkempt room full of patients on gurneys littered along its
length. I found Azra behind a curtained-off space in the middle.
She had a syringe in her hand; I thought she was getting it ready
for me. An old woman was squirming on the gurney, clutching her
stomach, riven with cramps; she gasped and croaked and mut-
tered, her eyes darting sideways, as though she were following the
trajectories of her pain. The nurse turned her over rather heart-
lessly and lifted her gown. I saw the shrunken ass, the ripples of
cadaverous skin, the red and brown blotches on her thighs; the
atrophied calves; the sores on her swollen, bluish feet. Azra
plunged the needle into her left buttock; within seconds the old
woman calmed down and the nurse turned her over. Her eyes
rolled up; her upper lip exposed toothless gums; her nostril walls
were paper-thin. It seemed to me she was dead, but Azra did not
seem concerned. She could tell the difference between life and
death. There, she said to the old lady, who could not hear her. You
should feel better soon.

We went to the office of the surgeon on night duty. There was
nothing that bespoke Azra was the one on duty, other than the
same low-heeled shoes under the desk. She checked my hand, turning and twisting it, ignoring my yelps and recoils; she switched on
the light box to look at my X-rays again, shaking her head. I reveled
in her worrying about me. Perversely, I hoped she would have to
operate on me; I would have been thrilled if she were to cut through
my weak flesh, all the way to the bone.

What do you see there? I asked.

I see what I don't want to see. You need to have that hand above your heart when you sleep. And you are probably walking around with it hanging down. You need to stay put and rest.

It was Rambo, wasn't it? I said.

What was Rambo? she asked, wiping my hand with a ball of cotton soaked in alcohol. The flesh felt nothing, but I could see she was gentle. My hand was dying. My hand was going to die first, then the rest of me, limb by limb.

It was Rambo who killed Rora, I said.

She pressed a pedal to lift the trash can lid and dropped the cotton ball in it; the can was empty.

It was because Rora knew that Rambo killed Miller, I said.

Who is Miller?

You know who Miller is. He is the American reporter Rora worked with in the war.

Her curls glistened under the blazing neon light. You could tell by her hair Rora was her brother.

Miller, you say, she said and shook her head. What did Ahmed tell you?

Rora told me the whole story. He told me that Rambo killed Miller because he was consorting with Beno. He told me Rambo got out of Sarajevo after the surgery disguised as a corpse.

That's the story he told you?

Rora had photos that could be used as evidence against Rambo, the photos of Miller dead at Duran's brothel. Rora knew too much. I could not figure out why he would risk his life coming back to Sarajevo, but I thought he had the negatives put away somewhere.

You are pretty smart, a true writer, she said. Great imagination.

And I think you were the one who operated on Rambo. You saved his life and he owed you. But Rambo must have decided it would be safer to get rid of Rora altogether.

Azra snorted, took her glasses off, and rubbed her eyes—which were an even darker green today—as though finding me annoyingly unreal.

You are right, she said. I did operate on Rambo. But I just patched him up so they could take him to a hospital in Vienna. Which they did on a UN plane, with a government escort and an attending nurse, who, frankly, we could not afford to lose at the time.

She put her glasses back on.

As for Miller, last I heard he was reporting from Iraq. He stopped by in Sarajevo not so long ago, gave me a call. He was on his way to a vacation in Paris. He asked about Ahmed. I told him he was in America and gave Miller his phone number. For all I know, he is still vacationing.

I find that hard to believe, I said.

That's the truth.

Who killed Rora, then?

A boy with a gun, she said. The police arrested him today. He wanted the camera, he wanted to show off his gun, the gun went off and he kept shooting. That's what he told the police. He was high as a balloon. He sold the camera and bought drugs. They found him asleep on the Miljacka bank. He could not remember at first what he had done.

I find that hard to believe. Rora knew too much. Things happen for a reason.

She was smiling, her eyes tearing up: my apparent foolishness and gullibility must have reminded her of her brother, of the time they had spent together, of the stories he had told her. She could see that he had enchanted me.

What else did he tell you?

He told me that your husband deserted you to join the Chetniks.

That's true, she said. My husband deserted me so he could shoot at me and my family until death do us part. That is absolutely true.

Well, at least something is true, I said.

Something is always true, she said.

I am going to stay in Sarajevo for a while, I said.

Stay as long as you want.

I can't leave just yet.

I understand, she said. I understand.

Did the boy take the rolls of film, too?

No, she said. Ahmed left them at home.

That's good.

That makes no difference at all.

I am sorry.

No reason to be sorry, Azra said. Let's take care of your hand now. You will need it for writing.

ACKNOWLEDGMENTS

I would like to thank Boro Kontić, George Jurynec, Alissa Shipp, Angela Sirbu, Chaim Pisarenko, Valeria Iesheanu, Iulian Robu, Vildana Selimbegović, Jovan Divjak, Peter Sztyk, Maggie Doyle, Tatiana, Franjo i Svetlana Termačić, Tanja Rakušić, Semezdin Mehmedinović, Predrag Kojović, Boris Božović, Reginald Gibbons, and—particularly—Nicole Aragi for their kindness and friendship. As my best friend, Velibor Božović is beyond thanks, but his mind and photography were indispensable and I must acknowledge that.

In my research, the people at the Chicago Historical Society were generous and helpful. *The Lazarus Project* owes more than the basic facts of the Lazarus affair (to the extent that there are any facts in a work of fiction) to *An Accidental Anarchist: How the Killing of a Humble Jewish Immigrant by Chicago's Chief of Police Exposed the Conflict between Law & Order and Civil Rights in Early 20th-Century America* by Walter Roth and Joe Kraus (Rudi Publishing). *Easter in Kishinev: Anatomy of a Pogrom* (NYU Press) by Edward H. Judge and *Anarchy!: An Anthology of Emma Goldman's MOTHER EARTH* (Counterpoint) edited by Peter Glassgold were also essential. Finally, the making of *The Lazarus Project* would have been impossible without the support of the John Simon Guggenheim Foundation and John D. and Catherine T. MacArthur Foundation.

That's it. Over and out.

Picture Credits

Photographs on pages iv, 10, 28, 64, 98, 122, 150, 174, 202, 226, 248, and 276 are courtesy of Velibor Božović.

The following photographs are used with the permission of the Chicago Historical Society: x, DN-0005942, Chicago Daily News, 1908; 24, DN-0005941, Chicago Daily News, 1908; 52, DN-0005898, 1908; 86, DN-0056693, Chicago Daily News, 1911; 114, DN-0000763, Chicago Daily News, 1904; 136, DN-0005931, Chicago Daily News, 1908; 166, DN-0068694, Chicago Daily News, 1917; 190, DN-0004009, Chicago Daily News, 1906; 216, DN-0071301, Chicago Daily News, 1919; 240, DN-0005897, 1908; 266, DN-0005871, Chicago Daily News, 1908.